Infinite Sum

By

Sheila Deeth

An Ink-Filled Stories Publication

Copyright 2016 by Sheila Deeth

ISBN: 978-1-949600-03-2

All rights reserved as permitted under the U.S. Copyright Act of 1976. No part of this publication may be reproduced or transmitted in any form or by any means, electronic or mechanical, including photocopy recording or any information storage and retrieval system, without permission in writing from the publisher. The only exception is brief quotations in printed reviews.

First published 2016 by Indigo Sea Press

First IFS print edition 2018
First IFS ebook edition 2018

Cover design by Sheila Deeth

Dedication

I've been telling stories since the day I learned to talk, and writing them down since the day I learned to write. I suspect I've been waiting to tell this story since the day a trusted adult first abused me. But *Infinite Sum* is not my story, and Sylvia is not me, for which reason I really should thank all the wonderful people who rejected my first attempts at this novel; Sylvia's feelings are just as honest as if they were mine, but I think her tale is much better told because it's hers. After all, I've been telling stories, fiction not fact, since the day I learned to talk. It's what I do.

I'm also enormously grateful to my mum. She has told me repeatedly, since the day I left home, that I ought to make use of my writing skills. Without Mum's constant prayers and encouragement, this story would never have been written. Next, I'd like to thank those generous friends who encouraged me with early reviews—in particular authors Catherine Cavendish and Paulette Maturin, and most especially mystery author Aaron Paul Lazar who applied his razor-sharp fine-tooth comb to the final edits of the text. Thank you so much!

I must thank Indigo Sea Press and Ink-Filled Stories as well, for publishing this second novel after Divide by Zero. And I am grateful—I will always be grateful—to God for teaching me forgiveness is not my job.

—Sheila Deeth

OTHER TITLES BY SHEILA DEETH
IN THE MATHEMAFICTION SERIES

- **Divide by Zero**—*a community divided by tragedy*
- **Infinite Sum**—*a woman close to breaking point*
- **Subtraction**—*the man who wasn't there to help*

ABOUT THE AUTHOR

Sheila Deeth is an English American, Catholic Protestant, mathematician writer, with a math degree from Cambridge University England and a life-long love of words. Her works include the Mathemafiction series of contemporary novels, science fiction and fantasy novellas, picture books, animal stories, and the Five-Minute Bible-Story Series. Connect with her online at www.sheiladeeth.com

INFINITE SUM

Readers say:

"Infinite Sum… is a beautiful work of art. Like a skillfully rendered collection of drawings, this literary masterpiece deals with one woman's life as she comes to terms with her disturbing past… a story to be savored, one sumptuous chapter at a time." *~Aaron Paul Lazar*

"The voices of both the adult Sylvia and Sylvia the child are clear and compelling, leading the reader, at times almost unwilling, to the final, satisfying conclusion."
~G Davies Jandrey

"A novel that is edgy and full of suspense, yet sensitively woven around the life of one individual, Sylvia..."
~Glenda Bixler

"Art and math blend in this beautifully written story of healing and forgiveness." *~Donna Fletcher Crow*

Sometimes memories add up to reveal a secret too huge to bear. Sometimes, instead, their sum forms a gateway to the future. And sometimes the difference can be determined by choosing your point of view.

Sylvia's memories lie buried in her past, but now they're pouring, red and black, into every picture she paints. Perhaps it's time for this mother of three to look behind the images and see what really happened in Paradise.

Infinite Sum

The Canvas

Chapter 1

"Don't try to decide what you're going to paint," says the teacher. Then I wonder; if I don't *decide* to dab my brush in paint, does he think some glorious image will appear unaided?

"Don't restrict yourself." But I'm bound by the page.

"Let inspiration arise from your subconscious. Set it free."

The teacher's voice rises skyward with his words. I watch him lift manicured hands, so very consciously and theatrically. But we're working in a warehouse, under a lofty ceiling of snaking conduits and tangled wires. Around us, deliberately inspiring objects are artfully displayed—paintings, sculptures, a vase of flowers, a crooked pile of boxes covered in cloth. Distant spotlights splash the walls, while layers of gauze and canvas tumble down in wild abandon. In the midst of it all, we painters guard our easels, proudly wearing our different shapes and styles, eagerly devouring the teacher's wondrous wisdom, and ready for art.

But my subconscious really doesn't feel like inspiring anything. My hand holds the paintbrush, level with my eyes, as if I'm measuring angles or judging the shade for some curious tone, while I stare pointlessly at flowers. Yellow roses, tipped and veined with red; I mourn them as they dangle over the rim of a blue glass vase. Their feathered heads promise magic in that precious moment before falling. And then, in silence, one lonely petal drops. I let my paintbrush dip and stroke its sunset onto the page and think, *yeah great; this is me, inspired by dying flowers.*

Colors, shapes of blooms and stems; I add them to my canvas, and my hands are painting fast. Wash blue with white for the vase's pure translucency. Bite my tongue and feel my lungs expand as breath swells fiercely through my head. I dip and stroke, streak and lie, bend and rise until my kneecaps ache. Red clings to tipping tips of petals while darkness piles its urgency behind, and angles bend with a flower's sharpening shot at eternity. Ruined lives are encased in the vase's delicate glass, and my fingers flash with ease.

"Let inspiration arise from your subconscious," the teacher repeats.

I'm in the zone. Then I wake and he's announcing it's time to go home.

The canvas in front of me is filled with red and black. Broken petals swell with decay, laid out on a layer of coal. Shattered flowers lie torn and dead and scattered, never to return. What did my subconscious have in mind?

*****

I'm a mom. I'm married, and I have three sons. I worked as a computer programmer before the kids were born, and I used to be a mathematician. But I'm also a wannabe artist who dreams in color and longed to be famous once.

Art, color, nightmares, and the subconscious; they're all a mystery, filled with possibilities of hope and change. But math is different. Math is real and solid, right or wrong, with no uncertainties. Art plays games, while math follows rules. Art soars, and math measures its path. Art takes you where you don't want to go. But math lets you stay unmoving, right where you are.

Measures don't change just because your mind gets distracted. Integers don't shatter and their edges won't cut. They're not sharp. Real numbers don't paint in red and black. And equations never land you in therapy.

There again, equations probably don't land you in art class either. But I'm giving my dreams one final fling before going back to work. I've promised Donald I'll get a job when Adam turns ten; use those hard-learned mathematical skills; sum those graduate letters after my name into a winning résumé, though I'm not sure they sum to me. Donald says pictures won't sum to anything, but excuses my time here because "You always liked painting," as if we're discussing a nice new shade of pink for the bathroom wall. Still, time's gone by and all I produce are sheets of stabbing red and angry gray. Black lines like prison bars don't pictures make.

*****

The teacher laughed when he saw my blasted roses the other day. "You obviously needed to get something out of your system, Sylvia." Perhaps he ought to sign on as an art therapist. Then my *real* therapist says, "What do you *think*, Sylvia?" while I try not to think.

Dribbling raspberry sauce on vanilla ice-cream after dinner for the kids; red bleeds its broken veins on white; rivers fracture and freeze and—I try not to think.

Walking the supermarket aisle where *feminine products* promise *comfort and freedom* and all that, I wonder why the packets are pink instead of bloody red. I try not to think.

Seeing a photo of my sister with her grown up sons, I remember secrets shared in the bedroom back when we were kids; park benches in the rain as we grew up. But we're strangers now who never really knew each other at all. And I'd rather forget; stuff memories back inside the closet again, like childhood paintings stacked in their boxes in the loft.

"No," says my therapist. "Dig those paintings out. This is meant to be difficult." So I'm tasked with bringing all my old pictures down; studying their colors, lines and pages; and trying to find out who I once was. "Then tell me what you think."

The house is locked and silent around me now. I've finished the washing. The furnace roar is done. The water-heater waits on stand-by again. And leaves aren't blowing against the glass in the living-room door. No rain drums the roof. I've done as I was told.

Those boxes of pictures sit on the bedroom floor, hiding their spiders, coated in attic webs of dust and gray. Their cardboard cartons are all misshapen though, making a lumpy

5

unbalanced heap. Faded writing wilts as it tries to proclaim their former lives—*Joe's Soap*, then something illegible *for all your postal supplies*. Black plastic frames lean against them, holding paintings from high school and college. And somewhere, buried in their hidden history, I know I'll find the pictures I drew last time I was stuck in therapy, when nearly ten-year-old Adam was just a tiny babe in my arms.

The doctor's voice repeats like a ghost in my mind, so confident and sure as he spoke back then. "It's just post-natal depression, my dear. It's just the baby blues. You'll get over it." Then Donald, trying to cheer me up, suggested, "Join an art class. You always liked painting." Nothing changes after all.

That first therapist, those ten long years ago, imagined I could paint my feelings and reveal their secrets on paper. I can't remember if I did, and I'm not sure I want to find out.

Crayoning Between the Lines

Chapter 2

Next week, at the community college, I paint a pastoral scene with farmhouse, fields and trees, a fence, a river, hills, the sun, and forests of endless green. There's too much detail in it, I know, but the images flood my mind and demand escape.

An azure sky with wispy clouds bids welcome, but it needs some depth. I touch my paintbrush lightly into black; add siding's shades of night and gray to white-washed farmhouse walls, and tint those windows red as evening falls. I need to paint the night-life too, dark creatures, glowing eyes... But soon my river flows too thickly like a trail of death and tears, until my picture's lamp-less. Broken town surrounds a dark canal in brick-red shades, grown thick as treacle beneath a starless sky.

"Not quite your thing, pastoral scenes?" asks the art teacher mildly. I smile. "I'm guessing you must have grown up in a busy city."

I didn't though.

The paper's brittle and cream with age, tea-stained around the edges, crumpled with dirt along a fold. A square of white, thickly outlined in gray, sits proudly over a field of crayoned green. The sky's blue stripe adorns the top of the page with a tennis ball sun, spiral-patterned where the crayoned yellow circle escaped its lines. Brown and white rectangles stand with jagged edges almost vertical, a fence made out of broken trees across the bottom of the page. Behind its bars, or between, an odd-shaped lump of blue balances on blobs of wobbly black. It's probably Grandpa's truck. A black lump next to it trails long straggly legs, looking for all the world like a giant spider.

We lived on Granny and Grandpa's farm when I was small, sharing their home until our own house was built. Grandpa was some kind of authority in town and owned lots of land all around. I've heard they thought of incorporating once and calling the subdivision after him, though with Grandpa preaching so much I used to imagine we were named Steepleton because of the steeple that stood on the white church's roof.

Jason Steepleton the Second was Grandpa's name, and his farmhouse glowed with an appropriately faded aristocracy—all white-planked walls, purple wisteria, dark windows, and painted doors in fields of green. It's all gone now of course, built over with matching boxes for matchbox families and cars. But the Steepleton place was a pretty big deal back then, dominating the skyline on its miniature hill, dark forest behind and blue skies overhead, gravel roadway winding under trees to the secret place where seasonal laborers lived. Grandpa was important, the son of an important man. My dad, *Jason Steepleton the Third*, could never quite live up to him. And my big brother's just a washed-out replica at number four.

Me, I was the little kid warily eying the woodheap in a corner of the yard, wondering what creatures hid inside. We had to pass it every day on the way in and out the house. I always imagined *something* was staring at me, though it was harmless of course—just a pile of ragged logs and planks stacked high against the fence near the old outhouse. In shadows or under clouds it seemed to grow, like a monster ready to pounce. Wind roared between its timbers. Then I'd crouch and hide, or take a flying leap to run inside. The lumber smelled alive to me, a cloying scent of dampness and rot overlaying green growing things. Bark dust crumpling like smoke in the sun left a sour taste in the air. Wood shavings dripped into crevices where snakes and spiders hid. Clouds of insects danced in spring.

"Silly Sissy," my big sister said, dragging me away as I stared, nervously entranced, at the wood and flies.

"Nothing to be scared of," said Daddy with a comforting hand at my back. "Hurry along."

Then Grandpa added, "Ah, the tales it could tell," fueling my imagination with visions of sermons and hell.

Grandpa was a real old-fashioned preacher-man. His voice was kind and quiet around the house, subdued and dusky like furniture waiting for Granny to polish it. But in church he put on a whole new persona as he donned his thick black robes. Fox-red hairs stuck out around his head making a halo in the sun. His arms would weave so his wide sleeves flapped like raven wings. And his voice would flow like a torrent. Thundering waterfalls of words, rich and dangerous, carried rocks and debris from Noah's flood. Death, sin, divide, conquer and save; the sermon would rise to a furious crescendo of sound. Then Grandpa would drip some final message into silence; awe and wonder magically turned into wisdom, and wisdom to joy.

One Sunday I decided I was tired of being Lydia's *Silly Sissy*. I wanted to be brave like the heroes in church, or failing that, at least make believe I had a chance to be brave. I steeled myself all through the layers of breakfast, greasy bacon, pancakes, syrup and milk. Then I slipped unseen to hide by the front door while everyone else finished their meals. I was determined to be bold and sure, grown up, and silly no more.

Fastening buttons and ties on my coat with perfectly deliberate precision, biting my tongue, biting my fingernails too, and stretching for the doorknob, I crept outside. It was Whit Sunday of course—I had to choose a special day for my big adventure, not just a regular Sunday of food and church. But perhaps it was Whitsuntide's promise of renewal that gave me strength.

The woodpile crouched, pale and ghostly in the early morning light. Gravel crunched under my feet, but I hoped the air's heavy weight might quench its sound and keep my enemy asleep. Then I stood, hands resting on white-clad—Whitsun-clad—hips in defiance, watching my nemesis, viewing the puff of rising air that symbolized devil's breath. The wood-pile's dragon taunted me while a ray of sunshine, arrow straight and shining, became my golden rocket pointing the way to victory.

Cold wood shifted and grated as I started my climb. Wood-fibers etched my palms. I twisted my fingers into claws while gritty splinters slid beneath my nails. Then I slipped and bent my knees to clasp the slope. I wanted to grip with my feet, but they flopped like useless lumps encased in foolishly shiny footwear, the pure white of my Whitsun attire getting lost under scratches and grime. My knees began to shake.

Big brother and sister were ready for church and came outside to wait while Daddy brought the car. They watched and whispered behind me, loud and proud, "Why's she always so naughty?" Perhaps they thought I couldn't hear. "She'll make us late."

Then the woodheap uttered a startled screeching cry and began to fall.

I hate that feeling of the ground giving way beneath me, like standing on top of a ladder in a dream while the steps turn into a slide, or looking at a painting I've finished and it's nothing like the picture I had in mind. My fingers shake and my stomach feels hollow again.

Logs tumbled while I sank and drowned in the mess. Splinters and snakes slipped under my skin. Dust rose in clouds while shuddering sounds fell to earth in a broken heap. And I hurt, body and soul, feeling betrayed by fate in my moment of earnest triumph. I lifted my voice in a helpless wail.

"Why's she so naughty?" Jason repeated at me, and, "Serves her right I guess."

"Silly Sissy," Lydia replied.

Mom came out and shouted about the mess and *did I know what time it was* and *why did I do these things*, but I didn't care. I just wanted to disappear, not be there anymore, not be anywhere. Then I heard the car halt on gravel, and listened to Daddy's footsteps as he climbed out. His voice was soothing balm to my bruises and cuts, like Granny mending me. His feet picked their way through the ruined heap, and his strong arms lifted me up.

"It's alright, little girl. Daddy's got you now. You're safe."

I snuggled deep into the smell of his shirt, feeling small as a babe and precious as a first-born son.

Mom snatched me away of course, cold air whooshing past my suddenly burning ears. She swept me back into the house and upstairs to change. I wanted my daddy and reached back over her shoulders to beg for him. But he was carefully buttoning his Sunday jacket over wood stains on his shirt.

Blood pricked my knees and Mom wiped it roughly away. Her lips made a bloodless line like a scar across her face. She pulled my dirt-soiled clothes off me, tutting at tears in the fabric, tucking broken threads back into hems and buffing the stains on my shoes with the palms of her hands. Luckily last year's red party dress was long enough to cover the signs of my crime. Mom tugged it over my head and I glanced in the mirror to be sure; a little torn, a little faded, but otherwise okay for the Whitsuntide parade. I wore tears on my face, and added to them all the while in the back seat of the car. Mom told me stingingly to *bee-have* and I ignored her.

Then we arrived. My sorrows dried and my bad mood vanished in the tune of the band's proud music. My feet bounced to joy of the dance, scuffed shoes and all. Then I pranced, head held high, along streets and up the long church aisle all the way to our family's bench, proudly forgetting my sin until Grandpa's sharp eyes turned to me. Then I dearly wished I could disappear again.

"Don't you have *any* of your new clothes on?" Granny asked when we got home afterward. Her voice sounded sad and she shook her short black curls too close to my face. I pushed her away, struggling to breathe in the thickening air of her powder. But I was still wearing one new item of clothing, so I pulled my skirt up high over my head to display the frilly underwear, forgetting broken scabs on my knees and streaks of blood still sticking to my legs. Big sister Lydia gasped in her sweet superiority, while Mom complained patiently, "Sylvia, my dear, we don't go showing people our underthings." Then Jason laughed in that odd, silent way he had, shoulders shuddering, face chiseled in stone. Granny spluttered indignantly, and Grandpa said I was a *tyke*.

Chapter 3

I liked being my Grandpa's *tyke*. It meant he'd excused my latest crime, and now I could move on. It felt like the name of freedom, forgiveness and hope. So when Donald brought a dog home as a surprise gift for the boys, a few years ago, I took one look at its leakage in the box, forgave it, let it out, and called it Tyke. He's a black-haired Labrador tyke, and belongs to the boys of course, but he thinks he's mine, which suits me perfectly fine. And he cries when I leave him behind.

Today he's probably crying at home as I paint a face like a bull's in the center of the canvas. Red eyes are rimmed with halos of black, and a russet ring glows darkly under yellowish horns. Billows of thick gray smoke obscure the rest of its features. Maybe it's just a red-eyed man in a hat, not an animal at all. I try to thicken the fog into the shape of a body but find I've slashed diagonal lines across in red and black, dividing my painted page into triangular rage.

"Bull in a china shop," says the art teacher, dripping his fake admiration. "Very effective, Sylvia. Lots of emotion too. A powerful piece, I'd say." He clasps his hands in front of his chest and bobs up and down as if praying. But of course, community college teachers are bound by contract to sound empowering.

I'd say my picture was rubbish, but I don't. I'm practicing a *gentler internal dialog* as ordered by my therapist. I don't even know why I've painted a bull anyway—I was planning to paint Tyke, the way he stared from the bedroom doorway at childhood's pictures strewn across the floor, the way his eyes seemed to see much more, and he lifted a paw in the air as if to bless me. I showed him my first crayoned picture of a bull, and he almost smiled.

Sticky blobs of brown crayon fill the center of the page—some kind of face I think as I turn the paper over and around in my hands. The image falls into place at last with a stripe of thick blue sky at the top, mirrored in green down below. The biggest blob is a bull's proud head adorned with yellow horns like broken moons. Blue eyes shine underneath—I guess I thought all eyes were blue, pale windows open to reflect the sky. Four black legs hang at the sides of my bull-brown lump, matchstick straight, with none of them quite reaching the ground's emerald stripe.

A two-legged, red-topped figure floats in the air beside the bull. It's very small, could perhaps be a flower, but I think it's my Grandpa showing me around the farm.

Grandpa was good at forgiving. He even preached about it. And being his tyke was much more fun than being Jason and Lydia's all too tiny *Silly Sissy*. *Tyking* was far less pointless than following my siblings into Granny's red parlor to play *Chutes and Ladders*, then hearing them scold me bitterly, "Shoo, Silly Sissy. There's only room for two."

At nearly four, going on more, with my brother and sister in school all day and no houses or families nearby, I really needed somebody to play with. Lots of children ran through the trees of course, in summer anyway, but they were farm laborers' kids, brown-skinned and black, and a Steepleton child mustn't mix with *the likes of them*. Granny and Mom might walk out bearing leftover food. They'd share odd words with the children's mysterious mothers, but I stayed inside. Not our type, not our color, they were offspring of temporary strangers, almost as scary as the beast that lurked in the woodpile.

So I walked alone around the farmhouse, measuring my domain with baby steps, making friends with wall-paper patterns on the walls, inventing magical castles under tables, and keeping watch for monsters hidden in closets. I gazed longingly at my siblings' books on their shelves, knowing I mustn't get them down or I'd be told I couldn't read. Lydia's gorgeous chest of art supplies tempted me, but my sister had already announced, "You're far too young to draw." Boxes of games enticed me with bright colors, pictures of models and wonderful scenes all painted on their sides, but I didn't dare touch.

My travels always ended at the kitchen where I'd watch Granny and Mom, their sharp needles mending, warm tongues wagging, clever hands reaching for hot dishes fresh from the stove—"Careful Sylvia. You'll hurt yourself." Then Grandpa would stroll in, carrying with him the warmth of the great outdoors, that slightly dangerous scent of murk and earth, and the twinkle of laughter in his eyes. And he'd say I was a tyke.

"Tykes don't sit around the house, Sylvia. They go out and do things."

Grandpa's hands would grab me under my arms, and he'd swing me high until the ceiling felt close enough to touch. I'd pretend I was an eagle looking down on the mussed up nest of his thick red hair. He made me big and powerful, strong enough to face the world and win, or even to sneak out of doors once in a while to challenge the woodpile.

I didn't climb the woodpile anymore of course—I'd learned that lesson—but I was allowed to climb and stand on fences and the gate. At that magical time in the late afternoon when Daddy was due home from work, when excitement thrilled the air, I'd fill my nose with the scent of dinner's *almost there,* and be on my way. The front door handle was too high to reach without jumping, but I'd pull it down, then lean my weight on my heels as I slid through the gap. Barefoot, I skipped alongside the gravel path, feeling grass and mud squish between my toes. At the gate I leaped up eagerly for the bar. With fingers hooked over the top and feet set just right, I could bounce to my heart's content. The wood sagged but was smooth enough not to leave its splinters in me. Meanwhile I picked away scabs from dried out bubbles of blistered paint. Dirt etched its way beneath my nails again. And finally that puff of dust in the distance, thrown up behind the car, would resolve itself into metal and wheels, and I'd shriek in delight, "Look, Daddy's back."

If it wasn't time to wait for Daddy, I'd visit the bull instead, climbing the first two rails of his fence and resting my chin on the top, but only when Grandpa was around to supervise. Mom and Granny said bulls are dangerous.

I liked to watch the ponderous swaying of the old beast's head. His eyes would flicker from me to the sky to the ground. His nose would flare as his mouth solemnly chewed and spat out grass. Warm air rippled above his back, smelling of dung, slightly sweet, mixed with dustings of green. Insects buzzed in fibrous clouds, and I'd laugh when he flicked his tale, a thick brown snake, to brush them away. Sometimes I stared into the bull's warm gaze, hypnotized while I watched small puffs of mist arise from his nose—such a very big nose. I longed to touch those yellow pointed horns though Grandpa said, "Be careful. He can cut you with them." And I wondered if the brown smeared on their ragged tips was blood. I wished I could stroke the dangling thing beneath the bull's swollen belly. I wanted to reach for the shape of its ancient tennis balls. "Ah, he's old," Grandpa said, following my gaze. "He was a terror in his day. Serviced the herd like a hero, that old bull." Then I wondered what *services* in church had to do with an ancient bull and a field full of cows but decided not to ask.

The bull followed me with stiff-legged gait while I wandered around his fence. His eyes, brown eyes, not blue after all, were wary, hints of red and madness in them. With twin dagger-horns I imagined him a native warrior, guarding his fort. Then Grandpa would tell me the world is God's fortress and we're all God's warriors, even Jason and Lydia.

The bull never charged after me of course, but he stared at me, watching suspiciously, making quite sure I understood that bulls should be taken seriously. Nobody ever told the bull what to do. Nobody laughed at the bull, not even Jason and Lydia. The bull was my friend and my guardian angel demon, a little scary like brother and sister, a little aloof like Grandpa, but happy enough to let me stick around.

Mom said I was like a bull in a china shop, but I didn't hear her right. I imagined my bull's thick legs and feet, stomping on dinner plates, *chopping* china like grass.

Chapter 4

This picture looks like some kind of five-barred gate. White crayon is striped over tangles of green, with squiggles above that might be leaves on the trees. And the sky—I was so proud of my skies by then; I'd learned there isn't really a streak of blue overhead, so I covered the paper with crayon right down to the ground and beyond, blue on blue, into the thick blue stream behind Grandpa's barn. Blue water meets blue heavens in a smooth blue band, as if I was trying to figure out how to keep them apart.

Later I learned the sky's not blue at all, just a bluish shade of gray. And water's not a reflection. It has thoughts all its own.

"You can't let her wander out there on her own. It's not safe!" *Not safe, not safe.* I hear my mother's worry in memory.

Jason and Lydia had just got home from school, bike-bells shattering the afternoon peace, and gravel clattering from beneath their wheels. Metal clunked as they threw their trusty steeds down by the gate; Jason's tall, chunky and black, Lydia's childish and red. Then I, the too-young-for-school *Silly Sissy*, ran from the bull's square patchwork field to meet them. Grandpa strolled behind, while Mom stepped out from the doorway to block our path.

"I wasn't near the bull," I complained, ducking under Mom's arm behind Jason and Lydia. I dodged into the hall and wondered if perhaps I'd get to play *Chutes and Ladders* today after all.

Grandpa didn't escape so easily. Mom rounded on him as he walked into the house. Words spilled out although I couldn't catch their meaning, something about children and safety and never and no, as if the world outside might lose me and the old bull bury me.

"Nothing untoward," Grandpa muttered grumpily, stomping muddy feet on the doormat and lifting his eyes to solemnly wink at me.

I scrubbed my feet on the carpet, hoping they wouldn't leave a mark. When I looked back, Grandpa had his head bent low. He stooped so he seemed no taller than Mom, back bowed under an imaginary load. Sunlight glinted in the shadows of his hair, turning its brownish red into an autumn glow.

"Nothing's going to hurt that little one, Savannah. The bull's too old. Past it. You worry too much."

I could see Mom wasn't satisfied. She blocked the hall with arms akimbo, hair like a yellow halo in the afternoon sun. Her hands were planted firmly around the waist of her summer-blue skirt. "It's a bull, Jason," she intoned, each word a solitary bullet shot from her mouth. Maybe she said "It's not the bull," or "It's bull." I'm not sure, though I tried hard to listen. "I want her protected. I want her safe." I should have been pleased, but Mom said she wanted all of us safe and there was too much to think about or too much out there to hurt us, or something like that, and I felt confused, tied up in her words. "For heaven's sake, I can't watch them all the time. We need a home of our own."

I slunk away down the hall.

"You can't hide her away from everything." "She's not a baby you know." "She's got to learn." "She's a child."

I didn't care.

Well, I cared about the child bit I guess. Being a *child* was fields and forests better than being a baby. Maybe little sisters who are *children*, not babies, just might be allowed to play at *Chutes and Ladders*. So I bent my ear for my brother's and sister's voices to gauge their mood.

Gentle murmuring drifted from the parlor, Jason and Lydia's usual hiding place. The door stood ajar, letting the room's pale light drift dustily into the hall. "She's not," I heard Jason muttering, while Lydia's high voice answered quickly, "Of course." *Not what, and who*? Were they talking about me?

I pushed the door, and stepped across the threshold of a picture book.

Granny's parlor was curtained in thick red brocade. Sunlight slipped through the dusty window like weak blackcurrant juice, dripping over tables and chairs onto the floor. My brother and sister smiled brightly at each other from matching faces with shining teeth and eyes. Lydia lay on her stomach, draped over the plummy purple rug. Her feet waved in the air, with clean white socks encased in smooth black shoes. She rested her pointed chin on cupped hands, elbows digging into the carpet, while gossamer hair spilled like silk over her shoulders. Then she turned to look at me.

"Out, Sissy!" she spat through thin lips twisting from smiling to fury in a moment. "You can't play here."

Why not? They were playing. They were children and I was a child. My mommy just said so.

Jason faced Lydia across a *Monopoly* board. Cross-legged, he angled his knobby knees out to the side. Gray pants stretched tight beneath a sagging white shirt. Neat buttons marched to his tie, and his head bobbed restlessly on top. Bright eyes wavered wetly behind wire-framed glasses while his fingers plucked threads away from a buttonhole, pulling, twisting, winding. He'd tear the button off.

"You need to go now, Sis," he said quietly, insisting on adding an explanation as if to comfort me. "We're playing a game, see, and you know you can't join in." Dear serious brother.

Why couldn't I play? Why didn't I ask them why? Why didn't I ask my mom to make them let me join their game? But Granny would call her away to the kitchen, she'd run, and they'd kick me out again, so what was the point?

The game board lay between my siblings, its checkered squares surrounded with bright-colored cards. Dice squatted enticingly in the middle. Silver models stood nicely centered in place. I knew you could play *Monopoly* with three people, even four or five, but not with me. The piles of pastel money reminded me I was too young to count. Stacks of cards pointed out that I couldn't read. Glaring eyes and red-flushed cheeks declared I wasn't wanted. Lydia's glaring eyes; Jason just looked sad, like he always did.

They used to ask all the time, why was I so naughty, but what else should I be if I couldn't belong? And now I would *naughtily* wander the house in search of secret places where I wasn't meant to go.

I stared through the hall's gray gloom with watering eyes. A curious scent in the dust drew me to a door. Tight closed, it hid Granny and Grandpa's private room, the place where they slept. I chewed my lower lip in determination and turned the handle, sneaking inside with rebellion guiding my feet. Then I stood on Granny's flower-patterned rug, gazing around at spider-web lace, pink cushions scented with soap, pink powders exuding the sunshine of Granny's perfume. The air was quiet and still. The bull lowed achingly somewhere beyond the window. Birds sang and their twittering sipped like water on glass. Then the door handle clicked.

"Sylvia. What are you doing here?" Grandpa's voice trickled deeply like the stream, not angry, not sad, not preacherly, but strange.

"I just…"

"You're not meant to be in here."

"I know. I'm sorry Grandpa." The sudden depth of his voice had frozen me in place.

I felt the air slide past my cheeks as Grandpa walked to the bed. Springs creaked their protest when he lowered his weight to sit on the brocaded cover. Then he opened his arms and I ran, eager to feel the comfort of his welcome and forgiveness. At least one person wanted me around. Strong hands tugged me up and positioned me safe in Grandpa's lap, legs dangling either side of his knee, my face pressed to his chest until I leaned back to stare into his smile. Grandpa's leg felt bonier than I'd expected, not soft and smooth like Mom's. Still, I swung my feet as if I were riding the bull.

"Poor little thing." Grandpa's face loomed close, his warm breath blowing the scent of grass into my mouth. Red-gray hair shone in the pale pink light around ruddy cheeks, blue-gray eyes, and bright white smile. "Everyone sending you away, are they? Not letting you play with them?" Grandpa's fingers played with my hair then stroked my cheeks and danced along my arms. Meanwhile I nodded, sucking my lower lip, feeling goose bumps and not quite sure yet if I was in trouble.

We stayed still for a while, except for Grandpa's fingers trailing circles around my elbows. Then I started to squirm, afraid his steady breathing and the rocking of his knee would send me to sleep. His eyes looked heavy, lids drooping like the downward curve of his mouth.

"Ah well, never you mind." Grandpa sighed then slid me down to the floor, helping me adjust my skirt and heaving himself to his feet. "Let's go help Granny in the kitchen shall we? She might let us bake a cake. Will that make you feel better?"

"Yes Grandpa. I guess."

Chapter 5

A gray snake curls at the side of the page but I think it's meant to be a road. It swirls lazily through fields of green under endless cloudy skies. Near the middle of the page, a square gray box reflects the same dull shade, its boundaries marked with smears of thick red lines. Black windows hold burry specks of pink, like faces peering out to see the world. Smoke rises from a small square chimney on the roof, its plume paralleling the journey of the road as it too crawls off the page.

A pink fence decorates the grass at the bottom of this picture—perhaps I couldn't find white crayons this time, or maybe I'd soiled them coloring over red. The brown blob off to one side might be the bull. Next to it, a family of seven stands proudly arranged. Mother and father are recognizable by the yellow of Mom's long hair and Daddy's gray. We three children look like a set of jugs, tall, middle-sized and small, all yellow-headed with bright red smiles, though my hair should have been much darker than my siblings'. Black-haired Granny forms a tiny figure next to an enormous Grandpa topped in red. Granny's curls are like a darker version of the scribbling smoke from the chimney, but Grandpa's hair is a halo. He stands guard, brown as the watching bull, arms akimbo like a broken triangle. My first family portrait I guess.

We made pastry, not cake, those days when we raided the kitchen to bake together. Grandpa let me turn lumps of dough into models before he baked them. I molded a bull from washed-out edible clay, loving the cool clean dampness of uncooked pastry against my palms, soft with the sheen of oil squeezing over my fingers. Then Grandpa squashed all the pastry together in a ball, patted it flat and let me paint oozing layers of strawberry jam. Next, my sweet sticky fingers rolled our platter into a sausage. Grandpa wielded a triangular knife, slicing pinwheels and laying them flat on a black tin plate to go into the oven. Sweet scents filled the kitchen and house as we watched the clock hands turn. Then we pulled out the tray, spread cakes onto plates, and smothered them all in sugar, while the honeyed air grew cloudy with white powdered snow.

"And what do you think you're doing?" Granny asked, coming in from the yard where she'd been digging vegetables.

"Making cake, Granny."

"Making a mess. Shoo. Get out of here."

Soon the house smelled of dinner, rich with the brown scents of meat and gravy, and bright with fresh vegetables. Grandpa retired to his office where yellow lamps illuminated sheaves of papers on the big wooden desk. I knew I mustn't follow. Lydia and Jason were playing in the parlor still, while Mom hummed in her bedroom, another place small children like me shouldn't enter. I drifted along the corridor with the dust and slipped upstairs.

We children slept in one long room under the eaves of the farmhouse. It looked like a bedroom made for Goldilocks' bears. Three beds stood in a row against the sloping roof. A small round window at the top of the stairs looked out over forest, fields and fence, the yellow barn and the big brown bull. I stood on Jason's bed, resting my hand on the windowsill, and trying to make out the flies buzzing around the bull's head. His feet pawed the ground, and I wondered if he missed me. Workmen tussled with hay at the door to the barn, yellow paint and yellow nature fighting for dominance. I knew the workmen would be shouting but I couldn't hear the words. Manuel was my favorite I thought, because I liked his smile. But another called José played guitar. And others, with even more exotic names, sang songs, wore bright colored clothes, and danced all night. I watched them shovel feed up onto a pile. Then

Grandpa, who must have gone out again, drove his tractor along to help them, and I turned away.

I had to scramble over Jason's bed to get into the rest of the room. Toys lay strewn across the floor—mostly mine—and games were stacked in their boxes on the shelf. Clothes hung from pegs, the room too awkwardly shaped to house a closet. And the floor beneath was carpeted in red. We each had separate rugs next to our beds, Jason's blue, Lydia's pink and mine green, while metal bedheads promised magical rides to mystery. I imagined the rugs like flying carpets, Jason's carefully tuned to fly over water, Lydia's over fire and mine over land.

My bed occupied the shadowed spot in the middle of the row, where sunlight never dallied. And Lydia's was pressed against the far wall. I climbed on her covers so I could kneel at the other round window and watch for Daddy's car. Fields spread out below me, green and gray and brown. Beyond them the patchy darkness of Paradise Forest hovered like a green mist over the town. As I watched, a cloud detached itself, small and determined, kicking up gravel and stones. Daddy was coming home.

"Daddy!" I shouted, bouncing off the bed, sending covers sliding to the floor. I rushed downstairs, forgetting, as always, that Lydia would see the mess and know who to blame. My feet thundered, even without shoes, clattering and banging while flailing elbows hammered against the wall.

Outside, Daddy's engine rattled its distinctive sound in the yard. I'd not even reached the door. No standing on the rotten gate to wait for him today. "Daddy, Daddy, Daddy!" I shrieked, struggling to push my way outside, then throwing my four-year-old self at his legs as he staggered along the path. Gravel crunched and cut my flying feet. Green grass scents blew thickly around my nose. Granny's flowers bloomed, winter pansies in the rain and cold, or golden sunflowers under summer's glow. Then Daddy hugged me in this, my one bright moment of his undivided love. Afterward he strode ahead of me to the door and I stared at his back. My feet stung and my eyes filled with longing while I listened to the bull's siren song.

Daddy's home. No one could call me *Silly Sissy* now or cut me out of their games, because Daddy wouldn't let them.

Chapter 6

*R*ed crayon swirls in the center of the page with yellow and orange ripples shading to black. Thick gray smoke pours up into a rich blue sky, while triangular flames shine bright as Christmas tree lights. The green earth below is muddy where crayons have mixed—all colors merging eventually to gray.

The mysterious José played his guitar in the barn. Trilling rivers of music poured out, that long hot afternoon at the end of summer. The grass was tinder-dry, and Grandpa had been watching out for fires, rushing with water to every faintest wispy sign of smoke. The air was leaden, heavy as an overcoat.

Five years old by then, I was a student in kindergarten and proud to go to school each morning, returning for lunch when Mom brought me back home in her clunky blue car. She sat in the kitchen now with Granny and Grandpa drinking tea from chipped mugs. "Should rain soon," said Grandpa lugubriously. "We need the rain."

"For the crops?" Mom asked. I could see she was trying to sound like she understood, picking at threads in her placemat while she talked, like Jason picking at his clothes.

"For the grass-fires." Grandpa snorted the way my brother and sister always did at me. "Don't want to see anyone burned out of their homes, do we?"

I sneaked away, hoping everyone thought I was playing upstairs in our room. But I'd gone outside again—Tyke Sylvia on the prowl. The bull munched grass, the noise of his teeth like the churn of a washing machine, and he looked up at me. White crescents showed wetly below the infinite brown of his liquid eyes, but he wasn't concerned. Neither was I. I sat atop the rickety fence, swinging legs that had grown perceptibly longer, humming contented replies to the buzzing flies. Sunshine grazed the back of my head. Cows lowed gentle music in a distant choir. And José, behind me in the barn, strummed his guitar.

A crackling background sound distracted me. It rattled somehow out of tune, out of synch with the musical rhythm of the lazy afternoon. Perhaps the bull was munching a twig or a stone. It spoiled the song though, making my mood swing wildly like his snaking tail. Happy sunshine, tasting of honey, was soured by the splintering memory I shouldn't be out here.

I shut my eyes to fume in bitter frustration while the crackling drew closer. Why shouldn't I sit on the fence by the bull? Why shouldn't I play outside on my own? Why shouldn't I listen to laborers sing in the barn? Why couldn't I join in? Acid rebellion tensed my muscles, unsettling my balance on the fence's beam, while music called with its gently soothing distraction, yellow paint poured over brown, enticing me down. *Come now. Come around. Come join in the sound. Come sing with the music and dance.*

Yes, I would sing and dance!

I filled my lungs with a rich deep draught of air. Surprisingly hot and gritty, it made me cough, but I ignored the taste. Jumping down to the ground in defiance, I headed away from the bull toward the barn's forbidden territory. Dry dirt puffed from my footsteps, while hair blew into my eyes, stinging like knives. Feathered fronds of grass tickled my legs and knees, all the way to my underwear, and rich cow dung blew smoke to fill my nose. Except cow dung doesn't really smell like smoke, and the soured air was making me cry.

I thought at first I just felt guilty for going where I shouldn't go. Crying before the crime might be a sign of growing up. So I turned back to the bull as if to ask his permission. But instead of finding comfort in my friend's unchanging presence, I heard his feet stomp restlessly, in time with his bellowing roar. The fence had disappeared in a smoky haze. Dust poured in furious clouds around the bull's stout body, making a halo of red churned with yellow and gray. Sharp horns pointed toward me, angled like swords, ready to probe and rip and tear me in two. My bull, my friend, pawed the ground again and gazed from reddened eyes. Smoke poured from his nose, completing his disguise as a monster even fiercer than the woodpile's demon. And his dragon roar set the afternoon alight.

Hooved feet thudded and scraped in front of me, and I froze, unable to move, so I couldn't escape. My bull was going to charge through the fence, I thought, through the gate, and run me down. My bull, my protector, my friend was betraying me! I screamed "Help!" and turned my shoulders away so I wouldn't have to see.

Of course, the bull was pawing the ground in fear, not anger or threat. If I'd looked properly I'd have seen red flames behind it, flickering in the trees. I'd have heard the engine roar of fire's approach. But, *Silly Sissy*, I was too involved in my own explanation. The danger was real. It just wasn't the old bull's fault, or mine.

José and Miguel raced out from the barn, shirts unfastened, dark hair damp, brown skin gleaming with the curls of black on their chests. I thought they'd rescue me like surrogate fathers, parents of brown-skinned children. I lifted my arms so they could sweep me high and carry me off on valiant shoulders. I'd be the barnyard princess, queen of the farm. But I still hadn't seen, still thought the bull was the only threat, and me the only one who might get hurt. Angry at the crackling sound's distraction, innocently blaming my friend with his snaking tail and looming horns, I was too young and I simply didn't know.

"Fire!" A blur of farmhands surrounded me now, all ignoring me. No princess after all, I trembled, lost and lonely, in their wake and turned away, invisible.

Black clouds had gathered in front of the flames in the trees. I struggled to see through tears that bit my eyes and watered my cheeks. I wandered to the bull's dark fence, ignoring the fact that I was walking toward the fire. I recognized he was still my friend, and I wanted to comfort the foreign fear in his eyes. I climbed warily, watching the smoke for signs of the fire's approach, watching the bull for the flame of his curious desires. But he stood still, improbably, like a statue with his head oddly tilted, staring down at the ground. Poor thing. He'd never meant to frighten me.

Men rushed past carrying hoses and pumps, turning aside around the fence as they rushed to the tree-line beyond. Buckets of sand flew like clouds in the air while other workmen hurried back into the barn. Farmhands passed huge water jugs hand over hand along a line. Miguel ran back and forth, taking command until Grandpa took over from him. I saw it all like a movie, black and white and gray, and imagined I heard the voiceover say, "But all was saved."

Our fire wasn't big as grass-fires go, and the flames were soon defeated. But I stayed behind to stare at my bull, offender, defender, friend and betrayer together. A patch of color in the grass by his hooves still demanded his attention. Then I watched it grow legs and a tail; a farmyard cat, hiding near the bull's sweet benevolence, arching its back in thanks before heading for the barn.

Afterward I'd tell my brother and sister how flames reached the sky and were tall as a house, how smoke made the air turn black, and rivers of lava flowed from our small-town volcano. They didn't want to hear me, so I crayoned a swirling picture of it for them. They believed me even less.

When everything was quiet, the farmhands went home, back to their hidden cottages under trees beyond the barn. Guitars and music were forgotten unless they played in private to their dark-skinned dark-haired wives and dancing children. I watched them leave and wished they'd play for me. I could dance. I could eat at their tables, and watch them button shirts over sun-browned chests. I dreamed princes and crowns, but they weren't our kind of people, though Grandpa told me we're all princes and princesses in heaven.

"Even the bull?"

"I'm not sure bulls go to heaven."

"Then where do they go?"

When Grandpa didn't answer, I imagined the other place, hell, filled with fire-breathing yellow-horned bulls, all pawing the earth and gazing through maddened red eyes, and I felt sad. I really wanted my bull to live forever in heaven with me, or else on earth. When you're small they're kind of both the same.

The excitement was well and truly over, except for the scent of dirt and smoke in the air. Jason and Lydia already knew I was simply telling stories—they hadn't been there. With hardly any fire damage there could surely have been no danger, so Mom said to Daddy. But I closed my eyes and saw the bull still watching, pawing the ground, with smoke on his horns. Grandpa said scornfully, "What do you know about it, sweet town-girl Savannah? Fire could have took it all. Where would you be then?" He harrumphed bitterly. "You and your *waiting for a house of your very own to live in.*" Then Mum pulled threads from the cuff of her blouse as she sat down.

Hot meat, hot vegetables and mashed potatoes, all were served on china plates when we ate our dinner that night, as if the fire had rendered mealtime precious in its demise. Grandpa said grace, thanking God that the grassfire was so quickly and cleanly extinguished. Lydia and Jason tittered foolishly and I smiled behind my hands. I knew more than they. But Grandpa didn't thank God for how cleverly I'd saved the world by shouting out for help. He praised Granny's cooking but not my efforts with pinwheel pastries, red-striped, nicely stacked on a tray to be served for our dessert. He said he was glad we had enough money to pay for laborers' wages and food to eat. And he hoped we'd all be well-behaved, giving honor to fathers in heaven and on earth, forever *Amen.*

As always, I listened carefully to the words, weeding them for traps. I wondered if I was well-behaved and if honor meant children must always do as they're told. Will doing as you're told make you a princess? And why should the poor old bull have to burn in hell? He never meant to hurt me.

Chapter 7

*T*his next picture's drawn on clean-edged pure white paper—I must have made it in kindergarten or school. The image is clearly a cat with long tail arching over its back. Looping curves of its sinuous body contrast with the sharp-edged triangles of its ears. I think the spot of gray in front might be a mouse with its tail trailing behind, cat's paw like a boot held over it. The cat's colored brown, with blobby spots of red and black and yellow. It looks a bit like a leopard rendered cubist style. Blue eyes—I'm not sure why I still thought everyone's eyes were blue—I've drawn them almond-shaped and wide, much too human, with white at the sides, but I was only a child.

I watched through Jason's round window each night as laborers closed up the barn with its huge double doors. And I resolved, if I wasn't allowed there on my own, I'd just have to make Grandpa take me one day. But in the evenings it was always too late, too cold, or too dark. And in the daytime the barn was filled with business and work. "There's too many things going on, Sylvia."

Still I pestered him. "When will you take me?" Until he gave in.

It was the day after the fire. The afternoon sunlight stayed long, but the laborers had been given the day off, and the barn door was closed. Daddy was at work. Mom and Granny were drinking tea in the kitchen from their favorite mugs. And Jason and Lydia were still at school.

Grandpa marched in from outside and announced, "Sylvia, I've got something to show you."

I just knew he had to mean the barn, so I leapt to my feet. It wouldn't have mattered if Mom had told me to stay. I would have run out into the yard with him anyway.

We strolled together, my tiny hand held in Grandpa's sweaty paw. My feet ran at top speed next to his slow steady pace. Then I began to skip, swinging from his arm so I could fly. The air still smelled smoky, as dust and ashes rose like mist from the ground.

Grandpa unlocked a small secret door at the bottom of the barn's wide entrance. His key rattled and scraped before it turned. Then hinges squeaked and we walked through from sunshine to dusty shade. Hay-bales were lit with slats of light coming through long gaps in the wall. Yellow brightness slanted over shadows, like prison bars in reverse, gray and smelling of mold.

"Just give me a moment, Sylvia."

I stood still, awed by the size and the clouded intensity of it. Then I turned to see Grandpa lifting a long heavy beam of wood from the double doors behind us.

"What are you doing Grandpa?"

He leaned forward, pushing and heaving, until the doors began to separate. Sunlight poured in, dispelling shadows, turning dark to light. Strands of straw fluttered golden in the breeze. A spider trembled on its crystalline web. Wooden slats slid and vibrated over stones and grass and hay.

"Look," said Grandpa, turning me back to gaze where the hay-bales lay.

I saw nothing at first except straw and a shaded rack of tools. But Grandpa tugged me forward, further into that forbidden place, whispering urgently, "Come and see." So I came and I saw.

A small brown cat lay nestled in a broken bale of hay. Green eyes glowed ethereally in the dusty light. A delicate pink nose twitched restlessly, heart-shaped and sweet, while tiny ears switched direction from side to side, as if to capture every sound. The long thin body lay sleekly splayed, paws outstretched, stomach flat on the ground like a burst balloon, fur smooth as chocolate. And tiny speckles, like lumps of pastry dough, lay in front of it, some black, some cream, one white. The big cat mewed and shifted its position. Then the dough-lumps moved with it.

"What?" I asked.

Grandpa pointed to a tiny pink nose peeking out beside the cat's fur. The air around us hummed with gentle mewling sounds, while the cat's tail tapped on the floor and feeble paws scrabbled.

"She's got kittens," Grandpa replied.

There were kittens in our barn!

I begged my mom for days to let me keep one but she always said no. Granny insisted, "This house is for people, not animals." So I had to be content with wandering down to the barn with Grandpa each day, avoiding the workmen, watching the kittens grow, and always being careful not to get too close. Grandpa said the mother cat might reject her babies if I touched them, and nobody wants to see small children turned away. But then, just as they got old enough to play with, all the kittens vanished.

"You can't keep wild things inside, Sylvia. They needed their freedom you see," Grandpa explained, tossing an empty sack to the corner of the barn as his wet boots squelched on straw.

"Then where did they go?"

"Somewhere safe."

Lydia said the kittens were dead and I wondered, do cats go to heaven, and red-eyed bulls to hell? But Mom said the cats had all gone back to their dens in the forest or burrows by the creek. I began to dream of being old enough to leave the farm and meet them. Perhaps we'd play together with black-haired black-eyed children under the trees.

It was a pleasant dream, and I really was going to leave the farm soon anyway, just not the way I planned.

Chapter 8

I should call this picture Still life without silverware. A cup, saucer and plate take center stage. They're meticulously outlined though not quite right, while faint ovals are sketched in a curious border around the edge of the page. I think I was trying to learn how to turn circles on their sides. Pink flowers grow around the rim of each china shape, but the perspective's all wrong, as if the pictures are projected on invisible screens. Green leaves grow like vines. A yellow tablecloth hangs in the background, shaped like a jagged diamond, with a hint of rectangular windows and blue sky hiding at the top. There's no drink in the cup, nor food nor crumbs on the plate, and no silverware. And no people, no cats, and no bull.

It's strange how some things look so enormously present when they're not there.

None of this world was ever meant to last. Mom and Daddy were having our new house built on land that used to be part of Grandpa's fields. Not the fields where the bull and cows lived, nor the fields where long grass grew from the mud by the creek, but further away, north of town, near a village called Paradise. I remember Lydia and Jason laughed when Mom told us the name. Daddy smiled and kissed Mom's face, a solemn kiss with his hands pressed next to her nose. He made Paradise sound like heaven.

Daddy drove us out there to look at *how things are going* one weekend. I'd started elementary school by then, not just kindergarten. I was proud of my six long years, and weekends meant significantly more than before. But I didn't know what *things* Daddy was talking about, or where and how they should be. Tucked in the middle of the back seat of our car, with Jason and Lydia wedged tightly on either side, all I knew was we were taking a road trip, and road trips were meant to be fun. If only the siblings would stop pestering me.

Lydia's elbows were almost as sharp and bony as Grandpa's knees, and both my siblings had fingers that pinched my sides like needles. If they'd had horns there'd surely be blood on them. If they had fur it would stand on end while they hissed and spat at me.

The road trip took us through town, past Grandpa's church and the High Street shops, and out into the forest. Those twists and turns under the trees would have made me feel sick, even without Jason and Lydia tumbling on top of me all the time. But we came out into sunshine eventually. I opened my eyes to another tiny church next to a garage and a row of bright-colored shops.

Daddy drove around a corner between brick towers which Mom proclaimed were *the entranceway*. I caught the first letter of Paradise on a sign and felt proud of my skill. But it was hard to see around Jason and Lydia. Scenery flashed by in windows of gray sky, snatches of trees, and patches of shiny brick. Then Daddy swerved onto a muddy verge and the car juddered to a halt. We all piled out.

The air around us was gray with dust and oil. A grid of buildingless squares stretched out across the ground. Gooey mud clung to our shoes, its texture like cowpats, its juices exuding the slightly sweet stench of hay bales and stewed grass. I wondered if Mom would insist we wash our footwear before returning to the car. Then I wondered where we'd find water.

White picket fences bounded the squares of the grid. All clean and rigid, they didn't look at all like Granny and Grandpa's weary rails—more like pictures really.

Of course I simply had to climb the nearest gate. Mom and Daddy shouted that I should get down.

Behind the fence, a hole in the ground was filled with puddles of water like a bathtub when the plug's pulled out. Big brother Jason walked heel to toe around string-bound lines of brick as if measuring them. "He'll do well, that lad," said Daddy with a wide glowing smile. Lydia leaned on the car and drew pictures of how a lonely clump of trees might seem when they were grown, and I kicked stones. Mom found some future neighbors to chat with, everyone studying their own fenced plot of land, everyone dreaming a house that might be better, bigger, taller than everyone else's.

Leaving our car to the dripping rain, we wandered pseudo-streets all crazily bare, with poles sticking out of muddy holes, wires hanging from boxes, red-brick boundaries, and the whole world measured and patchworked into a quilt. A chunk of quarried stone hunkered down at the base of those two towers we'd driven past. They looked smaller now, more like shrunken sheds or the playhouse at school. I spotted the letter *P* for Paradise again but couldn't read the rest, its script too smooth and swirly with loops and lines. Lydia proudly proclaimed, "It says *Paradise Mansions*, you Silly Sissy." So we might live in a mansion one day! Not that Granny and Grandpa's place was small, but I imagined the sort of mansion you see on TV, all white curved staircases with rooms like concert halls, and servants of course. It wasn't what Mom and Daddy had in mind, but they weren't telling us anything.

"Let's make an afternoon of it," Mom said as we wandered back to the car. I wondered how we might make it a morning since we'd set out after lunch. But Lydia shushed me when I tried to ask. I was used to being shushed.

Daddy unlocked the car and grunted as we all piled in. Mom snorted, staring at stinky mud-shod feet. And soon we were heading back toward Paradise, the village, and back toward home. But Daddy's blinkers clicked as they flashed, and gravel sprayed again as Daddy turned the car onto a wide gray parking lot. Lonely and eerily vacant, the gravel expanse occupied a clearing under trees outside the church. This

Church of Paradise seemed an ugly stone-built place, with too-tall twisted tower and too-small windows. I liked Grandpa's little white church, back in town, much better.

Jason and Lydia tumbled from the car like TV characters, all blond hair, bright smiles, and perfect behavior, with clean clothes billowing in the breeze. Even their shoes seemed almost shiny despite the mud. Meanwhile I straggled behind, dark-haired stranger somehow sneaking onto the film set. I scratched lines with my feet in the dirt, dragging wretched heels and toes, leaving trickles of earth behind. When I looked back, a black-robed figure was waving from the church door. "Mom," I said, but everyone ignored me.

Paradise was scarcely even a village back then. A gas station gable hunkered low over squat lumpy tanks up the road from the church. The tiny row of shops hid under matching roofs. White-covered tables decorated the curb outside a red-helmeted restaurant, and rain dripped its puddles down on them. Mom whisked a menu into the air to keep her head dry. Then we staggered through the heavy glass door, setting a distant bell tinkling to announce our presence.

Lydia and Jason marched straight to a table with a view of the street. The rest of us followed and sat down, though the space they'd chosen was too small. Knees and elbows bumped awkwardly, and my precious siblings kept poking their fingers at me to make me squirm. Then a girl with mint-scented gum in her mouth asked what she could get for us. She looked scarcely older than Jason, and wore a nametag that spelled c-a-r, so I giggled and foolishly pointed it out to Lydia who proudly informed me, "Silly Sissy, she's called Carla."

Drinks arrived in thin glasses and white china cups, balanced on a silver tray with a plate of cookies, jug of cream and sugar dish. "Don't break it. Don't spill anything," said Daddy, his hand hovering over mine as I snatched for my snack. Mom stared at me and muttered, "Bull in china shop." I finally figured it out; she meant *shop*, not *chop*.

Daddy repeated his injunction to take care while I tried to bend my fork—well, why not? It was metal. Removing the silverware, he set it beside his plate, his face a mixture of patient amusement and annoyance. Then he asked for a straw so I could drink my soda without holding—without dropping— the glass.

The waitress, C-a-r-l-a, brought straws for everyone, and pointed to a tray of trinkets by the cash machine, "If you want to buy anything..." So Jason and Lydia rushed over, picking up tiny tractors and trailers, hair ribbons, plastic farm animals and rainbow-colored bouncing balls. I would have played with them too, but Mom wasn't letting me out of my seat.

Lydia came back with a hairclip shaped like a sleepy blue cat. Jason didn't want anything, but he'd found a plastic bull for me, so I was happy. Then we finished our snack.

Traffic rumbled while we ate. Water splashed. Machinery grumbled and whirred on the building site. Men in bright yellow hats walked by and whistled through the window, while the waitress preened. Daddy said, "No," when I tried to whistle too.

"When will we move in?" asked Lydia, chasing cookie crumbs with the end of her spoon, while her other hand fingered the hairclip in her hair.

"End of summer," said Daddy. It seemed like an eternity away.

Chapter 9

*T*his one's definitely drawn on school paper, square-edged, thick enough to hold its shape, white enough for the colors to still look bright. It's a picture of a hand but, behind the fingers, the page is filled with pale rectangles, piled and angled like magnetic letters fallen from the fridge and strewn on a gleaming tabletop. Small squares like stamps lurk in the corner of each colored patch, while squiggles of fake cursive writing squirm together in well-measured lines. And then there's the hand, thick, red, and blotchy, covering the center of the page. I probably drew around my own fingers to make its shape, marking the edges with a wide black crayon and filling the center with layers of glue-like red. I'm kind of impressed that I'd finally learned to crayon between the lines. But I'm not sure why the hand should be bright red. Red and black? Perhaps I was angry about something.

Daddy's *end of summer* seemed forever away, until, all too suddenly, it was all too soon. I'd made friends in school by now—real friends, not bulls or cats, or Grandpa or black-haired children disallowed. I even got to visit other people's houses once in a while. I'd learned that plastic plates don't break, that I wasn't too young to play Monopoly after all, and that everyone else's siblings were pains as well. I was growing up, seven years old at last, but I was growing up here, at Granny and Grandpa's house, not somewhere else. I'd managed to forget it was all going to change.

Mom and Daddy started reminding us that we'd be moving soon. "Keep your room tidy. Put your toys in their boxes at night. Pack your clothes in your case." And I hated it. School was so much more fun than home these days, since there I could pretend nothing would change.

One Saturday, Grandpa sat me down at the kitchen table with a box of crayons he'd got me for Christmas—or was it my birthday? Christmas and birthdays came so close together I could never remember which. He set a stack of cards in front of me. They looked the same size as envelopes, not really made for pictures, and my waving hands scattered them across the cloth. Grandpa sighed and gathered them back together.

"What are these for?" I asked.

"For you," he said. "You can crayon a picture for each of your friends on these. Then we'll write your new address on the back. You can even put a pretend stamp in the corner. That way everyone will know where you live when you've moved. You'll be able to keep in touch with all your friends."

I liked the idea of coloring, but couldn't quite understand what Grandpa meant. Wouldn't everyone know where I lived anyway? Didn't grown-ups always know? But Grandpa said, "No. You'll be in a different school after the summer. You won't see these friends every day and, if you don't tell them, they'll never know where you've gone." *Never* sounded like a very long time, and *gone* sounded terribly final.

But Grandpa had to be wrong. He must have mixed me up with Lydia. She was about to start Junior High, so of course she'd go to a different school after summer. But Jason was in high school already. I already knew he wasn't going to change schools. So of course, neither was I.

I still colored my pictures though, since drawing was always fun. I drew a bridge like the one over the creek at the back of the house. I drew a farm, a barn, a bull, a cat, a cow— I'm not sure how many other things, but I filled the back of each of Grandpa's cards with pictures of home, and I had plenty of friends to give them to. When I finished, I colored tiny stamps with numbers and faces on the other side. Then Grandpa helped me write my new address.

Grandpa said I should take the cards to school and hand them to my friends. But I thought I was so much cleverer than he. I wrote my friends' names, oh so carefully—so proud I'd learned my letters and could do it without help. Then I dropped the whole sheaf of pictures into the mailbox at the supermarket.

"What did you do that for, Silly Sissy?" asked Lydia, seeing me waving empty hands while Mom loaded the cart. "You can't send letters."

"Yes I can." I felt proud and pleased with myself. "I'm telling all my friends where I'm going to live."

"But how did you buy stamps?"

"I drew them, Silly."

"Silly sissy."

Lydia had that look on her face, the one that meant she was sure I might understand if I only stopped to think. So I stopped and thought and struggled not to cry.

"Never mind," said Grandpa when I got home. "You can still tell everyone your new address and make sure they remember. You can do it Sylvia." He didn't use his loud church-voice, but he demanded my attention and made me believe him.

I can do it. I can.

I recited my new address endlessly, everywhere I went, "1359 Paradise Mansions, Paradise." I whispered it in my friends' waiting ears until no one would sit near me anymore. I shouted it to mothers as they drove their cars from the curb. I tried to write it down on notebooks and hands, though the wealth of letters and numbers sometimes confused me. I saw it blinking on lighted signs in my sleep.

On my last day at school, Lydia's last day too, we sat on miniature chairs in the hall during an endless *end of year* assembly. Lydia's class was at the back with mine packed nearer the front. A gramophone played music for the graduating seniors. Lydia marched forward with them, hands outstretched for her gift of a small blue dictionary with golden letters on the front. We stood to sing the school song, out of tune. We promised to stay safe. And we marched back to class. No one played music for me or gave me a gift.

"What do you want to do with your final afternoon?" my teacher asked.

Chairs rattled and scraped as everyone scrambled up and ran around the room. Some played Monopoly. Some read books. Others sat and listened to a story. Me, I got the crayons out and made a picture of letters all bearing my address—small rectangles with squares like stamps in their corners and squiggles of writing underneath. I started to cry and the drips made circular splotches on the page so I stuck out my hand. Then I crayoned in black around the shape of my fingers, coloring the middle thickly in bright red crayon, like the bleeding of dreams. Nobody looked at me.

When the bell rang it was time to go home. "Yes Miss, I'll keep safe." I smiled and waved. Then, "No Miss, I won't be here next year." She gave me my picture and said it should remind me of her.

My home with Granny and Grandpa wouldn't be here next year either. I still didn't know how to make any sense of that.

Chapter 10

A black car squats in front of a bright red house under purple sky. A black-haired, pink-faced child stares out from a round yellow window somewhere upstairs. A red-haired man and black-haired woman stand in the open doorway. The car is filled with people.

It's a picture made out of squares, blobs and circles, none of them quite in the place you'd expect them to be. But it's not hard to see what I intended to draw. Without perspective, people's faces stare side by side from windows of the car, two faces in front and two behind. They all have big red smiles, while the people in the house have blue dotted tears like extra eyes. The inside people have mouths set in narrow straight lines, and the pink-faced child upstairs raises thin arms in anger or celebration.

"I don't want to live in a mansion," I shouted, seven years old and futilely furious. I stamped my feet on the dry earth of the path, raising clouds of dust that wreathed my knees. "I'm not going. I won't go."

Lydia was already in the car, staring out the back with a frozen white face. Her only spot of color was the blue cat hairclip over her eye. I thought she must surely be as angry as I. After all, we'd been promised five more weeks at Granny and Grandpa's house to get used to the idea. Now, all of a sudden, we had to leave straightaway for our strange new mansion in Paradise.

"You'll do as you're told, young lady," said Daddy, his voice as deep as the gaping hole in my heart.

I screamed, "I won't go," and flung myself down on the grass, flailing my arms and legs with wild abandon, ignoring the sudden pain of sharp-edged stones on elbows and knees. Daddy reached to pick me up, and I scrambled to my feet, chasing to the bull's white fence in an attempt at escape. Then I was swooped into Daddy's arms, and I forgot I was big, felt just like a toddler again. The woodpile stared at me.

"Why's she always so naughty?" echoed in my ears.

Daddy hugged me, and Mom held me close, but I squirmed valiantly while they maneuvered me, like a badly wrapped parcel, into the car. Lydia's rigid knees dug into my back as I tumbled over her. She grunted and a swift dig from her elbow jammed me down into the space between her and my brother. Then Jason wriggled further away, staring straight ahead, face miserably blank, as if he knew no more about this than I did. Meanwhile Mom climbed silently in at the front, refusing to look at anyone. Daddy gave Granny a brusque and helpless hug and we drove off.

There was no handshake or hug for Grandpa, who stood and watched from the door. And the bull didn't even wave his head or tail to say goodbye. From waking up with five weeks to go, we were gone in the blinking of an eye.

I remember crying nearly all the way to Paradise. Lydia and Jason held their hands over their ears. Mom and Daddy ignored me rigidly. But nobody shouted at me. Somehow that was the most awful part of it. They should at least have told me to be quiet.

Rattling gravel under the car gave way to paved roads' rumble and engine's roar. I recognized the old white church—Grandpa's name on the notice board—he was preaching tonight—but we didn't stop. I wondered if we'd be back there on Sunday, or was our church to be discarded and lost, left behind like the doll I always carried and had somehow mislaid, now we lived somewhere else.

Fields gave way to houses with well-tended yards and footpaths outside. Shops opened their doors. Strangers walked with children in buggies and bags hanging low to the ground. We passed a play area with swings and slide—it looked new, the wood still bright and clean; and I almost stopped crying, just for a moment, imagining how I'd really like to climb—and climb and climb, destroying woodpiles and saying goodbye to my Grandpa and my bull. But Daddy drove on, and on.

The town center bustled with cars and vans lurching out of side streets and stopping in random spaces by the road. Brakes shrieked and Daddy jerked the wheel. In the back, we three flailed wildly from side to side, elbows and knees intertwining, me bawling still. Then we were out in the fields again with thick trees shading the sky while a ribbon of water bubbled and splashed over stones.

At last we passed the dull gray blob of the church of Paradise. The road became dusty with gravel again. Stones rattled against the sides of the car; I wondered if Daddy would shout loudest at me for crying, or at strangers for leaving such a mess on fresh blacktop. I drew my arms and legs closer to my body, trying not to touch, not to annoy Jason and Lydia. Then Daddy swerved and stopped. Mom said, "We're here."

The yard in front of us was a mess of broken bricks and weeds. Dried-up mud marked the pathway to a door—no paving stones. And the *mansion*, our long-promised castle, was just another boring house after all, with brick walls, wood-framed windows square and blind, and a front door painted white. Mom and Daddy grabbed cases from the trunk and marched inside, but we three children stayed wandering over rubble, looking around corners, inspecting bricks, and taking care not to trip. I found a fountain in the back yard but it wasn't working yet. The naked cherub looked ugly and out of proportion with arms outstretched, knees bent and a pile of broken stones under his feet. Behind him sunshine reflected from wide glass doors. When I pressed my nose to the glass, I saw Daddy in our strange new living room, waving out at me. "Come in, Sylvia," he shouted, and the glass rumbled, making his voice sound distant, underwater.

Back at the front of the house, I felt oddly dismayed, exposed to anyone who might pass, though hid from cupid's gaze. The door creaked as I pushed my way inside. Then I crept down a long dark hall, following voices to the kitchen. Perhaps it would all look lighter another morning but, for now, this house felt like eternal night.

Dark wooden cupboards lined the kitchen walls, offset by red counter-tops. Mom emptied a box of food, laying out packets and bottles in complex rows. I watched her for a moment then followed my father's voice to find him in a study just like Grandpa's, an imposing room whose walls were paneled brown and layered with shiny bookshelves waiting to be filled. A gloomy leather-topped desk crouched in the middle of the floor like a giant spider ready to pounce. Behind it an archway led to the dining room where straight-backed chairs stood to attention around a glowing wooden table. I waded across the thick carpet, feeling lost, and trailed my hands from solid wood to the flower-woven tapestry on the sofa's arms. Cupid had his back to me but I waved to him anyway. Then I heard Mom climbing the stairs and I headed after her.

No gorgeous white bannisters here—this house wasn't like a TV mansion at all. My fingers slid on soured cherry rails, and the straight steps released me to a passage that felt so narrow, we kids almost bumped into each other as we went from room to room.

There were five bedrooms upstairs, one for each of us so we wouldn't have to share anymore. "It's time Lydia had her own space," said Daddy, lumbering upstairs behind me. A huge dark frown seemed to carve his face but perhaps it was just shadow. He stepped into each room, plunking suitcases down on new beds with new brown covers. Everything smelled of shops and dust and cleaning stuff.

Lydia's and Jason's rooms looked out over the front of the house. I saw the ribbon of broken road from their windows, the car parked lumpily beside it, a low wall fencing us in with a small wooden gate. Mine and the spare room overlooked the bricks and windows of neighbor's homes—I swore I'd keep my blinds down all the time. But Mom and Daddy's bedroom, with a secret bathroom all its own, looked out over the back yard and fountain and naked cherub. Lucky them.

"Off to your own room now, Sylvia. You know our bedroom's private."

I walked out sullenly and closed the door, then stopped with my ear to its wood. I guessed Mom's tears were private too, and I didn't know why she was crying.

Sitting on my bed, sulkily refusing to unpack my waiting case, I repeated my quiet refrain in desperate undertones. "I don't want to live here. I don't want to live here. I don't...."

"Hush now," said Daddy, swinging my door open wide. "This is your home. Get settled in."

Then Lydia walked past with a sway and a smirk, announcing, "I'm never going back."

I shrank in dismay. *Never* going back to Granny and Grandpa's house! What was wrong with her?

Chapter 11

A stack of crayoned drawings waits to be peeled apart. Each one pulls colors from the last until they lie like fallen leaves on the floor, stained with mud perhaps, or washed away with rain. I remember making these, one after another on the shiny kitchen table, because there was nothing else to do in this place where no one lived but us and nobody knew us. My skies regressed to infantile lines of blue at the top of each page. Circular suns played like a cherub's broken smile underneath. And the story's told.

Three people fill the center of almost every page. They look like a perfect family. No siblings of course, but maybe Mom and Daddy have vanished too. This mommy's head's adorned with tight black curls when my mother's hair was blonde. The father wears a halo colored richly reddish brown. They're not quite Granny and Grandpa either since the mom's dressed in bright red skirts instead of Granny's pastel colors. The father wears Sunday black instead of faded jeans.

The child, always a girl, wears a bright red smile in each of these false images. She's dressed in a triangular skirt and her legs jut out at singularly improbable angles. The background might be a neat white house, a fence, a field full of cows. She's riding a horse in one of the pictures, with surrogate parents looking on. Perhaps it's a bull. And here she chases blobby brown sheep and cows, or cuddles a cat and a doll.

The crayon's thickly layered like glue, childhood anger poured into colors on the page. But I was always careful to keep between the lines.

Mom and Daddy went back to Granny and Grandpa's to pick up Mom's blue car. They didn't offer to take us with them. Jason was left in charge, and I was young enough to ignore him so I sat crayoning at the bright red kitchen table while nobody watched. I remember taking my red crayon out, testing it nervously on the sacred surface, wondering if anyone would see if I scribbled there, then hiding my shame. I pressed my nose to the smooth tabletop before scratching my signature off. It smelled of wax.

Car tires rattled on the gravel drive as Mom and Daddy came back. I didn't rush to meet them, just peered anxiously around the kitchen door, watching what they brought, somehow imagining Granny and Grandpa might climb out of a box and shout *Surprise.*

More drives to and fro led to more boxes, cases and plastic bags all piled up in the hall. Lost toys sat on top, but not my missing doll. I didn't complain though, just drew more pictures, making sure the dark-haired girl with triangular skirt was never alone. Jason stayed in charge, solemnly reading in the gloomy living room, the pages of his book making that scraping flapping sound as he turned them over. Lydia stayed upstairs and I half-wondered if she was crying but didn't want to find out.

Soon the final trip was done. Daddy trailed upstairs carrying odd-shaped loads. Our bedrooms were swiftly adorned with their colored rugs again but still looked wrong. The walls were painted too bright with the shades of false smiles. Jason's room wasn't ocean blue like his rug but dark and haunted as a midnight sky. Lydia's pink had terracotta shadows as if the room had seen too much sun. And my glowing green was darker and harsher than any forest floor. Lydia and Jason cut pictures from magazines and tacked them up. I peeked in to look when their doors were left open and saw posters of pop groups with twinkly lights and shiny guitars all staring at Jason's new bed. Lydia had images of pop stars too, but only the guys and always with drippy smiles. Still the walls all looked wrong, too straight and square, and they smelled of dust and paint.

We hung our clothes in yawning cavernous closets, trotting from door to door to share out garments, mistakenly thrown into the wrong plastic bags. Then Lydia began to beg for a shopping expedition. Not Monopoly? Not crayons and paints? New shoes and jewelry were suddenly essential supplies to my dear big sister, and Mom and Daddy couldn't seem to deny her anything. Rushing from their unpacking, they drove into town with scarcely time to breathe and demanded again, "Watch Sylvia, Jason. We're taking Lydia out."

"What, now?"

"Yes. Now."

My brother stood on the corridor outside his room and stared at me. He was really tall by now, stooped like a nervous question mark with his eyes fixed on the carpet as if some secret were hidden there. "Better go downstairs."

I asked him why. I felt lost.

"I dunno. Play Monopoly maybe?"

It seemed he was genuinely taking me under his wing, so I rushed to agree. But Monopoly with Jason proved pretty boring after all. His calculations took too long, and somehow he was winning, right from the start, even when he was telling me what to do. Soon I left him to read his book again while I crayoned more pictures.

Lydia grew out of both of us in the space of a short car ride.

Chapter 12

There are two little girls in this picture, one blonde-haired and one dark. They stand hand in hand with triangular skirts colored pink and blue. Matchstick legs wear matching green socks and black shoes. Matching faces wear blue eyes and bright red smiles.

Nights were dark in our new home and I missed the steady breathing of brother and sister to comfort my sleep. Every sound seemed amplified. I lay on my back, hands clasped over my chest, ears absorbed in listening to my panting breaths. Meanwhile my limbs tensed ever tighter, ever ready to leap out of bed. A sudden hum was just the fridge. Heating and cooling whispered as air vents clicked. New-made metal window-frames expanded and contracted—Daddy explained it all to me as soon as I first complained and added, "Go to sleep." But I couldn't sleep.

Untangling myself from the covers, I pushed my pillow back against the wall and scrambled to the floor. The blind was closed at my window, casting shadows in thin strips of gray like a jail. I picked my way carefully around unfamiliar furniture and pulled the cord. Cold glass felt smooth against my face. Lamp posts stood guard along the road, but the streetlamps weren't hooked up. Black sentinels, they had no weapons to defend. Neighbors were yet to move into their homes and fill their windows with light. Squat monsters, square and made from bricks, stood around us, hiding the stars. Shadows gathered along the path, not of trees and bulls but of rigid, cruel straight lines. Meanwhile the house hummed its own scary tune and I felt so alone.

With everyone fast asleep, with no one to see, I tugged my pillow and covers behind me and crept to my sister's room. There I lay down on her floor by her bed, listening to Lydia's steady breaths while my frantic heartbeat slowed.

"What are you doing here?" Lydia squawked with the gray of dawn, the house still dreaming.

I heard history in my head—"Why is she always so naughty?" So I didn't answer, just trailed back to bed, smelling sawdust, new carpets and paint, shivering in the cold.

"You'll settle down when you start school," said Mom, but I'd yet to truly realize I wasn't going back to my old school. I needed that small hope.

Jason borrowed Mom's car one day to drive to his high school registration. "You take care," Mom warned him and he nodded nervously. When he came back, his face under yellow hair was a startling white and his lips almost blue. He shook as if a bull had charged after him, and his breath smelled sour as fear. Jason, my hero, who I still believed would drive me every day to my old school, never dared to drive again until he left college.

I remember hushed conversations. "You must." "You can." "A Steepleton never gives up." They were followed by, "I can't." And finally, "I won't. Do you want me to die?"

Mom took Lydia to her registration day at the Junior High. Lydia wore her smartest shirt and jeans, with the blue cat clipped into well-brushed hair. Meanwhile I wore tee-shirt and shorts and drew pictures at the kitchen table, while Jason read another book. When they came back, Lydia twittered about hair and nail varnish and shoes instead of classrooms. But my own registration was cold dark halls filled with strangers calling names. I knew no one. Why was I here? "I want to go to my own school, Mom. I want Jason to drive." Then I remembered his white face and frantic words; I didn't want him to die. What did that mean?

"This is your own school."

Mom's hand was sparse comfort in the echoing hall, but I lost even that when she made me go off on my own. "Get your picture taken, Sylvia. Join the line. And look at all these children. Make some friends."

I'd already made friends, and lost my letters to them in the mail. What's the point if your parents are going to move you away?

The girl next to me had short blonde hair and didn't want to talk to anyone. I wondered if something was wrong with her, but she looked okay, walked okay, and knew where to sit and stand and how to smile sweetly for her photograph. I found myself smiling back at her and was glad to find she'd waited for me afterward.

"You new too?" she asked in a voice as soft and thready as a twittering bird's.

I said yes.

"Will you be my friend?"

The question threw me and I wasn't ready yet, so I said I didn't know.

"Well. Will you pretend to be my friend? My mom really wants to know I've made some friends."

I could certainly relate to that. So we walked together to where a pale thin woman with straggly hair leaned against the wall. "This is my friend," the strange girl announced.

"Oh that's wonderful, Sharon." The mother turned to me. "And what's your name?"

"I'm Sylvia," I answered, staring at Sharon's face, hoping I might remember who she was when school began. I didn't bother introducing her to my mom.

Chapter 13

The big yellow rectangle's got to be a bus. Square windows along its side are filled with round faces and bright red smiles. Two girls dance on the roof. Two more stand in front, and another two behind. There's no green ground, no black road, and no blue sky. The bus and its children just float on an empty canvas, defining life in a vacant world of their own.

That first day of school I dawdled over breakfast and packed my bag so slowly I almost missed the bus. I'd thought before that riding on a school bus might be fun. Now I stared at its yellow bulk, looming down the empty street. "Please Mom, will you drive me?" I begged. But my feeble pleas didn't work. I ended up sitting in a cold lumpy seat every day, crouched over my backpack, squashed between a tall boy chewing gum and a waif of a child who kept humming to herself. I hated it and couldn't wait to leap out into the sunshine when the bus stopped. Then I stood alone, not knowing where to go. Lacking any better ideas, I helplessly followed the humming infant.

Nothing looked the same as I remembered from registration. They could just as well have handed out timetables in a shopping mall or church instead of here. I couldn't find my room and couldn't even find the right corridor, not even with a map. I couldn't remember my teacher's name. I didn't know what grade I was meant to be in. I wanted to go home from this alien world, all filled with voices that knew where they were going and what they were doing. Thumping backpacks and banging feet danced a merry tune, excluding me. Then a hand grabbed my arm.

"Sylvia. Hi! Remember me?"

I had a friend at last!

The first class started with everyone told to draw pictures—summer vacations, family, places we knew and things we cared about. I drew my favorite doll, which was still missing, still at Granny and Grandpa's house. Sharon drew a picture of her cat. Then I screwed my paper up and threw it in the trash while Sharon showed hers to the teacher. What's a picture worth when you can't have the real thing?

We did math, which I was good at, and writing, which was okay, and then some more art. We did PE too and I ran like the wind, wishing the cows and the bull and the cat could see me now. Would they run with me? Would they smile and carry me home? I dreamed the soothing scents of the farm and smelled school dining room food.

Needing something to say while the class chattered, waiting for their teacher, I told everyone that I loved art and loved drawing pictures at home. Then I crayoned thickly with layers of black and red before tearing my pictures apart into ragged strips. My fingers ripped and peeled around colored lines, then I lined the bin. The teacher had put my red and black image of a house on the classroom wall, but I pulled it down, dropping pins on the floor. Then I stamped on it, and threw it away. I dumped my notebook too, and broke my pencil in two. Meanwhile Sharon, for some curious reason, insisted on staying by my side. She said I was strange but she was still my friend.

At last the teacher called my parents in. She took the screwed up balls of paper out of the wastepaper bin, all that homework I wouldn't hand in, all those pictures I'd torn and thrown away. I squirmed on my tiny tin chair feeling cheated as if she'd violated some sacred waste-bin privacy. Mom and Daddy hugged their knees on tiny chairs too, but they weren't hugging me.

"You can't throw your homework away, Sylvia. You can't throw your classwork, your pictures, your artwork… you can't. You mustn't. You see?"

Mom and Daddy listed so many things they said I couldn't do, as if just words defined obedience. Their disapproval hurt. I'd hidden my feelings on paper to protect them, but it wasn't allowed. So now I hid myself as well, losing my rebellion in fake compliance. I made new drawings, the same as those I'd done at the kitchen table when we first moved away. I planned a different family, different home, different set of parents with only one child. I dreamed of Granny and Grandpa and me, and no one could complain because nobody knew who I was anyway. "This is my family," I told my classmates who thought they might be my friends. "This is my house. I'm lucky. I live on a farm."

I pretended to be Sharon's best friend as well, until pretending became who I really was. Laughing, happy, innocent Sylvia who always had an exciting story to tell, kept three cats and a bull in her back yard but couldn't invite anyone home because of the gnome spitting water from its magical fountain, and because it was too far.

My brother and sister had never attended this school. No one knew I'd created a tissue of lies to hide behind. No one needed to know. Meanwhile I told myself the fairies had given me to the wrong family.

Water-colored

Chapter 14

Donald's very patient with me. He asked what the mess was all about when he came home from work that day, when I'd brought the pictures and boxes down from the loft. Papers were spread across the bedroom floor, and the ladder still stood against the wall, with spiders' webs and dust trodden into the carpet. Donald flung his jacket over the bed while I explained it was all my therapist's fault. "And you said I should go to her." Which made it Donald's fault too so he sighed, closed the blinds and changed his clothes before carrying the ladder out to the garage for me. I could see him trying to process the thought—mess vs. healing—and he really wants me to be healed. He just can't fathom why I wasn't properly fixed ten years ago, why two years of therapy have somehow come undone.

I imagine the numbers flickering behind Donald's eyes: Taxes, mortgage, salary, years; and how many times are we going to end up here? What percentage of our lives will be spent with his wife telling secrets to strangers while Donald has to pay for the privilege? What percentage of his income? He's good with numbers and I'm good at reading his mind.

I'm good at sorting through memories too, and I spend an hour a day on these pictures, like the therapist told me to. I've even dug out my old Santa tin to store the pages in after I've looked at them. When I open it, the smell of crayons hits my nose, reminding me of the farm. I used to keep all my brilliant sticks of color in a cookie tin back then. The lid closed in the scents, so I'd taste that concentrated sweet, waxy staleness on the back of my tongue whenever I opened it. Then I'd crayon my dreams to my heart's content, maybe even staying between the lines.

The cookie tin's painted with bright Christmas scenes, all brushed in high school acrylics with scratches beginning to tear the colors away. Santa and his reindeer ride around all four sides, with the front reindeer's nose almost touching the back of Santa's sleigh. Indigo sky twinkles with stars and snow; russet fur ripples with muscles; and moonlight shines in ribbons of silver and gold.

The sleigh's filled with presents of course, in packages, blue, green, and yellow, with ribbons and bows only hinting at treasures inside. On the lid, Santa's face smiles with cherry cheeks and azure eyes, hair white as snow. He holds a kitten under his chin, nestled in the fur of his beard, and its eyes are blue too. The whites of cat-fur and man-fur combine, so only ears and eyes and paws and a hint of a tail remain. I remember painting this tin—in high school, I think.

There are hints of wings behind that beard, an angel's wings perhaps. My guardian angel cat, that Mom so despised, lives in disguise on the lid of a Christmas cookie tin waiting to be filled with broken crayons. Or with broken pictures. Or with me.

The pile of boxes wobbles in the closet as I tidy up. Crumbling cardboard threatens to collapse under the weight of it all. I wonder if I might fail beneath the memories. Maybe that's why I only spend an hour a day in there.

But now the thud of Tyke's tail on the doorframe brings me back to the present. He smiles his doggy grin, all teeth and drooling tongue and quivering chin, and I check the time. The boys are due home from school. They'll want their snacks.

Adam's backpack slams against the wall as he comes in. He shouts *Hi* to the dog and says nothing at all to me because I'm just his mother. But I remind myself to *practice a gentler internal dialog.* He doesn't speak because he knows my love, because I've given him enough security to trust me over the years. Now I give him cookies and milk as well, remembering when the smell of crayons was part of his coming home. He does his homework in front of the TV now though, with plastic refillable pencils, pens and calculator in hand. He's growing up.

A second bus rumbles along the street. Brakes shriek. Voices shout. And another key turns the lock. Too big for cookies, the older boys demand grilled cheese and bags of chips instead. And cans of soda. I want coffee. My skilled hands prepare for everyone's needs. My steady hands carry the tray. And my busy hands lay their food in front of them, while I restrain myself from complaining at their taking me for granted. That *gentler dialog* reminds me I always wanted to take care of my kids. But it wouldn't hurt for them to thank me once in a while. *Even* he *said thank you, even then...*

I paint a small girl's *gentler internal* smile onto my face when Donald's car turns onto the drive.

Chapter 15

I remember my first watercolor set. It was a birthday present, sent through the mail, wrapped in brown paper and shiny with sticky tape. Mom wasn't even sure she'd allow me to open the parcel when it arrived. She put it behind the telephone and told me not to touch it. So it stared at me, with postage-stamp eyes, like the monster in the woodpile, daring me to disobey. Then Daddy came home and swooped to my rescue again.

"It's addressed to her. You've got to give it to her," he said, which was exactly what I'd been telling Mom, though my voice was higher and whinier.

Mom picked the parcel up, holding it at arm's length as if she thought it might grow teeth and bite her. Then I clutched it to my chest.

The return address was Granny and Grandpa's farm. I hadn't seen them, not once, since the day we moved out. But at least I now knew they'd not forgotten me. The parcel warmed my memories and sang with the song of the bull, for all that paper and string were cold and the only sound was a rattle. Then I opened it.

I remember the smooth metal case sliding silkily from its shelter in the cardboard sleeve. Its weight felt satisfying and firm in my hands, while white-rolled edges enticed me to pry them apart. A fractured rainbow of rectangular colors and shades awaited me, all neatly labeled with names like *gold* and *amber* and *burnt umber*. I wondered what umber was and why we'd set fire to it. But mostly I wondered how soon I could start to paint.

Twin paintbrushes lay like swords in their scabbards, sharpened and ready. Empty squares of milky white offered the chance to mix what paint blocks had so carefully rendered separate. All I needed was water and paper to set me on my way. And newspaper, to keep the kitchen table clean.

I rifle through the first few pages of watercolor images. *A long grayish face with triangle nose, half-closed eyes and pointed chin is topped with red hair. It's got to be Grandpa. On the next sheet, a plump visage smiles with lips overly bright and cheeks vivid pink. Granny would have laughed at this one. Mom's portrait has an oval face surrounded by long yellow curls. Her mouth smiles slightly but her cheeks are pale blue ice. And Daddy's picture is thickly gray on gray, iron hair matching flintlocked eyes, and lips in a narrow zippered line. Then there's Jason, painted so Dad's stone combines with Mom's yellow and blue. And Lydia.* It's Lydia's face that holds my attention the longest.

I've given her skin tone a yellowish pinkish hue—peach and salmon perhaps, or else the ubiquitous flesh with something brighter added. The colors are layered and over-layered on her cheeks, crinkling the paper while roughening its surface with dust from too many brush-strokes. A long thin nose is outlined in coffee-brown. Champagne hair, almost cream, frames the narrow face and tumbles onto shoulders encased in green. Blue eyes, flecked with yellow and green, stare from black lashed outlines under creamy brows. Carmine lips hide half a smile, not quite in place, and a row of teeth are carefully outlined in black. Lydia's sharply pointed chin stops just above a small cross dangling from the rigid V of her necklace.

I'm going to turn to another page when something makes me look closer. *A shape I've dismissed as blue dust over Lydia's eye turns out to be a tiny rendition of her hairclip shaped like a cat. The round head and arch of its back disguise two wings sprouting over her ear. I've used brighter colors here than everywhere else, as if the cat's small figure were what really mattered, big sister Lydia simply incidental. But I've painted it so tiny it's almost a secret.*

Looking closer again, I think I added those wings to the cat much later, with different paints.

I begged my mom, "Can I try them out? Please?"

She said it wasn't my birthday yet. So I begged again, and again and again, and eventually Mom sighed, brushing dinner's half-chopped vegetables onto a tray, and sending me upstairs to get paper from my room. When I came back, Mom had spread newsprint over the table and placed an old plastic cup full of water in the middle. "Here you go, and watch you don't spill. And don't get your milk confused with your water either."

I laughed happily, all tears and frustrations forgotten. Then I asked, "Can I have a birthday party? And can Granny and Grandpa come?"

I think that's when I picked blue ice for the color of Mom's portrait.

Chapter 16

*T*his next picture's a birthday cake. It fills the center of
the page, with yellow icing, a purple number eight, and
straight pink candles topped with triangular fire. It
would be a perfectly ordinary image, except for the black line
tearing down the middle like inverted lightning. Its angles cut
the cake, the candles, and even one of the flames, as if I were
making a jigsaw but forgot to cut out the shapes.

"We weren't planning on a party this year. No," said Mom
in measured tones.

"But couldn't Granny and Grandpa come?"

"Not if you're not having a party."

"But I could have, if they come."

"But they're not coming."

Mom's eyes looked blank and her voice took on a dull,
intractable timbre, but I couldn't stop. "Well, can I go there
then, to Granny and Grandpa's house? Can I go to see them? I
want to say thank you for my present."

Mom always liked us to be polite and say thanks. I was
sure this had to convince her, but it didn't. She still said no.
And I knew I couldn't have a real party, not a real
schoolchild's party, because I didn't have enough friends in
this strange new place. I played with Sharon and some other
girls, but none of them knew where I lived. They still thought I
came from a farm with cats and a bull, herds of cows, singing
troubadours, and a fountain with naked spitting gnomes. I'd
have surrendered my secrets and invited them all to
our *mansion*, if I'd only believed it might persuade Mom

and Daddy to let Granny and Grandpa visit. But I knew it wouldn't work.

I didn't even tell anyone at school when it was my birthday. Of course the teacher knew, so everyone sang to me and gave me cards in school, and the floor refused to swallow me. But I said my parents were too busy farming to give me a party. "Maybe next year."

After school, Mom promised, "We'll have our own little party. Don't worry dear," while I sulkily dipped cookies into milk.

"Like what kind of party?" I moaned.

"I've made you a cake."

I pretended not to care.

"And Daddy and Jason and Lydia will be here."

"Daddy and Jason and Lydia are always here." I raised my eyes in challenge. "I want Granny and Grandpa."

When Mom said no again, I grabbed my nice new paint box from the kitchen counter and stormed upstairs. "No painting in your bedroom," Mom shouted. But she didn't follow me, so she'd never know. I swiped old newspaper from the pile in the hallway and promised to be good, keeping my milk glass firmly in my hand.

Upstairs, I spread the newspaper over the green mat by my bed. I glugged the last of my milk and filled the glass with water from bathroom. Dregs in the bottom turned the liquid cloudy, but I knew my paints would change its color again. Then I put my *Do not disturb sign* on the door and set to work.

It felt strange trying to paint while lying on the floor. Crayons can color from any angle, but painting's constrained by gravity. I needed to reach into the glass with my brush without spilling water everywhere. Milky or paint-colored liquid on clean new carpets wouldn't endear me to Mom, and, for all that I really didn't care, I didn't want her to punish me by not giving me my cake.

Mmmm. Cake, I thought, painting an oval in the center of the page. I painted just with water at first—well, milky water—

so mistakes wouldn't show, and I made sure to keep my outline as cleanly round and symmetrical as I could. Afterward I filled the shape with canary yellow buttercream, mixing in a touch of burnt umber for the sides, so they'd seem to be in shade. I'd been thinking how to make colors all day, and how to make flames and people look the way they should. No people on this cake of course, but I planned to light its candles one by one.

Struggling to choose between ruby and fuchsia for my cake's bright number eight, I finally combined the colors in one of those blankly inviting white spaces. Then I carefully added eight candles, burning my age, trying not to get the page too wet behind the flames. Finally done, I laid the picture flat on my bed to dry, got out my homework and started reading my book.

The front door banged when Lydia came home. She was already climbing the stairs when I realized I hadn't washed my paint glass yet. I rushed to the bathroom to deal with it, but Lydia stopped and saw me of course. "Oh yuck, Silly Sissy. What have you been drinking now?"

"Not drinking," I said, then swallowed my guilt. *Wrong answer*.

Lydia peered into my room. The kitten hairclip glared at me where her hair dangled over her forehead. "Bet Mom didn't say you could paint upstairs did she."

I knew, just knew, big sister was going to tell on me. But instead she smiled and gave me an unlikely hug, almost spilling the cloudy brew down her skirt. "Never mind. Happy birthday, Sis."

I stared in amazement and felt myself start to smile back as she retreated to her room.

Fresh-washed, the glass went on my nightstand, ready to pretend it had been left there all day. I shoved the stained newspaper into my backpack to throw out later. Then I followed shyly into my sister's room. *Better catch her now*, I thought, while her mood was good. I had a question that really needed an answer.

"Lydia?" I asked, nervously.

"Yes, Sis." The blue cat seemed to smile when she looked up.

"I just wondered. Why won't Mom and Daddy let Granny and Grandpa come to see us?"

Lydia frowned and the cat slid down the side of her face. She chewed her lip, as if I'd presented some especially difficult math problem. "I'm not meant to tell you."

"How d'you mean?"

"Well, something happened, and it's kind of a secret I guess. Mom and Daddy are really, really mad."

I stared, confused.

"So am I," Lydia added, wagging her head so the cat-clip started to dance.

"So are you what?"

"I'm mad at Granny and Grandpa too. And nobody wants it to happen again."

I had to ask what happened of course. But Lydia rolled her eyes, her good mood dripping like dregs of painted water from paintbrush to floor. "You wouldn't understand, Sylvia. You're too young. I'll explain it when you're older."

Of course, that was the wrong thing to say to a birthday girl. My face flushed warm and red, and my foot stamped the ground. Then I told her my sister I hated her, before storming away again.

Chapter 17

*T**here's a picture here of a house torn in two by zigzag lines; another of a blasted tree; another of a bull, its smoky head and horns to one side of the black-drawn barrier, while an incongruous red car waits on the other; the bull's long tail looks like a snake about to attack. Another page is filled with lightning strikes, all different colors, but all of them ending in black.*

"Lydia! Sylvia!" Mom shouted up the stairs. "Come on down, and keep an eye on dinner. I've got to get Jason."

Lydia was instructed to watch over the food in the kitchen and turn down the heat if pans boiled over. I was meant to help her. But we were used to the system by now. Nothing ever went wrong. Nothing ever spilled. And nothing was ever quite right. Warm smells of dinner leaked through the house, tinged with papery newness and the scents of too much space, never quite achieving the comfort and seasoning of home. Perhaps store-bought vegetables just couldn't pretend to be as earthy and fresh as Granny's from the yard.

We sat in silence in the kitchen, watching steam coat the windows while night fell outside; each of us assiduously ignoring the other's gaze, and pretending to do homework. I'd brought my paints back down with the milk-and-water glass, so I practiced straight lines and zigzags and blending colors into black.

Daddy came home while we were on our own. Cold smoke blew in with him from the bleak outdoors—the taste of fall. But the billowing air carried the grimy oil of soot and cars, not the clean green scent of winter on the farm. A quick "Happy

Birthday, Syl," and hint of a hug, then Daddy was off to his study, closing the door with a faint and final click.

When Mom and Jason arrived, I climbed from my chair, put my books and paints away in my backpack, and stared at the empty kitchen table. It didn't feel like anybody's birthday now, just another long boring evening after school. Only the paintbrush in my hand and the cards and pictures in my pack said anything different.

"Put your stuff in your room," said Mom, so I hurried upstairs. I stood the cards on shelves near my bed, then took them down and hid them away again. But when Mom shouted, "Dinnertime!" I still felt a catch of excitement in my throat. Maybe there really would be birthday cake, and maybe it really would *almost* feel like a party.

Lydia and Jason had gone downstairs before me. I slouched on the steps, running my hand slowly along the rail, while feeling the carpet's fibers under my toes. The dining room door was still closed, so I paused for a moment with my fingers wrapped around the knob. Then I took a deep breath and went inside.

Everyone was sitting around the polished table, eager eyes focused on the door. They'd been waiting for me. They smiled for me! They said, "Happy Birthday!" and pointed their hands to my place, where stacks of presents had materialized by my plate. The curtains were closed against winter's dark. The lighting was bright and cheerful. And the room felt cozy and warm, almost festive enough to make believe we had something to celebrate.

Jason leaned to hug me with awkward straight arms as I sat down. Daddy wrapped me close and loomed over me. Lydia smiled, and Mom served food. But I wished, oh how I wished Granny and Grandpa could be there, to make it all perfect. Then I made the mistake of saying so.

"They're not coming here. Not ever," said Mom, tight-lipped again. She almost dropped potatoes onto the cloth instead of my plate.

My mouth fell open in anger or surprise. I couldn't measure *never*, couldn't work out when it would end. Even if Granny and Grandpa had done something wrong, like Lydia said, surely Mom was going to forgive them eventually? Was it even possible, never ever to get the chance to say *Sorry*? It sounded scary, especially since I'd just been painting in my room and was waiting to be found out.

"Give it time. Give it time," said Dad, though he mumbled and I wasn't sure who he was talking to.

Jason pulled at the button on his shirt until it fell off and rolled across the floor. At least that gave me an excuse to move so they'd all stop staring at me. I jumped down, scrabbling in the carpet as if I were a dog. Then I placed the button next to Jason's plate and scrambled back to my place, burying my red-rimmed gaze in food. Dinner was good, all my favorite things, and cake was very good. But I wasn't going to smile if I could help it.

They sang *Happy Birthday* while I blew out my candles, and I kept my secret this time, not letting anyone even try to guess what I wished for. Because, after all, *telling* means your wish won't come true and, with this wish, *telling* would mean they'd start shouting again. Afterward I went upstairs and opened up my paint box on the bed. No water? *Who cares*? It really wasn't a problem.

I sucked the end of my brush to make it wet, then swirled it fiercely around on the black paint block. It wasn't fair that Mom and Daddy were splitting our family like this. Not fair. Not fair.

More zigzag paintings followed, and next time I looked I'd split my picture of the cake in two as well.

Chapter 18

Eventually, I learned not to ask. When Christmas came, it went without saying we wouldn't see Granny and Grandpa. They wouldn't come here. We wouldn't go there. And the two extra places I laid at the table would be swiftly cleared without a word.

We didn't see Granny and Grandpa for Lydia's birthday, nor for Jason's. Mother's Day came and Mom wouldn't even let me send a card; nothing for Grandpa on Father's Day either.

Jason graduated high school without inviting them to his party, though I did see Daddy slip a photograph into a secret envelope. I began to wonder if Daddy was seeing Granny and Grandpa behind everyone's backs. Did they have a wall filled with pictures of us that he'd spirited away when Mom wasn't looking? If I painted something for them and left it out, in his office perhaps, would Daddy find it like a parental Santa hiding gifts for Christmas? But I didn't dare ask.

And I changed schools again, without graduating, again, without accidentally mailing any prettily colored cards with new addresses on them, and still without telling Sharon I didn't live on a farm. Of course, there'd be no convincing my new class mates that I lived anyplace but here, since they'd all be neighbors, and the school was Paradise Elementary, newly built, just down the road.

I painted my school, but I'm pretty sure I must have painted it at home. I don't remember the teachers asking me what my picture meant, or calling my parents for a conference. And I don't remember them appreciating my imagination either.

A long low building fills the center of the page with a neat little clock tower on its roof. Above, blue sky holds the usual yellow sun and a few white clouds. I've even added some cloud-like reflections in windows along the building's side, with large rectangular doors opening wide beneath the circular clock. It's all fairly normal and true, except for the way I've depicted the faculty and kids.

Four lines of animals approach the doors, one from each corner of the page. Eagles, dragons and robins fly down in a colorful V across the sky. Meanwhile, cows, sheep and horses march up from the road. A smiling red bull guards the doorway with a blue cat on his back and yellow horns, as bright as the shining sun. But the horns are tipped in red and seem to drip, a puddle of blood on the ground perhaps, slipping into a waterfall.

Paradise Elementary was built on ground that, like everything else around there, used to be part of Grandpa's fields. With yet another clean white picket fence, the building looked like an elongated shed in search of a farm. It served the children of Paradise Mansions, Paradise Court, Paradise Street, Paradise Road, and all those other heavenly places. The kids from the Church of Paradise went there too, and it should have been heaven, but it was just a neighborhood school. It should have been easy for me to make friends, but I wasn't even sure I wanted them. After all, I'd only move to Junior High in a few more years and lose them again. Nobody measured up to Sharon, who lived the other side of the park and wasn't changing schools. Nobody measured up to the friends from my first school, whose names I'd already forgotten, who'd all forgotten me. Nobody measured up.

I toss the picture onto the pile and turn to the next one in the box, *a painting of a church. But this church's walls and steeple are splashed red and white. It's not the Church of Paradise. I've painted the same lines of animals though, in an X across the page. The same bull guards the arch-shaped door, with the same cat balanced on his back and the same sharp horns.*

"Life's a balance," said Pastor Bill in his sermon one day. "A balance between enjoying what you have and reaching for more; between always doing exactly what you're told and thinking for yourself; between liberty and law; between forgiveness and sin,…" I can't remember all the examples he gave, but I remember that moment when suddenly I felt as if he were talking just to me. A balance between the forces of good and evil it seemed, the devil snarling on one shoulder, while angels whispered promises on the other; bull and cats perhaps, both trying to show me the path. But the bull was my loyal friend and the cat had claws. What did that say about me?

Small children waddled like ducks to the front of church and the pastor commanded, "Now, stand on one leg. Show your mommies and daddies how well you can balance." They couldn't, of course, and everyone laughed as they tumbled and rolled on the floor.

"Because life's *not* a balance," Pastor Bill explained, sending the kids back to their seats. "God didn't make us to struggle and fall. He made us to choose His path, to love, and obey. So we do as *He* says and enjoy *His* liberty and follow in *His* way."

Meanwhile Lydia muttered, very clearly and quietly, as if talking to me, "And who do *we* obey?" Mom and Daddy nodded their heads, that sage way they always did in church, as if their lives were perfectly holy, good and balanced, and not going back to the farm were just a fact, not a decision they'd made.

Pastor Bill showed us a marble now, small and black, held over a smooth plastic track. He placed the marble carefully in the center, then nudged it to one side. "We choose which way to go," he said, as the track began to tip, and the marble to roll. "Then God does the rest, like gravity." The marble fell and clattered into a cup.

Sermons on forgiveness had me wondering what it was that Mom and Daddy couldn't forgive; what kept us from the farm? I still felt nervous I might offend them equally one day. Would they cast me aside like a discarded grandparent? Would Lydia?

But I couldn't ask my sister anymore what had offended them. The lovely Lydia had become my friend, and I wasn't going to jeopardize this sudden joy.

Two beds stand side by side on the page, one pink and one green. A blue cat sits on the pink bed's pillow and a red bull on the green.

Two desks stand side by side in the next image, one with a blue cat guarding its sheaves of paper, the other with a bull.

In the next picture, two girls wear pink and green. Pink girl has a blue dot in her yellow hair. Green girl wears yellow horns over browner curls.

Maybe it was because Jason had gone to college and she was lonely. Maybe Lydia was worried about moving to high school soon. Maybe she just felt sorry for me because I didn't have any friends. Whatever it was, my big sister seemed to suddenly decide I was human. We even went shopping together sometimes. She admitted I was her sister when she met her friends in town. And she was the one who asked Daddy if he could move our beds into one room. "After all, we sisters like to talk, and we'll sleep better that way."

Daddy set up both our beds in Lydia's room while moving our desks into mine. Now we had our own upstairs office, just like Daddy's downstairs. We put the *Do not disturb* sign on the door and left it there. And we talked... about boys, love, marriage, art, high school, junior high, how to make friends, how to win at Monopoly, fashion, shoes, jewelry, hairstyles, Mom and Daddy... The only things we never talked about were our grandparents and the farm.

Chapter 19

I've found a hand-sized painting of a posy of flowers, just right to stick on a birthday card. It smells of Mom's perfume, even after lying in the bottom of a box all these years. I remember sprinkling drops on it and wondering if they'd stain. The flowers look like they're covered in yellow rain, so I guess they did.

It was Mother's Day again.

Bright and clear, and right on time, the sun's rays shattered the darkness of our room. Birds twittered like flutes above the rumble of traffic on the main road through Paradise. Then two pairs of bare feet thundered in an avalanche on the stairs. Daddy offered to help in the kitchen, but Lydia and I were old enough now to know what we were doing, not like on the farm where we'd made breakfast for Granny and Mom, and left a mess of everything over the floor.

We carried the trays upstairs ourselves, balancing cards and flowers and chocolates, with cups wobbling and rattling, pale tea sloshing its russet stream into the saucers. Mom looked pleased. She reached up from her bed to hug and kiss us both. Then Daddy chased us out the room so they could dress in peace.

Downstairs, we cleaned the kitchen up, putting everything back in its place. I still felt kind of sad that we weren't wishing Granny a Happy Mother's Day. I stared at the phone, as if I could will it into ringing, wishing Granny might ask to hear my voice. But I wished in silence. I was older now.

We could have walked to church, but it was windy so Daddy drove. At least, I assumed that was why he was driving.

We parked on the gravel parking lot, between the church and school, and held our hair and hats against the breeze as we rushed for the church door.

Tiny kids offered miniature bouquets to all the moms, frail flower stems wrapped in chunks of aluminum foil. Lydia giggled when I held my nose, but the church foyer smelled thickly of chemical roses, enough to drown the scent of candles and anything else. I guessed they must have sprayed perfume on all the flowers, and the fragrance clung like glue to the back of my throat. As soon as the singing started I found myself coughing, then Lydia slapped me on the back. I breathed into a handkerchief during the sermon and couldn't wait to get out.

Of course, Mom simply had to bring her flowers home, so we opened all the windows in the car and felt colder than if we'd just walked.

Daddy was talking, trying to tell us something while he drove. But the rush of air, outside and in, made it hard for us to hear. We just said *yes* to everything and thought we'd be okay. Then Mom turned around as if she didn't believe our replies. I watched her mouth open and close and wished I could lip-read, but we both nodded our heads solemnly, laughing behind our hands, and said *yes* again.

"Okay kids. It's time," said Daddy into sudden silence as he pulled up by the gate.

Time for what? What sort of okay did he mean? And why wasn't he parking on the drive?

"Your Mom and I are off to see Granny, like we said."

Except we hadn't heard one word in three. I nearly hit the roof of the car in delighted surprise. We were going to see Granny and Grandpa, at last! "Yippee!" I screeched. "Can we make a present for her?"

Then Mom turned around again. "You're not coming," she said.

"Yes we are." I felt stubborn enough to imagine I could speak for both of us and get my own way. But Mom stared pointedly over her shoulder at Lydia, who sat like a statue next to me, hands clasped so tight on the church bulletin the paper was crinkling up.

"It's okay," said Lydia, her voice too small, her face too frozen to care. The blue cat wobbled in her hair, though her head seemed perfectly still.

"You don't have to. That's what we were telling you. We're happy to leave you at home."

"It's okay."

"You could stay with…"

"It's okay."

"But are you sure? I don't want… *We* don't want…"

"It's okay."

My knees bounced as they spoke. I felt half excited, half dismayed, and wondered why they wouldn't listen. Lydia had said it was okay, and I for one would *not* be okay with being left behind.

Eventually Mom sighed wearily. "If you're really sure, but remember you don't have to."

Daddy started the engine again.

Chapter 20

There's a painting of the farmhouse here, done from memory I think. Purple wisteria hangs over the door. Gray and white stripes rise up the walls and fade into charcoal shadows under the roof. Windows are dark. The front door's closed. And I've chosen the angle just right to show Jason's window-under-the-roof where his bed used to be, a smoothly drawn circle centered under the eaves. The grass is green. The sky is blue. And nobody's home.

It was a strange and silent drive. Daddy whistled and moved his hands so confidently on the wheel as if nothing could be wrong. Mom sat clinging to the flowers in her lap with one hand, while she twisted her hair with the other. Morning sun streaked silver into strands of thick blonde curls. She shook her shoulders, tossed her head, turned back and forward again, then faced the open window with an empty gaze. Those overly scented blossoms from church were rapidly crumbling to dust.

Meanwhile Lydia sat frozen as the cherub in our pond. She didn't look like she was angry or scared, just like she wasn't really there.

I leaned forward eagerly in my seat, pressing my face into the back of Daddy's neck and trying not to bounce too high with glee. I wanted to shout, "Look at that bird," that squirrel, that tree; look at everything. And look where we're going!

"Very impressive," Daddy would say, while the words tumbled out of my mouth. The two of us pierced the fabric of silence with proud determination, and just for once I, the naughty one, was firmly on my daddy's side, rescuing him, instead of him rescuing me.

The gravel road to the farm had been paved since we left. Our wheels hit fresh blacktop with a roaring swoosh, and Lydia snapped awake then froze again, her face still fiercely turned away from me. Mom stared straight ahead.

Soon I could see the white wooden fence around our old front yard. The farmhouse stood behind it, laden with flowers and draped with greenery, surrounded by fields laid out with perfect mathematical precision. The bull turned around to face us from his pen. He must have heard the car; I couldn't help wondering if he'd remember me. Then I saw Granny, small and dumpy, black-haired, and smiling her welcome from the doorway as we parked in the drive. No signs of Grandpa, but at last we were home!

Daddy marched us all into the house where we traipsed across Granny's hallway, feet echoing, eyes peering out through rosy shadows of dust-laden air. I realized I was taller than before, or else the pictures had moved lower on the walls. But the living room was just as warm and red as I remembered with its thick purple rug. A glorious fire crackled in the hearth, filling the air with hints of flowers and smoke.

We sat on chairs like visitors, prim hands over prim knees. But I couldn't stand the straightness of it all, so I slid to the floor. Then I rolled forgotten fibers of the rug between gummy fingers, stared at the fire, and imagined pictures of cats and bulls all chasing around in the flames. Mom and Granny scuttled off into the kitchen to make sandwiches. They chatted contentedly, tossing occasional questions like breadcrumbs back through the door. "Mustard, Jason? Do you still not like lemon grass?"

Meanwhile Daddy relaxed in the rocking chair and smiled expansively. Lydia finally consented to get some paper and pencils out from the cupboard to play with me. And Mom brought trays laden with food.

The china plates had always been for visitors, not for us. It felt wrong to clasp one in my lap over tightly crossed knees. The little cakes all perfectly arrayed made me feel like a perfect stranger; and Lydia didn't help, nibbling her portion like a proper young lady and answering questions with flawless diction and delicate wry smiles. Yes school was fine. Yes she really liked her teachers. Yes it was strange not having Jason around. And yes our new house was nice. Yes, it had been a while.

I grabbed another piece of cake, stuffing my mouth too full so I wouldn't have to speak, and wondering how Lydia's words could taste so sour though they sounded sweeter than icing on a birthday cake. Then Grandpa arrived.

I heard his hand on the doorknob first, a tentative rattle instead of the well-remembered thunk of his sturdy fist. I wondered if he'd somehow forgotten how knobs should turn. Moments later the door opened wide, and he looked like a ghost, staring from the hallway's night. His head hung low and his hair was whiter and thinner than I remembered. He'd lost his russet glow and his eyes, when he raised them from the floor, were empty, rheumy and dim.

"Come in then, my Jason," said Granny. "Sit down."

So he shuffled forward, passing me on the rug without meeting my gaze, his gait the weary tread of an elderly man who needed his chair.

Upholstery creaked when Grandpa sat down but I wondered if it was his knees. They stuck up sharply in front of him, like tree-branches bent before breaking. He propped his hands on top to still their unremembered trembling. Then he accepted a plate of sandwiches from Granny, assured her solemnly with grating voice that they were surely delicious, and started to eat. He still didn't look at me, even when I bounced off the floor and stood in front of him.

"I want to go out for a walk," I announced, stubbornly sure that that my Grandpa was bound join me.

He raised his face to me then, and almost smiled. But something was wrong with his eyes, as though the lights had burned out inside his head. Meanwhile everyone else's eyes burned silent disapproval at my back, so I turned around, snapping my hands to hips defiantly. This wasn't how it was meant to be. This was wrong, all different.

"I want to see the bull, and the barn, and the cats, and everything. This is boring." I tried to stamp my foot, but the carpet's thick warmth rendered the gesture irrelevant.

"Well, you go on out then, Sylvia," said Granny. She smiled peaceably, while Grandpa dropped his gaze back to the floor. "Lydia, why don't you go with her?"

Really? Lydia might go with me into the yard? That seemed unlikely from past experience. The shopping mall was more my sister's habitat. But she unfolded herself from her chair and reached for my hand. When I looked into her eyes, I saw no lights there either. The blue hairclip seemed more awake than she.

"Are you coming, Grandpa?" I asked over my shoulder, while Lydia dragged me out. I knew he'd want to be there to show me around.

But everyone said, "No." Not loudly, not like they were complaining even, just like it was a well-established fact.

I saw Grandpa droop in the chair like a sack of potatoes, half-empty, dregs left behind after cooking the meal, while shadows grew like weeds under the crown of his wispy white hair.

Chapter 21

I walked with Lydia to the fence around the old bull's pen. Newly painted, its rails shone bright and clean against the green. The bull stood stolid in the middle of his field, but he knew I was there. He recognized me and stared with dark beady eyes, dipping his heavy head into a bow. Long horns swayed from side to side.

"I can't believe you always wanted to come out and talk to this beast. He's just a huge great hulking brute," said Lydia, unimpressed. She didn't climb the fence. Her pretty skirt might get dirty.

"He's not a brute," I answered. "He only looks like one."

"Yeah, well things aren't always what they seem."

That was just what I was saying, wasn't it? Lydia looked worried though, eyes half-closed under a heavy frown, as if the sunshine was too much for her. So I jumped down and suggested we go see the cats, in the barn, in the shade.

The secret entrance was jammed closed. But the wide wooden doors invited me. They didn't seem half as heavy as before, which was just as well, since Lydia made no move to help. I lifted the bar easily, enjoying my extra inches. Then I dug my heels into the ground, tugging until the ancient hinges creaked.

Dusty darkness welcomed us inside. Long straight cracks in the wooden walls cast shadows like prison bars across the floor. The nest where the mother cat had her kittens was gone, leaving an empty bath of hay. Straw and cobwebs hung limply from ceiling and walls. Broken bales jumbled across the floor.

Then something small scurried over my foot and vanished into the dark.

"A mouse!" Lydia shrieked and turned to flee, but I grabbed her arm to still her, while a cat streaked through the doorway in eager pursuit. Soft paws pattered lightning fast on straw. White fur flashed. Long tail swung like an eager snake. And tiny eyes—I almost imagined they were red—flashed fire.

Lydia sighed and said she really wanted to go outside again. But I clung to her and whispered, *Here kitty, kitty,* under my breath. If the first thing we'd seen had really been a mouse, I wanted to watch how a cat might stalk her prey, and I wanted Lydia at my side.

"Shush," I told her, tugging her forward to see. We peeked over the top of a wall of hay, while strands of straw scratched our knees.

The cat had settled an innocent-looking paw on the mouse's tail. Gentle purring vied with creaking timbers and the sighing wind, but behind it we heard an urgent squeak repeated, sharp as nails on a blackboard. Cats' claws are sharp like nails I suppose.

The mouse struggled forward and back, scrabbling on tiny legs as far as its tail would allow, then swinging around to try again. I wondered if the tail might twist off eventually. Did it hurt? But the cat seemed to smile and suddenly released its prey, settling back on its haunches to observe. I saw the mouse stretch warily and gather its strength to run. Then a white paw plunked on the center of its back. A loud squeal announced the tiny creature's defeat.

I'm sure at that distance I couldn't see eyes or expression, yet I thought I did. The pretty cat was sweet, soft, furry, musically voiced, white as an angel but cunningly disguised as devil, now eagerly engaged in the torture of its prey. I couldn't tear my gaze away, but I thought the devil-like sharp-horned bull would be kinder. He'd just stamp down on a mouse and be done. Then I said, for no real reason except to torture my sister, "We could paint that."

Lydia had closed her eyes. "No thanks." And we walked away.

My bull still glowered from his pen, head lowered, ready to sleep or charge at me. I watched his hooves paw the ground, listened to the grating sound they made on cold damp earth, and saw his massive shoulders stoop as his head swung from side to side. Then he huffed a spray of dust from his nose and stomped accusingly until I looked away.

We could have gone back into the farmhouse then. It was home or had been home for so many years, and would surely welcome us. But it wasn't the same. Visitors' china, a different kind of dust floating in the air, the smell of Granny's cakes but no dinner tonight. If we went upstairs, our bedroom in the eaves would whisper with ghosts, but they wouldn't be ours. Empty boxes might wait to entrap us. Hangers on rails would rattle under shadows of who we once were. Then Granny would shout, and Grandpa would sit white and silent in his chair, and it wouldn't be right.

I must have painted him from memory. This picture's so different from the one I made before.

Thin strands of hair wave white against a halo of dark. Rheumy eyes are hooded, almost closed. The mouth droops low in a narrow line twisted at the edges. Hunched shoulders almost hide the neck, and the shirt-collar's sternly starched, its sharp-edged corners open and cutting the chin. I've painted a cross at Grandpa's throat because he always wore one. But I'm not sure if I saw one around his neck that day. The nose is too big, a little too red, and the nostrils a little too hairy, flaring and wide. Dark lines on his cheeks all draw downward, down down low.

It looks like a face made for burial though the man was still alive.

"I don't hate him you know," said Lydia, as we swung our legs from our perch on the bull's high fence. She'd finally stopped worrying about her skirt.

"You don't?"

Lydia took a long slow breath before she answered me. Her fingers twined together in her lap, and she rocked, precariously balanced on the rail. "No, I don't hate him, not really. But I don't forgive him either."

"Forgive him for what?"

She jumped down dismissively. "I'll tell you when you're older."

So I'd have to wait. I would soon be ten but, in Lydia's eyes, that wasn't old enough. After all, she was almost in high school now, proud of her advancing years while I wasn't even ready for *junior* high.

Chapter 22

We met with Granny in town from time to time afterward. I remember she helped us shop for Lydia's gown when she was going to the Freshman Ball at high school. Lydia suddenly looked so grown up, and I felt so very small—well, small and dumpy—but she still included me in everything, asking me to help comb her hair, choose her makeup, and fasten Mom's borrowed necklace around her neck. The stones were the same shade of blue as Lydia's cat hairclip, but when I moved to fasten the ornament over her eye she pushed me away.

"No, I can't wear a silly little cat anymore. Not in high school. Why don't you take it?"

It was my first inheritance.

A blue cat lies asleep in the center of the page. It's curled around itself on a bed of white silk. Gray shadows paint their creases in the cloth. Lighter specks make tiny bright reflections, blue and gold in the shape of petals underneath. But a different brush, or an ink-pen, has added a tiny red eye to the kitten's collar and a faint shape of wings to its back.

"You look great," I said when Lydia was dressed and ready to leave.

"I know."

I fastened the hairclip over my ear and smiled at her. Then I trembled. "Don't get a boyfriend, will you? Please?"

She didn't, not then.

I flip through pictures of Lydia in her gown and wonder if I was dreaming my future, or maybe making plans to become a dress designer, when I painted all these. Then I come to another image of the pale blue cat. A band of silver wraps its throat, reminding me of Lydia's promise ring. Mom and Granny were ever so proud of that.

Granny still wasn't ever invited back to our house, but I knew Mom met her regularly, because she'd come home smelling of coffee or tea and Granny's sweet perfume. We all met at the coffee shop too, and when Lydia showed off her ring, Granny announced, "You're a woman now."

I tried not to let Granny hug me because I didn't like the scent. But I was a child, not a woman, so some small hugs were mandatory. Still, I asked, "Does being sixteen make Lydia a woman?" as I disentangled myself from Granny's grasp and pulled out my chair. "Or is it just 'cause she's wearing a ring?" It was a gift from church for Lydia's sixteenth birthday.

"Not the ring," said Granny. "That's just a symbol. It's the promise that matters."

So I twisted Lydia's blue cat *symbol* in my hair while she twirled the ring around on her finger. And another year passed.

Lydia's seventeenth birthday party was held in the hall at the Church of Paradise. She gave me a gorgeous hand-written invitation. It would be my first dance, which made me feel so grown-up. And boys were invited too! I wondered how Lydia had persuaded Mom and Daddy to agree, but I guess they thought nothing could go wrong because Pastor Bill was going to be there. The pastor even arranged for all the music—he said some new guy had just moved into town and joined the church. He was good with electronics, and he wanted to help out.

"An older guy?" Daddy asked suspiciously, while we stood discussing details before the date. Granny said the same thing when Mom told her about it over plates of fancy cakes and high tea at the illustrious Benson's café.

"Pastor Bill says he graduated high school a few years back, so he's older than these kids," Mom replied. "He works down at the garage, not far from church."

"Well, better make sure he's no cradle-snatcher."

Mom scoffed. "He's a church-goer, Mom, and Pastor Bill will keep an eye on things."

Granny harrumphed. "Yes, well." Her eyes looked dark and sad.

I've found more pictures of Lydia now, this time in a different gown. She stands by a mirror, admiring her reflection; sits on a chair while her fingers twist and turn at her promise ring; and steps through a doorway, casting a nervous glance back over her shoulder. I've painted her dancing too, with bright lights whirling around the page, faint shaded guys and girls in watery pastels pirouetting in her shadow.

One final image has Lydia dancing on a stage. She's holding hands with a long-limbed guy who faces away from me, dark hair like a tiny waterfall covering his neck. His knees are bent in narrow jeans, and Lydia flies in the air.

I wasn't sure what to wear for Lydia's party. I'd graduate from elementary school in the summer, and I was growing tall already, like a cross between a weed and a mushroom. But Lydia saw my concern and let me borrow a dress she'd grown out of—not her first-dance, Freshman Ball gown of course because that was too special. But it was a real gown just the same. It smelled of sophistication, the material flowed like water, and the pattern was as pretty as the coming of spring. Of course, the dress was too tight until Mom let out the seams, but I just told myself Lydia was too thin. With new high-heeled shoes, another of Mom's necklaces, a splash of perfume, and the precious blue cat in my hair, I felt as if I'd suddenly grown up into that curiously coveted womanhood. I'd need a *Promise Ring* of my own before long.

The idea was to dance the afternoon away, not the night, since even Lydia's proud seventeen was still considered young. But the sky was gray and shifting to black. Wind cut like ice on my back as we crossed the parking lot. I couldn't shiver in case I looked scared, and I really wanted to pretend that I belonged. I was tall enough, just a little too dumpy and fat.

When I teetered on the gravel, Lydia gripped my arm. "Come on, Sis." She steadied me and the music soothed my nerves. It drifted, warm like the hall's yellow lights, setting the bare trees dancing. Touches of winter's late frost trickled like snow.

The hall was warm with the sweaty smell of perfume, young bodies, sweet food, wet wood and electronics. Voices vied with a steady beat that thumped from ceiling to floor. It wasn't the most acoustically perfect place, but it sounded great to me. Clattering plates rang on heavy wooden trestles—the same long tables used to carry Mom's cakes at her incessant church fairs. Glasses made of plastic rattled loudly but nothing would break. Feet danced their vague uncertain steps as couples wondered how close they dared to stand. A red-haired teenager took my hand.

And I did it! I danced, balanced like glass on those strange high heels until I kicked them off and went barefoot. My skirt swung smooth as silk around expertly twisting hips and knees. My feet stepped forward and back and side to side while my body swayed. I waved my hands and swung around and rested my head on the red-haired boy's firm chest. Then we danced some more. I could get used to this.

Meanwhile Lydia was dancing with everyone who asked, somehow always at the front of the hall, somehow always catching the eye of the stranger with the music and the mike.

"One final dance with the party girl," our *older-than-these-kids* DJ announced, after Pastor Bill flashed the lights for closing time.

Lydia leapt onto the stage and grabbed the microphone. "Dance with me," she breathed like a movie star, taking the DJ's hands and pressing them to her side. They shuffled a slow sweet song, bodies close, while the rest of us stared. Lydia nestled into the stranger's shirt, he with his arms snaking smoothly around her, his chin resting ever so softly on top of her head. Dark hair and light. Good and evil, I thought. The bull and the cat. Everyone clapped when he let her go. Then the music finally stopped.

That was the day my Lydia met her Troy; the day I lost her.

Sketched

Chapter 23

I tell the therapist I'm halfway through looking at all my pictures. Shouldn't she be pleased? Shouldn't she say, *Well done Sylvia,* or something like that anyway?

Instead she just looks at me. "And?"

"And what?"

I think she's going to leave me hanging, but she speaks again, her voice so low and throaty I have to stare at her lips to be sure I catch the words. "And after the pictures? What will you do next?"

I smile and explain I'll still have the paintings in frames to sort out when I finish with the boxes. Isn't that what she intends? But I feel proud of myself, having tidied half the contents of those cardboard cartons away. Pictures and memories, crayoned and water-painted onto their pages, they're all safely stashed in fancy tins, with Santas and Guardian Angel Cats and carolers painted on the sides. I'm doing really well. Doesn't she agree?

She smiles serenely and asks why I'm telling her this.

"Because you told me to look at the pictures," I say.

Then she nods, but the line between her eyes still looks like a question mark.

I wonder if she might ask me something a little more specific. Ask me where the tins come from. Or what's a *guardian angel cat* perhaps? I'm sure I haven't mentioned them before, and they're kind of important to me. But instead she sits, cool and relaxed, languidly catlike herself, almost purring behind her desk while I perch and fumble with the fabric of my skirt. I wish I'd worn jeans. I feel like a mouse and check her hands to see if she's painted her nails. The silence drags on.

"It's been quite fun really," I say, when the air grows too heavy to breathe. "Donald's getting tired of finding pictures all over the floor, of course." She doesn't respond. "It's not like he's complaining. He'd just like to know how long it's going to take." My tongue moves too fast. "You know? How long it will be until I can pack them away and say I'm okay?" I struggle for breath. "He says the insurance might not cover enough. Says I need to hurry up. He says..."

Then her gaze says I'm filling space with empty words, so I pause for thought. Those next pictures are all so boring though. I glanced at them last night. They're done in pencil, black and white, just sketches, nothing more. Perhaps she'll let me skip over them?

"Why are you telling me this?" she asks again, like a cat releasing me just prior to the end, leaning back and waiting before she reveals her claws.

"Well, I just thought..."

"Why aren't they in color?"

Then I realize I've brought the black and white drawings into our meeting with me, and I've laid them on her desk. "They're just..."

I know she's going to read some deep meaning into black and white if I don't stop her, but I'm too late—she's already rolling the questions out like bullets. Did I leave out the colors to hide my feelings perhaps? Did I sketch what I didn't want to admit? Did I use a pencil because I couldn't bear the permanence of paint? Do I want to erase something? Do the thoughts hurt too much?

"That's not it," I protest, feeling as though she's spread me out like pictures on a bed. I snatch at the safest question I can find and answer her. "I signed up for art when I went into Junior High, and we started off with pencil. That's why they're black and white. That's all it is."

I hope she might ask about me now, the academic, genius mathematician of the family. Will she wonder why I signed up for art? *Come on*, I beg her with my eyes. *Ask me*. Daddy did.

Of course, Daddy never listened to my reply. He complained almost as much about my art as he did about Lydia's Troy. *Unsuitable boyfriend. Unsuitable occupation.* Art was somehow similarly *unsuitable*, leading only to poverty.

I remember Daddy staring at me across the dinner table when I brought the forms for him to sign. "You've only so much time, only so many lessons, young lady," he announced with a pompous frown. "You shouldn't waste school time on hobbies like art."

"Why? What's wrong with art?"

"You should do science, math, real subjects, something with weight."

But weight just made me think of diets and nutrition, while Mom added, "English, Spanish, French." Big brother Jason, finished with college and painfully job hunting now, muttered something behind his hands while slender fingers twittered over his lips. I couldn't hear the words but I guessed, bitterly, *Why's she so naughty?* Sister Lydia smiled.

"Well, I'm doing art, so there." If they wanted to call me naughty I'd just rebel a little more. "If you won't sign, I'll fake your signature."

We were eating Sunday dinner after church, enjoying the chance to get the family together around the table. Mom liked things like that. She liked peace and quiet though, as well, which was how I banked on easing my unsteady rebellion. I stared, waiting for her to calm us all down. Then Mom explained, "It's only junior high, Jason; only two years, and she *is* growing up." So Daddy caved. Lydia smiled again, and the subject was done.

For a moment I thought I'd won my beloved sister back from her boyfriend. I tried to smile at her through the savory steam of a dish of potatoes. But then the parents started going on about Troy again. Platters clattered onto mats. Voices grew hard. And I couldn't smile anymore because I wasn't on Lydia's side. I hated Troy. It was about the one thing my parents and I could agree on, not that anyone asked. But my big sister going out with a garage mechanic just didn't bear thinking about. My big sister talking about possibly, maybe, getting married one day. My big sister belonging to somebody else.

So here I sit, years and miles away, dreaming pencils and art, when the therapist's voice breaks in and interrupts my memories. "So, you'll look at the pencil drawings for next week? And bring them in again?"

"Yes, I guess." I will if I really have to. And they're black and white because the teacher said we had to learn shade and shape before using colored pencils. Should I tell her that? Am I learning the shade and shape of memories as I search through this spreading pile? And will anyone really want to see what those pencil sketches hide?

It's a toaster. It has two slots on top, a shadow underneath, and a dent in the side. The window's reflections are twisted and bent, the sun like a broken arrow needling them. The cable's frayed.

It's a kettle. I like how I've smudged the pencil with my fingers to resemble steam. I've smudged the sides of the kettle too and used an eraser to create a faint illusion of metal's shine.

It's a chair with twirly wooden legs and a tapestry image, somewhat threadbare, on the seat. I've shaded some of the pattern out but drawn the rest with enormous mathematical precision. It looks like poison ivy surrounded by lines.

It's a table, square, solid and scratched.

It's a plate, where dinner waits to be eaten like plastic lumps of coal.

And this one's my mom. See, I'm learning. I don't just draw objects now with this pencil, black on white. The picture only shows Mom's top half though, bending over a bowl in the kitchen as she so often did. I've caught the way her hair hangs low, the shape of her hands, even her nails. I've caught something in the angle of her nose as well, but I haven't drawn the face. I suspect I chose where to place myself so I wouldn't have to tackle something too hard.

Here's Daddy, sitting at his desk. His face isn't turned quite so far to the side. The shade on his chin isn't quite right, but somehow it's got to be him. His jaw's firm. His eye looks clear. His skin's unlined.

Lydia sits with the phone to her ear in this one, legs curled easily underneath. Blonde hair whispers around her cheeks, a mix of delicate lines and erasered white. Laughing eyes look down, drawn just the right size, nose sweetly angled, chin bent warily low. It really looks like Lydia.

And this one must be a self-portrait I guess—it's not so good. There's no face on it, just a thumb-softened blur because, after all, I could hardly sit still and keep looking in the mirror while I drew it.

The pages fly, and now I'm back to flowers and leaves and a picture of our cherub's fountain, frozen to stillness in midwinter snow. He wears a glowing cap of white.

The seasons passed and I turn the page, finding pictures that must be of spring. But it's late and I'm tired. I tuck them all into their box so I can look at them later.

Chapter 24

Twigs stand in a vase, like flowers, filling the center of the page. Each strip of wood is ramrod straight, black outline shaded with roughened bark and dotted with sticky buds. The penciled branches bend and refract at the water, sharp edges clearly seen through crystalline glass. Buds are shaded with dots of gray and black, growth just beginning to curl the life into them.

The vase casts a shadow beneath it, diagonal lines in soft charcoal gray. In front, a single twig lies close to the observer, its bud on the verge of opening to the eye. The shadow beneath is dark and heavy, while fringes of leaf and petal are rendered clear and clean. Drips of water or sap stick to unfolding innocence. I can almost pick it up.

Behind this page another picture shows blossom gathered from a tree. Two pencils have been used again, one sharp, one blunt. There's no color in it but somehow I see the petals in delicate pinks and white. They cling, pale and fragile, to webs of emerald leaves and russet stems, then fall to the page where waiting shadows catch them.

Behind this one are pencil drawings stapled at the edge like a book. I don't want to look.

Eight years ago, that's when I made this book, when I stapled the memories closed so they wouldn't fall out and fall open again, so I wouldn't have to see them. So what do I think I'm doing here, now?

I was a young mother of three small boys, working through depression with the therapist our doctor sent me to. *Been there, done that, worn the tee-shirt*; that's for sure. So if this was meant to mend me back then, why am I looking again?

"Imagine the cupboard where you store your sheets and towels," the therapist told me. Will this new one say the same? I had plenty of sheets and towels and washing of course—just no time to do it all and no inclination. "Imagine your memories stored like that, all squashed and disorganized. You meant to fold them when you hid them away but you must have been too upset. So we'll fold them better now."

I remember wondering, even as she spoke, did I hide the memories because I wanted to, or was it just that nobody wanted to see?

My therapist seemed so sweetly, safely alien and foreign; petite behind her wide flat desk, exotic with a small red dot between her eyes. Glossy hair and perfectly painted fingernails made me think she would never leave anything untidy, not in her office, nor in her life. Those nails made me feel safe, unthreatened; they were too pretty to be claws.

"Depression's what happens when your memory closet overflows," she told me in soothing, sleep-inducing tones. "The door swings open and everything falls out. All those memories you don't want to think about, falling all over the floor."

She assured me I could tidy them up and fold them all away, then shut the door again. I think I must have painted that image somewhere—a mess of cloth and clothing descending hopelessly from a door. I expect I'll find it soon, as I tidy through all these papers on my floor, as I do what my dear *new* therapist tells me to do. But I'm not such a young mother now. The strands of hair around my face are lank, and I'm sure there's a hint of gray. Middle-aged, that's me; and I'm old enough to work through this thing carefully. Or old enough to decide for myself I don't want to.

I couldn't decide anything for myself back then. I was too unbalanced to ask what I wanted, so I did exactly what the therapist told me. I tidied up my washed-up dirty linen and shut the door until, eight years later, it's falling open again.

The pages stare accusingly at me, sharp metal staples eagerly waiting to slash like swords at my hand. The paper feels limp and worn with age but still has the power to turn my heart to lead, my breath to dust.

Snow touches the tops of trees in an innocent forest-drawn scene. I've outlined branches in sharp black pencil and shaded the sky underneath with blunter gray. Shadows glide where spring holds winter's return at bay. Frost rims the edges of leaves in the undergrowth, all crisply clear, while darkness haunts the gaps between tree trunks. One shadow seems to move and separate itself, near the edge of the page. It looks almost like a figure stepping forward, stepping aside. Perhaps it's a man.

I sit, barefoot, on my bedroom floor, with aching back and thighs. My childhood art lies scattered like discarded bedding around me—unfolded towels at my finger ends all soaked in memory. But the pages are made of paper and their creases stay straight and sharp. No mountain of welcoming cloth in a jumble where I can lay my head; these pages lie like frozen autumn leaves, not petal spring.

Sweet Tyke rests beside me, his breath making gentle snores, chin drooling on paws. I place my hand on his head and wait for energy to inspire. Then I decide. I'm not going to bother to try to turn the page. I'll take this stapled collection unseen to her office again. Let her tell me what to do with it.

The cover is dusty, faded, and smells of damp and age. Trees and leaves and shadows weave their dance. It's Paradise Park, a picture of Paradise in spring. And I was a Paradise artist wandering, thirteen years old in the spring of my fourteenth year.

"I used to carry a sketchpad around with me, and two pencils," I say, sitting on the edge of the therapist's sofa again, knees pressed together, hands in the air, satisfying a nervous need to explain.

She smiles and asks, "Why are you telling me this?" but I keep talking instead of trying to reply.

"I kept one of my pencils sharp, so I could do shapes and edges and make things clear. And the other was blunt for shading. Then I'd sharpen the blunt pencil and switch them around when I needed to."

"Yes. Indeed." My therapist steeples her hands so they look like a church guarding the confessional while she waits for more words.

But I've run out of ideas. I still haven't shown her the pictures of course. I still don't know if I will, but I've nothing to say and silence stretches out, blends black and white into its own shade of gray.

"You're looking through your pictures?" she asks, because that's what she told me to do. That's why I carried them down from the loft. That's why they've been scattered all over my bedroom floor. It's why I have to pack them away in their tins and cardboard boxes every night before Donald comes home. It's why I'm always late with dinner. It's why I have this stapled book in my bag.

I nod agreement and the back of my neck starts to ache while a lump fills my throat.

"Really looking," she insists. "Not just hiding them away." I almost nod again. "And you've hit a snag?" So I nod decisively, even my shoulders beginning to burn with shame.

"What's the problem, then?" the therapist asks and I wonder, *what indeed*?

I reach down for the bag that rests catlike, doglike perhaps, against my knees. The therapist pushes her tissues across the table to me. They're bright and cheerful, like paper petals in a pink, spring-colored box. But I'm not bending down to cry this time. She's read me wrong. I sit up, holding the stapled sketches out, all tidy, tidied, images from *then*.

"Have you looked at them?"

I shake my head. Why doesn't she take them from me? "I want you to instead."

"Why don't we look together?"

I hold the book and it feels like a leaden weight. I wish it would somehow fly from my hand to hers. Then she might look and analyze while I gaze around the room. I gaze anyway.

Blue curtains frame a window lit with shades of sunshine and warmth. Paintings hang all colored and bright on the walls, all framed just right. Bookshelves stand loaded with straight-spined filigreed volumes, organized by topic, name and size. Earth-toned rugs cover the floor. A slightly spicy, soothing scent drifts lazily on the air. But my shifting gaze tries to glide past the therapist's face and I'm suddenly caught.

She stares at me, eyes watching through that clear summer blue that always seems so deep and so unsettling. Her warm face glows like an afternoon in fall. Gray curls of hair make a frame of winter's ice. I look for wrinkles and lines but her expression gives nothing away. Is she frowning? Is she happy? Perhaps I'm not very good at sensing emotions, or perhaps she has none.

I watch the therapist drop her pale wrists down to rest on the table. I hear them knock lightly on wood, and the sound makes me jump. The rumble of traffic through the window resettles me. *Was that the call of a bird?* Warm air starts to roar in the heating vents, and a plane flies overhead. The string of a desk lamp stirs. Beneath it, notes and notepads rustle, their edges curling to the artificial breeze. Then I let my sheaf of papers fall on top of them. I sigh, lean forward and place my hand on smoothly polished wood.

She knows the art of silence, this therapist. Is it the quiet of spring I wonder, waiting for life and hoping to come back to me, or autumn's fall and the call of winter's snow? My thoughts are wandering.

She knows the art of stillness and waits, hands poised and posed beside my picture book.

She knows persuasion.

I reach one hand to the tissue box while my other hand traces images in the air, nails like blossoms, fingers like bent twigs. The images are all black and white and gray, drawn with two pencils. Is that significant? One sharp, one blunt. Will draining all the colors away release me from their pain?

There's no escape. It's time to look at what the pictures tell.

The figure at the edge of the trees still watches, still probably a man, caught between sunlight and lamplight on the table. Is that a head maybe, a leg, perhaps an arm? But it's not clear. It could be someone slinking, hiding in shade. Or it could be just the way I chose to render the shadows of trees.

I turn the page, my hands on automatic pilot while my heart beats in my ears and my brain tries to freeze. The paper crinkles, old, almost brittle with age. The picture won't lie flat when I've opened it up so I press down hard, running my finger firmly down a new crease in the page. These memories have never been seen, since the day I stapled them. I don't want to see them now.

I stare at the window behind the thick blue curtain, at a gray patch of sky. But my neck feels hot and it takes too much effort to hold my head up high so I look down again. Hands on the table. Paper. Picture. Black and white and memories without words.

For all that the pencil's black and the paper white, the picture feels real, filled with shades and shadows and the coolness of green in memory.

Green trees rendered gray surround a pale ethereal center to this frame. Foreground puddles reflect the tracery of branches overhead. Rain is a slantness, left to right, in the way the lines are drawn. At the center, where the gray turns white, sunrays slant as well into sparkling waterfalls. Trees stand to attention, spreading from all four corners. I see their shadows faintly sketched behind the soft-drawn clearing. And a tiny figure stands perfectly centered there. She's too small for the picture though. If I try to draw it again I'll make her taller.

Slender arms stretch achingly toward to the brightened sky. Small face, upturned, is bathed in rivers of cascading light. The girl's long hair, huge backpack, skirt, legs, shoes are shaded all in soft-edged black.

A featureless smudge of white shows where her face should be, as if I changed my mind and almost erased her.

I wonder if the girl is me and perhaps I meant to erase myself. But the therapist doesn't ask and I don't say. Too cold to shiver, too curious to complain, too scared to stop and think, I turn the page again.

Warm air blows over my hands from the heating vent, ice over my heart.

This time the figure of the man is closer, approaching in front of the trees. He looks like a shadow untethered from the forest all around. Sun makes a halo behind his head with smudges of white on his shoulders, as if he's an angel in disguise, mistakenly dressed in black. He casts no shadow.

I turn the page.

I tried to show how fast the figure moved, with lines at his back; mooring lines for a ship perhaps as he strains to leave the page. The trees are rendered lovingly with lacework of branches and leaves. But the man, the figure, is a shadow, nothing more—no features, just a hollow blackness tethered by trailing lines.

I turn again.

This picture's filled with a face drawn too close to the eye, pencil dust still bleeding from the thickness of the gloom. Wisps of hair escape from a circular frame like a baseball cap. The chin's shaded in lines drawn straight as rain, a beard perhaps. Flat cheeks, sharp nose with nostril hairs—the head's tilted upward and the artist sees from below. Thick lips jut out. Black shadows hide the eyes under smooth-drawn lines for the edge of his cap.

I remember the angle, me looking up at him, while gentle breezes blew their scents of spring. Wind from the office's heating blows over the paper, rustling it, reminding me of leaves.

Another picture shows another face. This time the perspective's different; the position too. Parted lips take center stage as if the artist can't take her eyes from them. Lines and shadows hint at a tongue and teeth hiding between. But around the mouth the face has faded to patches of light and shade. There's none of that bright white left behind when an eraser hides the features—this picture looks more like the artist never saw or bothered to draw them. Black holes for eyes, pale lump of a nose, but everything blunt-pencil shaded around the clear-drawn, intricate, shape of somebody's bearded lips.

I stare at this one for a while, but still it doesn't come clear. The man—why do I think I must have known him? He remains a stranger on the page, well hidden behind the black and white and gray.

The next picture is nothing but hands. Clasped hands, empty hands, open hands, closed hands, blunt-nailed hands, short-fingered hands, but ever, only, hands. They pass through, over, under each other, ghost hands and solid together, some bits erased while others raggedly remain. Impossibly twisted hands. Hands everywhere.

And underneath, covered, hidden away, pale lines like broken memories scar the page. Something's almost invisible, drawn over and almost lost.

I see the girl from the clearing again, backpack, dark hair, short skirt, hands raised in the air.

"Do you want to talk about it?"

"No."

The next sketches are abstract, easy to ignore. I turn them over, one by one, waiting for something to spark a sign of hope. Sharp lines make shapes with eyes, nose, lips and tongues drawn into triangles and squares. They overlap, slide underneath, and peak from hidden edges, stop and stare.

In one there are just two pairs of eyes, one beetle-browed and dark in a rectangular box, one wide and white. Guilt and innocence bound or fated to unite?

Reality intervenes again when I come to a picture of a tree. *Tall trunk, wide branches—the bark's well-drawn, black-webbed with crinkled lines and layers of shade. The leaves— spring leaves—have grown from bud to green and form a glowing canopy now, no signs of snow. The ground is mixed, dry grass, damp earth, fall's skeletal detritus awaiting summer's cleansing rain. I admire the shading, the way I've mixed the pencils, blunt and sharp, to give a hint of shape without form, of light and shade without dark.*

A small white foot, that blinding, eraser-born white, extends behind the tree. You'll only see it if you look closely enough. Black shadows might be an arm smudged around the trunk. A hand's held higher on the other side—man hugging tree perhaps? Man hugging small white figure between his body and the bark? But you can't really see it.

"You can't really see it," I say to the therapist, my voice rasping and small. I'm only speaking because the silence has started to get to me. My finger has rested against that small white foot for far too long.

"You drew it. You know what's there," the therapist says.

"But you can't really see it, can you?" Man and child might just be accidental tricks of the light.

I turn the page.

Rain. It's a picture of rain, but the lines draw closer together in the center of the page. Diagonal shading forms two figures together—man and woman, walking hand in hand. What's wrong with that?

The next image is a bunch of flowers with two hands reaching toward it from the sides. One hand is rough, blunt-fingered, scratched and calloused. Work-worn nails have jagged edges, dark and rimed with black. The other hand, thin and questing, is almost a child's.

Bound together, arms around each other, tall man and shorter woman cling and hug in the slant-drawn shade of a tree. It's all done with shadows, dark and light with no detail, only the one blunt pencil washing shade over paper and life. There's a backpack on the ground.

Shape of a woman, pale, delicate, clothed in diaphanous fabric, fading light. She stands with arms upheld to a stormy sky.

Shape of a woman fallen, crouched on the ground.

I'm turning pages quickly now, too fast to press them down. If I let go, the book will close itself. But my hands are tied to someone else's law. I open, turn and open the page again. I have to see what image I'll find on the other side, have to search, look for more. My neck aches and my eyes can't move away. But I'm not crying.

Leaves lie scattered over the page, reminding me of the hands I saw before. But the hands were false, too many, too awkwardly drawn, their mystery obscure. These leaves lie clear and sharply veined, then squished into mud and soil, as if a figure's been lying there. As if...

I need those tissues, grab two at once and wodge them in my fist.

Leaves on the ground fill the next page too, and the next, and the one after it. But now there's one where I've scored straight lines over them, red pen, red ink, like a teacher declaring the picture's not good enough for the classroom wall.

Leaves and a patch of water reflecting light, not clear like a puddle, but sticky like glue, coating over the soft buds of spring.

I feel the therapist's cool hand over mine. She turns the page for me while her minted breath drifts into my eyes. The fresh taste cools the heat that's burning me, but I can't look up. I'm trapped, awaiting the end.

The final picture, sketched after more broken abstracts of hands and eyes and scattered clothes, is just a child. She sits alone, small girl cross-legged on the ground. Her arms reach down, pulling white socks over muddy feet. Dark shoes lie next to the backpack at her side. Buttons on her blouse are fastened wrong. Her skirt's too high, the fabric lying crooked over her thighs. But she's not so young. Not innocent. The shape of a woman's body worn by a child.

Dark hair hides her face. Dark shadows hide the trees. And mortal flesh keeps secrets silently.

A crocus blooms beside her.

"Spring," I remember my Granny saying. "When a young man's fancy turns to what a young man fancies." But *he* wasn't young, and I never drew his face. I was only thirteen.

Spent tissues lie like crumpled rocks around the spring-pink box.

Chapter 25

"You knew who he was of course," says the therapist, reading from ancient notes where I've told it all before.

I shake my head.

"But you must have known."

If I'd known, wouldn't I have done something, I say to her. Later, when there were those rumors of someone, a predator in the park, wouldn't I have told them what I knew? Wouldn't I have saved *her*?

I taste a lump, like dust and lichen broken from an ancient wood-pile, in my throat. I feel like I might choke. I stretch my hand and try to claim a bit more space to breathe. Then I see my pictures scattered on her desk. The staple's given way and set them free; I want to straighten them. Maybe it's the smell of old paper or mold from the attic that's making me cough. But I'll line the images up, pile them up, and the scent will go away. I'll tidy them like memories and close the book. Let bookworms devour as worms devoured the child.

I'm going to cry or else be sick.

"You must have known, Sylvia, so why didn't you say?"

I clutch my hands to my chest now, hoping to keep the tears inside, but my leg starts to shake. I want to stand and shout at her or run around the room. "I didn't know," I say, my voice rising to a squeak. I didn't know. I couldn't have known. It's really not my fault.

Slowly, red bleeds out from all the black around the room. The furnishings come back into focus again. Pale blue curtains—a soothing shade. Blue carpet, pink and blue patterns on the chair. Sweet scents in the air. Neat and tidy books on a well-ordered shelf.

I see in the therapist's cool blue eyes, she doesn't believe my denial, but she doesn't know. Her manicured hands are shuffling all my pictures again, not just the book. The pages are penciled black and white, pale shades of gray. She picks out ones where I drew people, and she spreads them in front of me—Mom and Daddy, Lydia, Troy.

"See how carefully you drew this one," she says, holding Troy's image out. I take the page and trace the lines with my finger, pleased that my hand stays steady and doesn't tremble. The storm's blown over, see?

A young man leans his body languidly against a wall. Long legs angle slightly outward, carefully balancing his weight. Narrow jeans, with twin holes drilled through the knees, hug well-muscled thighs. Cross-shaded fabric reveals the thinness of pockets, the shape of a wallet, and more. Troy's shirt hangs loosely over his hips, unbuttoned top and bottom. He holds one hand out toward the viewer, as if in the middle of explaining something important. Thin fingers stretch from the page leaving shadows behind.

I've sketched the tiny hairs on his chest with my specially sharpened pencil, curled and dark under the softly rounded chin.

"Look at his face."

I look.

Dark hair flops lazily over the heavy brows of Troy's hooded eyes. A narrow nose sticks out a little too far, too pointed but nicely shaded at the side. A tiny shadow hovers over his mouth. Cheeks are flat, the pencil lines smoothed with a finger to form soft planes then stippled over with stubble. Lips curl widely into a smile.

"The attention to detail," the therapist says. "Do you see what I mean? You have the knack, Sylvia. You really look, really see what you're looking at."

I lean forward on the sofa, hearing the springs creak behind me. I feel almost proud. My drawing really is pretty good. Then the therapist pulls together those once-stapled sheets in a loose-edged fan. I shiver. I don't want to look. Besides, she's making a mess all over her desk. The pictures will surely be out of order. I reach to tidy them.

"Stop that," she says in her short sharp *listen-to-me* voice, so I stop.

I'm trying to look innocent, like a child caught stealing cookies. I gaze around the room again, wondering what's outside the window—is the traffic piling up? But my eyes are drawn to pages held together like a booklet again, open to a picture of the therapist's choice. I can't turn away, but at least I can close my eyes. Dark. Red at the edges. I've shuttered them tight so I don't have to see.

Her hand touches mine. Then I feel paper, crinkled with age, resting on my palm, while my thumb is moved into place to hold it down. The staple pricks my skin. Bent edges shift to pull the pages closed, but they'll trap me inside if they do, so I open my eyes. Which picture is this?

Parted lips take center stage, as if the artist can't take her eyes from them. Lines and shadows hint at a tongue and teeth hiding between. But around the mouth the face has faded to patches of shadow and shade. There's none of that bright white left behind when an eraser hides the features—this picture looks more like the artist never saw or bothered to draw them. Black holes for eyes, pale lump of a nose, but everything else blunt-pencil shaded around the clear-drawn, intricate, detailed shape of somebody's sharp-edged lips.

"You really look, really see, and all you draw is his lips?"

"It's all I was looking at," I plead. "I didn't see him." Turning pages, shuffling through broken images, I try to show what I mean. *See.* Bright sunlight floods from behind him, dark shadows, quivering leaves, lines that indicate speed. I didn't see him.

"Or you didn't want to see."

Chapter 26

Next meeting she asks me to tell her what happened, using words instead of pictures. Why?

"Because then you might realize what you're trying to hide."

I'm not hiding anything.

"So tell me," she says, while I settle back on the sofa. "Tell me about the first time you met him. What was the weather like?"

"Raining."

But dryer in the forest I remember, and beautiful in that clearing when the sun came out.

The figure at the edge of the trees watches me. Sunlight blazes in front of him; shadows of trees and water loom behind. Is that a head maybe, a leg? Is this perhaps an arm? But it's not clear. It could be someone slinking, hiding in shade. Or it could be just the way I chose to render the shapes of trees.

I walked home alone from school that day. Bad idea, but nobody knew there was anything wrong in the park back then. It was spring in my first year of Junior High. I didn't feel like a new girl anymore. I knew my way around. And I could have caught the activity bus, should have I suppose, but it was always so crowded, rocking with noise and boys who'd stayed late for sports. I might not find a seat. After art class all I wanted was a bit of peace.

It was raining, I remember, that heavy spring rain that tries to wash the memory of winter away—rain that drips down the back of your neck and splashes up from the ground to soak your legs. The sky kept switching from thick gray clouds to glimpses of summer blue. There should have been a rainbow I guess, but then, my life was full of should-have-beens.

I should have been home earlier, Mom would say. Should have been doing my homework. Should have taken extra math not art. Should have walked with Sharon to the gates. I should have told them when I first knew. Should have worn a different skirt, a different shirt. Should never have gone out looking like *that* and especially not to school, and not to the woods. Should sing louder in church.

I could have taken the main path through the park. It was wide and well-lit, well-travelled, and went from the wrought iron gates up and over the hill. But puddles had turned its paving stones to lakes the night before. Small cataracts splashed with every step, and rain seeped in through the seams in my school shoes.

I'm not sure why I thought cutting through the trees would be any dryer, but I did it anyway.

Spring leaves caught the downpour, softening it, flavoring it with hints of minty green. The rain took on a slippery sound instead of incessant drumming. The ground was slick, soft and wet with mud, while autumn's debris lay scattered like pages of a book. I started to run, my backpack banging heavily, my arms outstretched for balance as I skidded between downed branches and withering trunks. Then I saw the clearing and had to stop and gaze.

Sunshine poured through a gap in the trees like a waterfall of light. It looked so impossibly beautiful, as if angels and fairies might invite me to their dance. I wanted to paint it there and then, except the rain would turn my paper to mush. Instead I ran toward the ethereal sheen, suddenly feeling my footsteps grow more sure and confident. I stood with my face turned up to the rain, its gentle sweetness tingling on the back of my tongue. Trickles of warmth trailed down my face. I stretched my arms, let the pack settle comfortably firm in the small of my back. I felt truly blessed.

I'm not sure when I realized I wasn't alone. A footstep sounded behind me perhaps, or I felt his breath in my hair. I don't know. But suddenly someone was holding me, turning me around and pressing my face to his chest. My eyes were closed by the gritty hardness of his shirt. My mouth filled with cloth. I thought it was one of the boys from school, someone from the bus perhaps, planning to frighten me. But I wasn't scared. The sun's sweet blessing had gilded me, made me strong.

"Did you see his face?"

I smelled oil on his clothes and heard his panting breath as if he'd been running. Then he pulled my chin up, pointing me heavenward. The sun was a halo behind his head, while his features all lay in shadow.

"No, I didn't see."

Then he started kissing me.

I remember his tongue was thick and tasted like dirt. I thought it might choke me, and I tried to push him away, but he just held me tighter. Then he started to lick around my lips, and his breath was sour like onions gone off in the fridge. He had some kind of beard I remember. His cheeks scratched like sandpaper, and his breathing cracked the sound of falling rain. Afterward I felt the weight of his chin on my head, while slick saliva turned to ice around my mouth. Then he thanked me and left.

"Did you see his face?"

"No. He was walking away from me. I just saw the back of his head."

"What about the next time?"

The therapist ought to be asking why there *was* a next time, shouldn't she? Why was I ever stupid enough to go back through the forest that way? I've asked myself. But I couldn't let some stranger scare me out of the peace of the woods, or deny me that special blessing from the trees. I liked walking there. I liked being invisible with no one around to keep complaining at me. I liked to wander where nobody else could see. And I wasn't afraid. He didn't hurt me. He might not even be real. Perhaps he held onto me to make himself real. Maybe that was all he wanted.

I guess, perhaps, a part of me really wanted to be held as well.

"Why?"

I wasn't blind. I saw Lydia and Troy sometimes with their faces locked together, arms octopus-twined so I couldn't tell where one ended or the other began. White-shirted Lydia hung wrapped in Troy's blue arms. Blue-shirted Troy was striped with Lydia's delicate shades of cream. Dark hair and light all blended around their heads.

I saw other kids kissing too in school corridors, girls locked between a guy's embrace and the faded paint on a wall, hands sliding over arms and waist and slipping under clothes, knees raised up high as if excitement made them reach for the sky.

All he'd done was kiss me, and nobody else was kissing me anymore. No goodnight kisses from Mom or Daddy now I was their big little girl. No boyfriend locking his lips with mine, like Troy in his truck with Lydia. Not even my sister's welcome kiss in the morning since she belonged to someone else.

I had my reasons, but all the same, the therapist really should ask more questions of me.

I've tried to show how fast the figure moves with lines at his back; mooring lines for a ship perhaps as he strains to leave the page, still reaching for me. The trees are rendered lovingly with laceworks of branches and leaves. But the man, the figure, is shadow, nothing more—no features, just a hollow blackness tethered by trailing lines that look like rain.

It was raining again that second time. I wasn't looking for him or even for the clearing, just rushing home, wet and weary after art. I saw the gap in the trees and wondered if the sun would shine again. I felt my feet slow down as if I were drawn to return and seek that image of beauty and peace. It was such a beautiful spot. I listened while birds sang summer to the raindrops' beat.

Then I saw him, just at the edge of the trees. I knew the shape of his shirt and the way he walked, heading toward me now, where last I'd seen him hurry away. I knew it was him when he stretched out his arms to me.

"Did you see his face?"

"Not really. He was moving too fast."

"But you saw the way he walked? Or the way he ran? Which was it?"

"I guess I didn't look."

"Well, try to look now."

He wore his cap too low and his collar too high, dark features sandwiched in between. His face was invisible to me. All I saw was the gray beard covering his chin. Clouds overhead meant I couldn't find his eyes.

"Who did he look like, Sylvia?"

"He didn't look like anyone."

"What type of person then?"

"None. No one. No." She seems to think asking questions might change the past, but I know it won't. I didn't see.

Of course, I know now who he was, but I still can't see him clearly even though I try. Staring through memory's like trying to pick off a scab when it's going to bleed. It hurts like stretching your body so far that your shoulder comes out of joint, like sticking your finger in your eye, or deliberately stubbing your little toe over again. Like seeing the bull and knowing he's going to charge? I can't see him and it hurts too much if I try.

"Sometimes you have to take off the scab when there's infection underneath."

I hear her words but I don't reply because I'm not infected; not infectious either. I'm just sad.

He sounded sad when he spoke to me that time. He hadn't thought I'd come, he said, but he was pleased to find me there. He told me he trusted me. Then he kissed me again.

"And what else?"

What else? Nothing else. Not then. Eventually he'd slide his hands beneath my clothes, just to hug me closer. Eventually his fingers would touch and probe. But not at the start.

I tell her how he squeezed my body between his own and the tree, how the bark felt crumbly but firm at my back, and tickled with tiny pieces breaking away. I remember his breathing, hot and heavy in my ear. I remember him shifting his weight against me, sliding his hands till we fitted together as if we were growing as one; how it used to feel when he touched me everywhere, like I was a painting unfolded and tearing apart. I tell her I didn't quite know it was wrong, because you're meant to respect and obey older people. They're wiser then you. And he meant me no harm. I knew because he said so.

It might not have really been wrong, I explain, because he hadn't done anything to me, not like the unnamed things Lydia's promise ring said she shouldn't do. And it might have been right because no one else was touching me. I needed to be loved. And because…

"But the last time?" the therapist asks me now, looking down at her notes as if she needs what she's written to give a clue what she should say. "You must have seen his face when he undressed you on the ground."

"I closed my eyes."

"You kept them closed, all the time?"

I remember the moment I knew I was going to fall. He'd tipped me back over his arm and my balance was gone. I could only pray he'd catch me, so I closed my eyes.

The sofa's firm beneath my legs, its cushion pressing into me as I squirm. I'm not sure if I want to stand, or push myself further back where softness yields and comforts me. I use my hands to shift my body. Then I fall, surrounded by memories pouring down like dirty rain.

"I didn't see him," I say.

"I think you did," the therapist replies. "I think you knew and you didn't say and you can't forgive yourself, but it wasn't your fault."

My mouth is filled with the memory of his tongue and the smell and taste and grittiness of dirt.

The therapist gets up from her chair, walks across the room, and fills a plastic cup with water from the sink. *How does she know?* Then she sits down again, gives me the cup, and asks how I felt.

I don't want to answer. I wrap my hands around plastic, wrap my tongue around the chemical cleansing taste, and close my eyes. Still, she's waiting. "I felt needed," I say.

Paper rustles on her desk. I risk a look and she's opened the book again, freshly stapled, smoothed flat and clean. She tells me to look at the picture I drew of hands. I almost laugh. *Needed* or *Kneaded* I think, imagining how the leather-like dough is kneaded to make bread. Fingers squeeze and press and mold like the past has molded me—like *he* molded me. But my laughter stalls like a dump-truck of garbage in my throat. I daren't let it out because it tastes like him. I sip water again.

"How do you feel now?" the therapist asks.

I feel invisible. My paper's worn too thin. Then I feel like a child in a clearing in that moment before strange footsteps sound and change my life. Blessed and broken. I can't go back, nor forward either.

"Would you have said? Would you have told everyone about him if you'd known who he was?"

I'm sure I would, but the more I think about it, the more I feel like I'm testing a broken tooth. My tongue starts to trip over words and dive into holes where the agony kills me. Would I have told? I really don't know. In a world where grandparents could be eternally unforgiven, would I have done that to him? I don't know what to say.

Then the therapist adds, "Keep looking through the pictures, Sylvia. We'll explore this one later."

The clock ticks on her wall, all ornate golden filigree and numbers as tall as small books. My time is up.

I pack my bag and grab a handful of tissues from the pink box. I always wipe my eyes now before I leave, and brush my hair back from my face with my hands. The door clicks closed with an odd finality behind me and the next patient looks up. Receptionist waves while patient pretends to smile but is really just glad I'm out of the way. Then I carry my burden of memories, black and white and shades of gray, in the bag Donald bought me for Christmas when he said my purse was too small.

At home I walk into the safety of my kitchen and feel suddenly lighter. Perhaps it's the weather. Maybe the rain's going to stop.

Chapter 27

I drop my bag on a chair and feel its burden leaving me. My lips stretch into a smile as I reach for the coffee jar. Bitter scents soothe me as the dark stuff brews, while the coffeemaker's gurgles compete with ticking clock. Autumn's last leaves are blown by bright spring breezes against the glass door.

I find some paper in the living room and a pencil on the counter-top, waiting for shopping-list needs. I have better uses for it now.

While coffee glugs, I hook a chair leg toward me and sit down to draw. It's just a doodle at first, human figures piled on top of each other, space-filling curves of arms and legs and thighs. I remember framing notes in my workbooks at school when I was bored, adding bodies on bodies with hands reaching down to the words I was meaning to write. They were secret pictures, not ones I cared to keep. So I roll this new page into a ball and toss it in the trash.

Coffee's ready, and I pour without sugar or cream, remembering sadly how sickly sweet I used to drink it as a child. Adding those glorious lashings of white on white, just like my daddy, I'd tell myself perhaps it would make *me* sweet. But at college no one kept sugar in their rooms, afraid the ants would come in. Cream went sour too fast, and I learned to drink my coffee black...

...left-handed, while my right hand's drawing pictures, and my mind's on other things.

Three figures sit together on a sofa. Hands on knees over torn jeans, they're clearly my sons—Thomas, Michael and

Adam; three peas in a pod. I shade their hair, Adam's curly, Thomas' straight and way too long, and Michael's neutrally normal. Then I think of three monkeys and redraw their arms, covering the ears of one, then eyes, then mouth. Hear no evil, see none and speak none I think, realizing I've managed to hide their faces again.

It feels good to be drawing. I wonder how long it's been since I last sat down with pencil in hand and no tasks on my mind. It's better than painting in front of a crowd, all waiting for teacher's advice; better than running out of black and red and hating the fire of an image gone cruelly dead. I sip more coffee, careful not to spill, and push the completed picture across the table. Done! Then I snatch another page, while my fractured mind starts wandering again.

Pencils and pens are made for job applications these days, for after-school schedules, lists of library books and student qualifications, names and addresses of friends of one son or another, notes to remind myself I need to buy milk. Meanwhile I've drawn a baby in the bottom left corner of a page, and a story starts to grow.

The infant lies curled up on itself, as if not yet born. Thumb in mouth, fist clutching an errant toe, eyes wide and bright, it could be any one of my sons but I think, from the mop of hair curling over its head, it might be Adam. Young Michael soon sits cross-legged next to him with a hand pressed over his baby brother's chest, like a cat with a mouse.

I remember the day we brought our youngest child home from hospital. We wanted to present him to his brothers and make it a good experience, so I laid a wide blue blanket on the floor and placed my precious bundle neatly in the center. Their level; safe; non-threatening.

Little Michael tottered dangerously close, so I held out my hand in protection, afraid he might fall. Then he squelched down onto a sodden diaper, reaching a small determined fist over his brother's chest. I wasn't sure if he wanted to squash him down or pick him up.

"What are you doing, little one?" I asked.

"Want baby crawl," Michael answered, with just the same confidence as when he demanded a toy car roll down a hill. What else would baby do? But Michael's sudden tug on his arm deprived Adam of the comfort of his thumb. Seeing my third son's tiny face crumple, I pulled my second son's urgent hand away.

"He's still a baby," I tried to explain.

Michael, with two-year-confidence, replied assuredly, "Babies crawl."

A third child stands now, behind the earlier two. His face is bent in serious observation of a toy held tight in his hands. Gray socks slide sweetly down his legs beneath pants too short or too long. And his tee-shirt's too tight. I think this is Thomas, but soon I find I'm adding more figures to the scene.

Thomas again, his straight black hair like a girl's turning up at the end. Beetled eyebrows slope in a deep worried frown, and his pointed nose is buried in a book. Beside him another, taller child crouches over the strings of a guitar. Adam aged nine?

In the middle of the page I find I've drawn three sons like a set of jugs, from shortest to tallest, from curly hair to straight. They might be dancing, each with his left foot forward and right arm back. Adam carries a guitar slung over his shoulder, Michael has his nose in a book, and Thomas holds a cell-phone to his ear.

I finish my coffee and think I could make something of this picture perhaps—my children multiplied into the seven or seventy ages of man. The figures in the center of the page should be colored, I think, to anchor past and future in eternal present. But my hand is still drawing while I wonder where colored pencils might have been stored.

More figures meander down the page on their way to the bottom right corner. They start to crouch, their outlines wavering and thin. I think this might be Donald bent over a computer. Maybe my father's the one with the walking cane.

And right at the end, tucked away, almost invisible, a man with an electrical shock of Einstein hair, face sunk in on itself, body curled like baby's with back of the wrist curled up toward his lips, this one could be Grandpa.

The colored pencils are in the dining room, tucked away behind a fruit bowl on the shelf. Adam probably used them to shade maps for homework and label the different States. I've refilled my coffee and drunk and refilled until three cups later I'm finished. The picture is done.

Busses roar, brakes squeal, and children shriek. The coffeemaker's silent, and a basketball's thump accompanies the clock's measured beat. Then a key grates in the door.

"Hi Adam," I call as my youngest son's backpack thuds to the floor. Shoes skitter and crash against the wall.

"Mom," he mutters, reaching into the fridge. Then he turns to look at me. "What are you doing? Hey, what's that?"

I'm not really sure I want him to see, but he'll tear the page if he grabs, so I hand it to him.

"Hey, that's us." He sounds pleasantly surprised. "Hey, Mom. That's not bad. I didn't know you could do that."

I think of the pictures so frequently left scattered on our bedroom floor with the door open wide. He must have seen them, but I guess he's never looked.

Chapter 28

I phone to cancel my next session at the hospital, because Thanksgiving's coming. The therapist suggests it might be a good time to take a break. "Get all those holidays and birthdays out of your system," she says. "Look through some more pictures. Don't give up. And give me a call when you think you're ready for me."

I can't decide if I'm happy or sad about this. Am I such a hopeless case she doesn't want to talk to me anymore, or am I cured? At least I'm drawing again, I think. And my drawings make me feel real, unlike those black and red paintings adorning the walls of the community art room. I don't even care if Donald thinks they're all a waste of time.

"Not that wasting time's a bad thing," he adds, lugubriously determined to sound generous and fair while he sits on the bed rolling his socks over pale waggling heels, one by one, before letting them fall where they will on the floor. "We all need hobbies, Syl, but there's more to life."

I don't earn money; that's what he means. I offer no help in the quest for college fees or retirement accounts. I'm a consumer of family resources when I ought to be a supplier—Donald used those words once long ago, though he hotly denies them now. I'm a waste of space—which he never said, but I hear his voice in my head.

"Are you sure you're cured?" he asks now with a worried frown, digging for slippers under the bed, while I pack pencil sketches in an old metal tin.

"No," I answer, shutting the lid and gazing down at the image on its surface where a cat curls happily. "She didn't say

I was cured. She just said I should give her a call when I need to go back."

"So, when will that be?"

"When I've looked at some more of these pictures I suppose."

I gesture at papers like autumn leaves covering the floor, and Donald sighs theatrically.

"I'm tidying them up." I defend myself from his unspoken complaint. "I'll make dinner in a minute."

Then he tugs me down beside him on the bed. "That's not what I meant." We sit like teenage lovers with wedding rings for promises, and I smell his closeness, his aftershave, feeling his breath on my cheek while his fingers rub against my arm. He tells me the pictures make him feel like I'm trying to become someone else and forget I ever met him, which makes me wonder which one of us really needs a therapist.

"I'm trying to find myself," I say.

"But what if you don't find you, and you become somebody else?"

"I'm me, Donald," I answer him. "I'll always be me. But I want to become a better sort of me. I don't want to be broken anymore."

He strokes his fingers lower than my arms. "I don't think you're broken."

The TV, computer, and Adam's guitar all compete to make the most noise and drown out the house. Three boys are locked in their private worlds, while we close the bedroom door on ours.

"Not broken at all," says Donald, kicking his slippers off again and setting his hands to undoing the many buttons on my blouse. He nuzzles my neck as the cloth pulls free and I freeze, feeling for a moment as if I'm coming undone. "Not broken," he repeats, and I wonder how long I'll last before needing the therapist again. Then I settle my fast-beating heart, remind myself we're married, and tune in to his game.

Close the curtains. Lock the bedroom door. Feel my husband's hands slide gently and kindly, so softly over me. Hear his murmuring love as he slips my arms from their fabric, pulls my blouse slowly over my head, and unclips my brassiere. He lets his fingers linger on my breast, circling the nipple until his warm wet lips bend down to suckle me. Then, slowly, he slides my jeans down the length of my legs, tucking his questing fingers under the waist of my underwear.

"You could undress me," he says, his voice thick with treacle. So I fumble with buttons but feel like a failure struggling with a simple command. The fabric of his smart, slick suit stands too firm. I'm scared to unzip him in case I do it wrong, but I smell him now. The scent of his desire. Then he moves and sighs and pushes my hands away.

We lie on the bed and he asks what I like him to do, but I don't know. He always asks and I never answer him. He wants me to tell him how to pleasure me, but I never know what to say. His body pleases. His love. The fact that he stays. The feel of him holding me tight like he'll never let me go.

I like his hands and his silk-smooth cheeks feeling hard, well-shaven, clean. I stretch like a cat where his cool bare skin rests evenly on mine. When his body rises, glides, hangs over me, I gaze into his eyes. Warm, laughing, happy, bubbling eyes, I shiver with delight and fall under their spell. Then he pulls my hand as if to make me touch him, and I retreat, wanting him to touch me.

We fumble, the timing never quite right and the missed beats always mine. The musky scent of love surrounds us, muffles the sounds of family and home. I wrap my arms around him and hold him tight when he wants to be free. I gaze into his eyes just at the moment when they turn cloudy and stop gazing back into mine. I feel his smile like warmth filling me, but he's ready to fill somewhere else. Then I welcome him, and slip and slide and glide to the rhythm of his tune. But his jaw turns slack. That's when I close my eyes again. I turn my head, stretching my neck, and press my cheek into the pillow. His loving and his warm embrace are welcome—he's welcome in me—but I won't look. He fills me, through and through, and I remind myself to smile.

The cat on the tin of black and white pictures smiles. Its lips curl in a secretive, catlike, nap-like grin. Its tiny teeth match the row of shiny diamonds along its collar. Green eyes stare lazily above a pink buttoned nose, and yellow sunlight forms the shape of a halo behind its ears. White paws and tail curl together in a comfortable ball while a soft blue cushion sags beneath the weight. Overhead, a flicker of light on black looks like angel wings aflutter on the white cat's back.

Chapter 29

Two figures walk hand in hand along a beach away from the viewer. A setting sun hangs lightly over their heads; its pale rays dominate the page. The thin-etched lines of a fine sharp pencil delineate shapes of hands and feet, while softer thicker shades fold clothes, form ripples in sand, and slide along the ridges and reflections of the sea. Splashes of color are added like afterthoughts. The sun's bright ball is orange, with streaks of faded red and brown forming a pattern of feathers in the sky. The woman wears blue shoes, turned white by water at the toes, and the man is shod in green. The startling white of an eraser's cleanliness surrounds the interlinked hands of my two walkers, revealing shining yellow in their rings. If you cut the picture in three, like a pie, the splashes of color, sun, hands, and feet, would lie each in a different part of the page.

This second picture just shows their hands with fingers intertwined. I've colored wedding rings in pink and blue. And I've always loved drawing hands, ever since I learned in school that they're supposed to be difficult. I love the shape of fingers, the patterns of joints lying so close to the skin, and the lines that can't be lifelines because they change—I've watched mine shift. And in pictures, I've erased them.

The woman's nails are buffed with an eraser's silken sheen. They shine while the man's lie blunt and hard against his skin. The background's darkened to rich soft-shaded gray with hints of reflections in yellow around the colors of the rings.

Another picture is centered in a frame of twining bodies. Arms, legs, hips, thighs, heads; each figure's complete, but tangled in a vine of languorous limbs. Darkening toward the edge of the page, these doodles remind me of how I used to decorate workbooks in school. But I've used an eraser to lighten the heart of the image, fading to white in the middle where two bodies lie. The woman is underneath, her legs drawn up, her hands reaching high over the man's broad shoulders. The man's chest faces the viewer and he wears an elated smile, the tip of his tongue just caught in line with his teeth. Blue eyes, red tongue are the only colors in this picture; the rest is black and white—not even any gray where lines are clear, bodies slick and smooth, and shadows just a case of repetition where the shape's twice drawn. Hair flops comfortably over the man's handsome face, a hint of shade on his jaw, square chin—I think it could be Donald from long ago.

And now a pregnant woman sits on a pale blue mat. The color's darker where her weight holds it down, as if there's something yielding, a cushion underneath. Her legs are crossed. One hand rests against the swell of her belly. Long hair floats, hiding her face. The blue mat's palely reflected beneath her bump. It mirrors the blue of the woman's eyes, the rest all black and white.

A mother feeds her son, but all you can see is the boy's round head, hair shaded brown, clasped to the delicate pink and blue of a breast. Smooth contours mold and melt with hints of a tiny hand clutching at air. But if you look closer the hand's not there.

Three bodies curl like kittens on a bed, mother, father and son. The child's in the middle, red eyes, the father's blue, the mother's green. Heads lie close together, parents' bodies curled left and right to keep the infant safe, arms touching his chest. The front of the picture has father's feet to the left, mother's to the right, and tiny infant legs lie in between.

Three bodies and a cat this time. I've finally managed one of those pictures where the image changes depending on what you expect. The green-eyed cat has red and blue jewels in its collar, tail curled from right to left, with wing shapes folded neatly across its chest. Mother, father and child stay hidden until you look at it right.

I look at it right, and I'm proud of it. But here's a change of pace:

A toaster again; it's different though; a family of five smiles out from the reflections on its side. And here an electric kettle steams with figures swirling in its gray-drawn heat. A vacuum cleaner hides a tiny infant in its bag. An open door reveals just a hand and a leg.

And now I stare at a picture built around a window suspended in trees. Vines tangle in and out through the panes. Pale green leaves float on curtains drifting gently in the breeze. But you can't see inside. Instead, where the curtains part, I've colored blue sky. All around are delicate blades of grass, thin stems of spring's new growth, thickened bushes and twigs. Inside and out—just a window—there's no house. But the sky's so bright!

Pastels and Papered

Chapter 30

I've run out of paper. Adam's given me all his spare sheets from school but I'll have to buy more. And I'm running out of time to plan for Thanksgiving. If I don't look up those airline prices soon, Donald will give up on me. After all, what's the point of having a wife at home if all she does is draw?

Mom's decided it's her turn to have us for Thanksgiving, not that I thought we took turns. We usually go to Donald's family because it's closer, then see Mom and Daddy at Christmas. But Lydia's oldest has just been installed as the pastor in Paradise Church. It sounds like he's doing some big Thanksgiving service; Mom wants us all to celebrate.

Adam is delighted with this news. He bounces around the house saying "Pastor Uncle Germ" even though we remind him Jeremy's not really his uncle; he's just his cousin. Meanwhile Michael sulks and won't look at me, because he'd rather stay home. And Thomas says nothing. Then Donald says we have to buy cheap tickets, an impossible demand, and I just want us all to sit near each other on the plane. I've searched the Internet for deals, watched the virus scanner's vivid green turn gray as I follow links with crazy names. But the flights are filling up. "We'll just have to pay whatever it takes."

I sigh. In fact, we'll be lucky to get all five of us on one plane.

Three routes all seem to cost about the same, so tonight I'll let Donald choose. Always supposing they're still available. Always supposing he doesn't decide we can't afford to go. But I want to go, I think. So I phone him, which I'm not supposed to do while he's at work. I ask if I should make the booking myself, before the tickets are gone, but he says no. It's a lot of money so I guess he doesn't trust me not to make a mistake. Then I decide to go shopping instead; I'll spend lots of money on food and washing powder and shower gel.

Tyke whines while I pick up shoes and coat and purse. I'll take him for a walk in the rain when I get back, but for now he has to be content with dog-treats while I rattle the car keys in my hand.

I think about drawing pictures of rain as I drive, of airplanes flying blind through thunderstorms, of downed trees cutting power lines, of floods crushing cars against buildings, or of airline tickets with the words all washed away.

The supermarket shines bright as day, while the parking lot hides, and plate glass windows pretend it's night outside. People wander the aisles carelessly, eyes not looking, ears not hearing, saying nothing to each other. Jumbled colors dance on the shelves. Reflections gleam from glass, and strip lights draw stripes across the floor.

My shopping cart's full. My credit card feels empty. But I see a box of pastel crayons next to a pile of sketchpads by the checkout, and I think I'm in heaven. Will Donald notice the price when I give him the bill?

I drive back home under skies still gray, but colors have leaked into rain. Puddles flash reflections of green. Traffic lights smile like flowers. I want to paint!

Tyke helps me put the shopping away by guarding the cheese and digging his nose in the bag where doggy-treats hide. Then he wants a walk, so I wander sodden paths outside, see red and yellow in falling leaves, a million shades of brown where they land on the ground, and tiny hints of blue in the afternoon sky. The kids will be home soon when I finally sit down, but I don't mind. I don't even mind that Donald will talk about flights. I get out the paper and pastels and feel my worries drain away.

Sweet scents assail me, rising from the box of colored sticks. They smell like play-dough and chocolate chip cookies, like sugar and spice and songs and all things nice. The paper's white, its fibers strong and smooth beneath my hands. The crayons slip like silk, soft and dry, almost powdery, like the memory of Mom's expensive makeup. I press a touch of gray to the page and start with the lines of a plane.

Bright white for the airplane's body shines, smoothly blending into gray. Windows are pressed with a fingernail along the fuselage, and a blurred blue pattern adorns the tail. The sky's a mixture of purple, yellow, and green with white highlights, all swirled together to form a thunderstorm. I add specks of red and green for lights that flash on the ends of the wings, with a thin white glaze in the windscreen where the pilot looks out. Then I use a kitchen knife to scrape at the tail, turning the blur of blue into a small flying cat.

Adam charges into the kitchen. I didn't even hear him come back. "Have you booked the flights yet, Mom?"

"No. Dad will tonight."

Soda splashes into a glass, and the bag of cookies crisps and crinkles while fingers dig down for treats. Sugar mixes with the scent of pastel crayons.

"Homework." I remind my youngest son as he rushes from the room, but he doesn't reply. Just laughs.

I smooth the swirls of clouds around in my picture, adding some blue then replacing it with black. Then the front door slams and the older boys get back. It's time to start dinner.

Thanksgiving is only two weeks away.

Chapter 31

The pastels call to me. I love their creamy softness in my hands, the way they layer on the page, their warmth as I rub my fingers over shades to smooth them together. I'm flying through this artist's pad.

Flowers make a perfect autumn picture, the contrast of bright blues and yellows on the stems with reds and browns of fallen leaves below. I've drawn an earthenware vase for them, that greenish gray that shouts 'ecologically sound' with ridges all around from the potter's wheel. Sunlight shines through a small square window in the top left corner of the scene, leaving a pattern of shifted panes on the ground. Edges of leaves are brightened by its rays, sharpened with the blade of a kitchen knife, and etched by fingernails with branching veins. The rest is pale, slightly blurred, except for a bluebell's nodding head and a sunlit daffodil.

"Have you done the packing yet?" Donald asks when he gets home after work. I thought the kids could pack for themselves, but he says we really can't trust them. I'll need to make sure they have smart clothes and button-up shirts for church on Sunday and Thanksgiving Day. Spare pairs of shoes would be good in case it rains. Thick sweaters and coats are required in case it snows.

We eat dinner at the table, and when things are cleared away I get out my pastels again, hiding the paper and new-formed image behind the crook of my arm.

Labels cover the suitcase's sides, bright colors for bright journeys to distant parts. It has an old-fashioned feel. The leather is mustard brown, scuffed with age, and the lock's made of brass. Clothes slip and slide through the open sides and pile onto the ground. A fluffy white cat lies comfortably on something soft and blue, shiny collar, red label, green eyes and just a hint of feathery wings across its back.

"Make sure you've got everything. Make a list," says Donald as he leaves for work on the Tuesday morning. The boys have tomorrow through Friday off school, and we're flying out tonight.

My guardian angel cat has its wings extended in wondrous flight. Front paws are poised, ready to pounce. His face bends low, and the cat's ears seem to twitch right out of the page. Green eyes are slitted to delicate lines, and a waving tail trails high with back legs hidden by the flying body. My guardian angel cat is ready to dive.

"Do you have to take that stuff with you?" Donald points at my purse which is tightly packed with books to read, toiletries and medicines, and packets of tissues and nuts. The box of crayons and sketchpad stick out where I've stuffed them down the side. I don't bother to reply.

At the airport we wait forever for our flight. I draw the snaking lines of passengers, the gaping maws of machines that check their luggage, rectangular doors to nowhere where they screen us for weapons and more, and seats at the gate arrayed in artificial lines, like zeros and ones being fed into a computer.

On the plane I draw plastic cups with jagged reflections from overhead lights. I draw the backs of strangers' heads and the sweet little child who plays peekaboo from the seat in front of us. He has a toothless smile and wants to keep his picture so I give it to him. His parents wave their thanks.

In the taxi I think I might draw blurry roads and lights and whispering trees but the page won't stay still.

When we drive past Paradise Park I put my artist's tools away and wonder what I'm doing here.

Then we arrive.

The air smells different in Paradise. The night has an angrier tang to it, but perhaps it comes from streetlights shining so bright the shadows turn blue. The grass is gray at this time of night. When I step off the path it crinkles and crunches underfoot like fallen leaves. I smell Mom's herbs by the front door to their house, thyme and rosemary, and I know she'll have used them somewhere in the food.

Daddy opens the door. He greets each boy with a solemn handshake as they try to maneuver their backpacks into the hall. "Upstairs," he says. "Last door to your right. I've put you in your Mom's old room." Then he tells Donald he thinks we'll have more space in Lydia's bedroom, as if two adults need to breathe more air than three fast-growing boys. "Jason's coming too, with Jeannie," he adds. So now I know who'll be sleeping in Jason's old room.

Chapter 32

I've drawn the Thanksgiving dinner table in Norman *Rockwell style. Food takes center place. The turkey steams, richly brown on its plate, with brightly colored vegetables shining from dishes to the side. Each bowl is lovingly rendered, even to patterns of pale pink flowers on the china from Mom and Daddy's ruby wedding gifts. The tablecloth is green and gold. The centerpiece, made of acorns and leaves and dried flowers, must have come from some church fair—I've never seen it before. And the family sits.*

Daddy plays the part of a grandfather with thin grayed hair and wary smile. I've placed him a little to the right at the front of the page. Mom as the grandmother faces him, perfectly pale and quaffed. Then lines of figures feed into the page from oldest to youngest members of the tribe, men and women alternating, and the boys sufficiently far away you can't tell who they are.

I finish my picture a day too soon, since it's still Wednesday, and Thanksgiving is tomorrow. Then I stand it, carefully balanced against Mom's fruit bowl on the dining room table. Jeannie says it's not bad, but Jeannie's always sweet that way. Donald and Jason are sitting by the TV sharing the newspaper between them. They look like they're enjoying each other's company, but probably neither of them has even noticed the other is there. And the children are upstairs.

Mom heads into the kitchen, offering to make coffee. Then thunderous hooves rush down the stairs, and boys raid her fridge for soda. "Don't drink too much of that," says Mom. "We'll run out." I catch a glimpse of their faces and see the thought of running out of soda is quite beyond the pale, so I offer to go shopping and buy some more.

My sister-in-law walks with me. We've both lived here before, and we know the streets and hills. There's a tiny supermarket still in the strip mall opposite the park. But Jeannie suggests we sit in the playground for a while before we go in, for old time's sake, so we cross the road and set off through the trees. A small sign designates our path *The Amelia Callaghan Memorial Walk*. I suppress a shiver, reading it.

Paving stones are damp from last night's rain. Wide puddles strive to devour the light, and I try not to let the water splash my legs. We pass the pond where lonely ducks beg for food. And finally we sit on a bench of sodden wood that smells of undergrowth. The forest looms so close. I could reach out to pluck memories from raindrops, hanging from leaves.

It happened here. Everything happened here, just through those trees, in winter and summer, or on one bright sunny day. I see the ghost of a fat man rushing down the hill. He calls for his dog while a mother calls for her child. Crowds gather and infants scramble all around. Teenagers stop their bikes. Ducks fly in terror from the pond while the red dog rushes out from trees and a white cat trembles behind. Birds flutter on trailing wings. And somebody screams.

"Are you cold?" asks Jeannie.

I realize I'm shivering. "Not really," I say.

"You must have come down here a lot when you were a kid."

But I didn't really. Lydia and Jason were so much older than me, and I didn't make any friends in school until we were all too childishly mature for swings and slides. I came here with Lydia's children when they were small. Young Jeremy would scramble up on the climbing frame. Little Jay would play in the sandpit on the ground, and Josh would whimper as a babe in arms. But behind those memories I still see the fat man on the hill, still hear the screams. It happened there, under those trees, not just to me, and it's time to move on.

A girl dressed in white dances alone in a clearing in a forest. Sentinel trees stand tall all around, their steep heads bent to protect her. Golden sunlight filters down, and the girl casts no shadow because she's really a ghost. All the darkness is held back by tremulous green.

I finish my picture after lunch but it still seems incomplete. Mom won't let me use her kitchen knives, so I scratch with the tip of a pencil, crush a splash of white into looming darkness, then shape a shining cat peeking out from beneath the forest green.

At dinner the boys sit together in a row and I feel another *Norman Rockwell* moment coming on. I draw them arrayed behind their plates, elbows on the table, dinner piled and bright with warm steam rising into their faces. Adam has music plugged into his ears. Michael's hair hangs thickly over his eyes. And Thomas has a forkful of food just passing between his lips.

I'm still adding the finishing touches on Thanksgiving Day, proud of the effect. Then Daddy says, "Time to go." So I look up, pastel crayon in hand. "Church? Thanksgiving? Giving thanks?" he adds. "Supporting your local pastor because he's your nephew?"

It's time to tidy up.

Daddy and Mom take the boys in their car, while Donald and I sit in the back seat of Jason's old wagon, and we drive down to church.

Chapter 33

The air's cold and smoky, not quite frozen, not quite damp. I feel small beads form on my hands and don't know if they're sweat or ice or water. Jason had the heat turned up in his car, and it was too warm.

Gravel crunches underfoot as we walk to Mom and Daddy's vehicle. We gather up kids, and I feel my hair start to drip. But the church's yellow sunshine beckons from the door. Jewels twinkle in stained glass windows and reflect on the dampness in the air. Organ music sips along the ragged edge of my hearing. I wonder if I'm ready to see Lydia, to cope with the whole of my family, all reunited in this place.

My nephew Jeremy stands in the archway at the church's door. He's incongruously dressed as a pastor in colored robes with batwing sleeves, plastic smile on his face to welcome everyone. "Happy Thanksgiving. Wonderful to see you. So glad you could make it. And you. And you." He needs a tape recording to repeat the words.

Air leaking out from the church smells of candle wax, but I remember how anti-Catholic Mom and Daddy always were. Surely they don't burn candles in there now. I smell damp earth as well, or vegetables perhaps. Thanksgiving and harvest festival must have been rolled into one. Has little Jeremy grown up to be a rebel after all?

Suddenly I'm remembering Grandpa's farm. The laborers would gather all the hay at harvest time. Its thick scent filled the barn, warm and sweet and musty somehow. And the smell of the bull, and the sound, head lowered, bellowing into the night. Cold air would trickle on the back of my neck as I ran to check the latest litter of cats—"Grandpa, are they okay? They'll not get carried away when they take the hay?" But of course they wouldn't. Then Grandpa would hold me tight in his arms and call me his funny little tyke.

Our Tyke's residing in a kennel for the weekend, with hay and straw and a little red roof of his own over his head.

"Happy Thanksgiving, Auntie Sylvia."

"Same to you, kiddo. I still can't believe this is you."

"This what?" Jeremy smiles that crazy innocent grin he had as a kid.

"This pastor, priest, whatever you call yourself. It just can't be you."

Then a wild voice shrieks, "Hello, Pastor Uncle Germ."

Jeremy ruffles the hair on Adam's head, spares a smile for my older two boys, then ushers us inside. "Mom's near the front I think. I'm sure she'd like you to sit with her."

For a moment, I think he's wrong. Mom's standing beside me. Then I realize he means my sister, Lydia. So we walk up the aisle, smelling candles and hay and oranges—they don't grow here—and I'd so much rather have stayed invisible at the back.

Mom walks or waddles as if she owns the place. Daddy strides next to her, ramrod straight, iron gray. My three sons follow and I see their heads turning eagerly from side to side, searching for something to laugh at or whisper about. Then Thomas slips away. He must have seen Lydia's other two boys—are they saving a space for him? He always gets on so well with them, for all that they're much older. I wonder if they've flown home from college just for this.

My brother walks with hands buried deep in the pockets of his coat. His shoulders slump—Daddy's first born son who could never stand up straight. Jeannie hovers beside him. Then Donald and I take up the rear.

When I move too close, my hand bumps into Donald's, and I want to be held. He doesn't take the hint. So I'm walking ever so lonely in a crowd.

Jeremy scurries up the aisle just as the service is due to begin. I see him slip behind a screen and remember there's a door back there. He probably still has some preparations to do. When he walks out, cool, calm and collected, he welcomes us all, sounding like he picked up a different voice behind the door. Pastor Bill, reincarnated in my nephew, is going to preach tonight.

We sing hymns and I almost remember them. We give thanks for food and drink, for family and friends, for jobs and houses, comfort and warmth. Why does everything always come in twos? We give thanks for health and strength but I feel mine's started slipping again.

Lydia looks great, still blonde with just the faintest streaks of gray. Her Troy's aged a bit but he's still as ruggedly handsome as he ever was. Jeremy looks the image of him, apart from the gift of red hair. But Jay and Joshua—I stare down the row to look at them more clearly—they seem more like my brother Jason and their grandfather, tight-featured and eminently right. Jay's inherited Grandpa's sharp pointed chin.

My fingers itch and I wish I'd brought my paper and pastels with me. I'd love to draw this place. I'd color the pulpit brown and black, add magical lights from the windows, and maybe draw some sunbeams shining down on Jeremy's head— perhaps they do on Sundays. Perhaps they make a halo, and he's a saint. I measure the space between table and altar, calculate the width of the carpet, and store all the dimensions in my brain. I should be storing messages from the sermon but I can't remember them. Something about thanks and giving and it's Thanksgiving. Boring, I think.

Back at Mom's I draw the church while Lydia sorts out drinks. The living room's crowded with all the extended family, everyone talking at once. I'll draw them next. I feel better again and I'm on a roll. My fingers won't stop and the pages fly.

It's a pretty little church with gray stone walls and lichen dangling from trees to roof to tower. Twinkling lights from the windows glitter as bright as blue sky overhead. Trees rise darkly green with touches of red for the promise of fall, and the undergrowth is brown.

It's the church as it looked when we first moved to Paradise, before the red brick schoolrooms and extensions. Or perhaps it's the church as it will always be, extending through time. Straight lines of schoolroom walls form delicate shadows, measuring an empty clearing in front of the door, and buried in shade. Sharp window edges gleam with hints of light in front of grey. Red bricks hide, almost unseen, behind the growing curtain of forest and trees. The new buildings stand pale as straight-edged ghosts against the old, and a white cat sits by the door.

"Yes, coffee would be nice." I slip back into my *Rockwell* mood as I sketch the family now, pastels trilling the fabric of inspiration. I'll start with my boys, then move on to Lydia's.

Three youngsters, ranged by height, sit on a sofa in the middle of the page. I've changed them out of their smart garments into comfortable tee-shirts and jeans. The image looks more authentic that way, though ragged blue is a little incongruous on Mom's flowered upholstery. A picture over their heads depicts a sweetly pastoral scene. Then I add a dog at Adam's feet and a white cat on Thomas' lap.

Three young men lean against a fireplace near flickering fingers of flame. The red-haired one has a glass of wine in his hand. The other two hold beers. A white cat's curled with its face turned to the fire, long tail twisted into a mysterious question mark. It's Jeremy's cat, lying on Jeremy's feet, very real and very much here. But the dog I drew is Tyke, who is very far away.

An older couple sits to the left of the page, facing a younger couple on the right. Both pairs are ensconced on flowered loveseats with twisted vines of green growing over their legs. In between is a low wooden table with glasses of wine all twinkly with light. The faces are recognizably Mom and Daddy, and Troy and Lydia. I've placed the cat over Lydia's feet, and

Troy is just wrapping his fingers around a glass. Daddy leans back, pontificating on some important point. They seem very relaxed.

This one's a picture of Jason and Donald, talking together in a corner. They look cagey, keeping secrets, like spies of old. Jeannie sits on a sofa down below them looking up. She might be the counter-spy, trying to hear while they try not to be heard.

Finally I draw one more Thanksgiving scene. This time there are only five at the table, mother, father, two little girls and a boy. The blonde-haired girl has a cat-shaped clip in her hair. The smaller dark-haired sister reaches a hand across the table. At first I draw her reaching for the casserole of peas. Then I change her aim, so questing fingers almost touch the cat.

Troy jangles his car keys. Jeremy says he'll walk. And Mom says it's time for bed. But I'll manage one more picture before I go up.

I sketch a set of keys on a table, while I'm waiting for the bathroom to be free. A guardian angel cat watches me from its link on the chain holding them.

Chapter 34

Christmas trees with colored lights. Christmas trees with snow. Christmas trees with presents down below.

Here's a Santa, some children and dogs. And here are three boys, warmed with magical glow.

Christmas trees by a roaring fire. And Christmas trees outside.

The Holiday season is over. I've drawn so many festive pastel trees, filling the pages of my pad until the white crayon's worn to a nub from sprinkling twinkling stars and splashes of snow. Some of the other crayons in the box have started breaking too, all split and cracked. Somehow they don't attract me quite the same as they used to do. Maybe it's because it's spring. Or maybe I've finally worked that angry art bug out of my system.

Donald says that's good. No more painting means I'm ready to work at a real job. Meanwhile I plan a party for our youngest son's tenth birthday—double figures!—but that's not *work* of course.

"You need to earn something, Love. Give yourself some self-respect, and give the rest of us something to lean back on." He leans over me and kisses my cheek.

"You earn," I complain. "I support. And I've got my self-respect."

"Yes, but." There's always a *but*.

I don't blame him though. Donald worries about the future; insurance, pensions, social security. I guess it's good that one of us has that sort of thing in hand. But me, I'm stuck in the present. I worry about children and homework and shopping and cleaning the house. I worry about not knowing where everyone is when they come out of school. You hear so much bad stuff about kids these days, getting kidnapped, doing drugs, or making stupid mistakes on the Internet. I want to be here for them, to know what they're doing, and to keep my eye on them. I think they need me, but Donald needs me too. He needs me to *work*. And I've promised I will. I've promised, as soon as our baby boy turns ten.

The trouble is, we're planning his birthday party *now*; he's been nine almost a year.

I remember how hopelessly I fell apart just after Adam was born. I must have spent a year, two years even, in therapy, struggling to hold myself and the family together. *Post-natal depression* the doctor called it, *like post-nasal drip*, but worse. I did everything they told me, followed all the rules, let everyone else make all the decisions for me, and I got better. I took my memories out of their box, then packed them away on the shelf, like fresh-washed towels in a closet. I tucked the pictures away in the attic, cleaned up my act, and told myself all was well. And it is. If I can keep the depression down to once in every ten years I'll be okay. The boys will be grown before the next one comes. They won't need me. *I'll line my empty nest with torn up pictures and scraps of memory; go live in a tree to confess how much paper I've used.*

We call the boys into the living room to discuss plans for Adam's party. They sit together, mathematically ordered on the sofa, and look just like the sketches I've made of them. I start to smile, but my hands lie still on my lap, no lingering artistry calling them to plant the scene on paper. No *Normal Rockwell* urges today. I'm good. I'm well. *Does wanting to make pictures mean I'm not? Does* not *wanting...?*

Adam wants to invite all his class to the party. Michael and Thomas complain they don't need to be involved; they'd rather play on the computer. Donald points out there's a limit to how many kids will fit in the living room. And finally we manage to agree. Adam will bring seven of his best friends home from school, and they'll stay overnight. Mike and Tom will invite one friend each, as long as they're guys—no girlfriends here—and we'll borrow sleeping bags from everyone we know.

So now I'm deep into planning, making lists, and counting pizzas in the freezer. I shove things aside in the fridge to make space for multiple cans of soda. Bottles are cheaper but they won't work. Teenagers, even nearly teens, and bottles and glasses don't mix. We'll need extra paper towels—extra toilet paper as well. And I'll need another list.

Suddenly I find myself all alone in the bedroom, with only Tyke at my side. We sit together on the floor. I stare at the white painted door of my firmly closed closet. Tyke stares too. The pictures are still in there. I imagine them falling, spilling on the carpet, piling up like windblown leaves against the sides of the bed, and spreading over me. I open my eyes to darkness where a blanket of earth and leaves smells of ancient mold and I can't move. I start to scream then feel Tyke's jaws on my hand as he digs me free.

Wasn't a cat there too? A white cat, just like Pastor Jeremy's Garnet, with silver-tone collar and small red jewel like an eye. There when the little girl… when he... when I...

It hurts to touch that place...

And now Adam's ten. It's party time.

The house is awash with scents of buttered popcorn and salty pepperoni. Adam's enjoying his pizza night, but mountains of greasy boxes and oceans of soda cans threaten to drown us. Stacks of rental movies sit by the TV to suit everyone's tastes, and there's microwave popcorn by the bucket. Not having any convenient buckets we're serving it in an array of my Granny's old wooden salad bowls.

Gunshots terrorize poor Tyke as he quivers on the sofa next to Mike. Explosions rock the walls. I wonder if neighbors are calling the cops, and Donald says he'll go work on the taxes in his office. I'm tired, and the boys don't need me, so I slowly drift away down the corridor. The bedroom beckons, but it's too noisy for sleep. Sighing, I decide to get out those pictures again. I leave the door ajar, just in case a popcorn disaster or exploding soda can demands my attention. Then I clear space on the floor.

The closet opens in front of me like a cavernous barn. It's dark in there. It doesn't smell of hay, but it's musty just the same; musty papers, clothes unworn awaiting the airing of some festival day. Memories stand, like hay bales, tidily stacked. Nothing tumbles out. No clothing slips and falls down from the rack. I dare the world to look through the crack in these doors and see who I am. And really, I'm fine.

And really... there's still unfinished business there.

With one ear listening for the boys, and the other trained on Donald clacking computer keys in his office, I drag old memories out again into light. Nobody shouts for me—*unneeded me*. But the boxes are falling apart, not so gloriously tidy after all. Ancient cardboard's worn with all this tugging and searching. Crooked surfaces sag, cold and damp against my hands. The scent of decay wars with popcorn and sugar, and wins. Flakes of brown like rust cling to my fingers; I'd wipe them on the dog, except he's too busy hiding with Mike on the sofa. I'm all alone with my pictures of guardian angel cats, Santas on tins, and scraps of forgotten dreams and memories. It's time to pick up those *painted* pictures at last.

The paper's dry and flaky; the images cracked. Scraps of color stick to my fingers, and Tyke wouldn't approve. I smile at the thought of a rainbow-painted dog, then rub my hands on my jeans. Powder plus water—that was how I painted these long ago. Now powder drips like colored ash with the salty taste of tears.

Donald frowns at me when he finally comes to bed. I think he was hoping I'd finished this pictures game. Now he wonders if I'm getting sick again.

Powder Painted

Chapter 35

Abstract triangles in red and green hide more than they reveal. There's a cat with odd-colored striations weaving across its stomach. Two pointed ears lie flat in one bright-drawn three-cornered shape. A nose peeks out from another, while whiskers, totally separate, whisper mysteries to the sky. A tiny tooth-lined mouth yawns over the shadows of skittering paws. Somewhere behind, a long tail waves and winds through triangles linked into a chain. It feels as if the cat's on the move, chasing around the corners of a maze, feeling the jagged reflections in mirrored sides, cutting magic from its eyes.

Our art teacher finally let us use real paint, halfway through eighth grade. It was powdered stuff that came in neon cans, like plastic cocoa waiting to be mixed with lukewarm water. But first she introduced us to color, with a pile of magazines dumped down on her desk. We had to pick a journal each and look for pictures we liked, then cut them up into triangles. It felt like a waste of good images, making holes in perfect lives.

Afterward we pasted our triangles randomly together onto paper. "Artistic license," the teacher called it, adding, "You're not doing jigsaws here." She ripped the page from our hands if we tried too hard to make things fit. "Choose your own designs," she told us. "Use your imagination." So we reshaped the past and created new possibilities out of it, gluing and sticking as if our very lives hung by the thread of her approval.

Finally the teacher opened up the precious paints, thick poster-colors arrayed in labeled pots, wide plastic palettes spread out like plates where we could mix them. *Contrasting colors* was the catchphrase now, designed to teach us that patterns shouldn't fade back into themselves. We painted pictures of chopped up pictures and spread them far and wide. Red and green contrasted well. But Sharon—my friend again, now we were in the same Junior High—insisted on saying my triangles looked too much like Christmas trees.

White glue smelled sweet as stolen treats. It molded thick as mountains and caves on the paper. Paints smelled like sugar except for blue which had some kind of savory undertone, and yellow was sour. The paper, *poster quality* our teacher said, was creamy white and thick enough so the colors didn't soak through. Our images were meant to stay supple and strong, but now they've dried out.

Sharon cut out a photo of a man in tight jeans with broad muscled chest, an ad for men's clothes. Most of the boys snipped pictures of girls in various states of *un*dress. I imagined the *pasts* they reshaped on their pages might bleed with misguided dates—the sort of dates that girls discussed with peals of broken giggles after PE. But future triangles with sharp-edged points boded ill for anyone hoping for love and a kiss.

As for me, I cut out a cat and wished there were kittens in the picture. Perhaps that's why I added those misguided lumps of colored fur along its sides.

So there I was, an artist in Junior High, but a secret artist, as hidden as the cat behind my triangles. At home I was the family's mathematician and brightest hope, with brother and sister falling from their wondrous pedestals. Poor Jason moped every time he came home and told us he hated his job. Dear Lydia didn't want to go to college, and hoped she might persuade Daddy to let her get married straight out of high school. Harried Mom was run off her feet trying to keep the peace. And me, I did everything everyone told me, obeyed all the rules, kept my head down, repainted myself, and dreamed maybe one day I might become Daddy's favorite one.

I didn't talk to him about still doing art. I didn't show him my pictures when I brought them home from school. I didn't tell him how the math teacher smiled at my doodles, calculating their patterns and helping me define the equations of their scope. I told him when I aced the algebra test though. I told him when my name got put forward for calculus, while everyone else was trapped in the geometry of shapes. I didn't tell him geometry felt just like art to me.

English was fun, but didn't offer much to talk about. Science made sense. History built a complex world-wide pattern of repeating shapes. And French took letters then turned them into words forever unsaid—we read long poems of love and passion, and dreamed. But I loved no one and only longed for peace and a quiet life. I felt no urge to get into trouble, no desire to waste my time on meeting people or making friends, and no need for social skills.

Meanwhile Lydia mourned her fate each night in upstairs privacy. Pale moonlight draped her in robes with the curtains' pink glow, scented her words with roses, and shadowed her fears. "I don't want to graduate, Sis. I don't want to be Daddy's paper cutout girl. I don't want to go to any of those colleges he keeps suggesting. I'll just stay here and look after you."

By spring she was busily announcing it all around the house. "I just want to get married to Troy after school."

Meanwhile Daddy replied, "Not while you live under our roof."

And I hid behind doors.

Daddy said Lydia was going to ruin her life. I guessed he meant she was ruining his, because how can a daddy be proud of his kids if they don't turn out the way he wants? I wondered if maybe, possibly, one day he might be proud of me. And I watched while college brochures migrated from kitchen cabinets onto the dining table. Soon schedules and application dates took the place of dinner plates. We had to eat in the kitchen for weeks while Daddy made Lydia choose. Meanwhile, the heavy scents of dinner piled over breakfast which piled over coffee grown stale in yesterday's pot.

"It'd be a waste not to go somewhere and study, Lydia. Bright girl like you. You owe it to yourself to make something of your life."

More cats, more splashes of red and green, are cut into jigsaw buttons with matching holes, scattered like puzzle pieces on the floor. There's a faint B minus at the edge of the page, so I guess it's not what the art teacher wanted from me, but I like the effect. It makes me think of an imaginary life falling apart. Or splashes of red and green ice cream.

On Graduation Day, Lydia wanted to go to the ice cream store. She'd share a *Spicy Peppermint* dish with Troy. But instead Mom and Daddy took her out for an expensive meal at Benson's. I stayed home and cooked frozen pizza in the kitchen. Big sister might be finished with school, but I still had homework and art.

Red cows munch grass colored vibrant green, mingled with sharp-edged flecks of azure sky. The way the triangles are cut and twisted, the sky's like streaking darts of ice, or arrows of cold fire. Flat shapes fit neatly to the edges of the page with white space painted faintly cream and a shimmering star in the center holding a bull with yellow horns and bright red eyes. A river of emerald blood flows from his side like a poisonous snake.

Lydia agreed to a compromise, and Daddy's dagger glances grew softer again. She'd go to university for him, but only the local one, across the park in town. She'd take classes in art for herself, live in the Christian dorms near church for Mom, and go out with Troy to movies every night. And I'd stay home, alone.

Cats with cow's faces stare from shapes of mirrors shattered and torn. Cows with cat's noses wander, swishing their snake-like tails across the page.

"You should use some other pictures," the teacher said, "not just animals." She wrote another B minus on the image I'd so carefully made.

"But everything's gone," *or everyone*, I complained.

I imagine the therapist might look at these and ask, "What do they mean, the cats and the bulls?" But I know they just mean Grandpa had cats and a bull and I loved him still.

Chapter 36

A *t first sight there's nothing wrong with this picture beyond a slight sense of unease. I'm using black for the background, and I've painted a bright red cat in profile in the center of its dark surround. The tail stands high, tense, wary, waving maybe. The back is arched and the cat's legs poise in delicate mid-step, front paw just raised, head turned to see where it lands. Green eyes shine bright. But the cat in this picture has four ears, or two ears and two horns. The end of its tail is corded, thick and strong, sinuous as a snake. It may just be cracks in the paint, but I think there's a tiny forked tongue flickering between those bright white teeth, triangular teeth with flecks of red on their ends.*

Nothing's wrong with this picture except the whole thing's wrong, innocence and evil, comfort and fear combined; beauty and the beast.

There were rumors still of someone stalking women in the park. Daddy told me I must never take the short cut from school. I never intended to anyway. A policeman had talked to our class, his message veiled with threats and nothing specific because, after all, you mustn't give the wrong ideas to teenagers. I saw the way boys looked at us, and I knew they had more than enough ideas to go around. Teachers said *be careful* and *walk in twos*. Pastor Bill said we'd all get *promise rings* as high school gifts next year.

There was a graduation dance at the end of eighth grade, but I didn't go. Sharon did. Her big brother arrived to escort her just as school was letting out. I thought he looked cool. But I didn't want to dance. I saw girls in bright skirts stream down the corridors, flesh pressed against flesh, lips turned and locked to other people's mouths. I saw boys leaning their girlfriends against walls, and I imagined tree bark scratching its lines along my back. The thought of another guy's tongue between my lips made me feel sick. Roaming hands made me want to stare into somebody else's face and run away, both at once. I imagined dancing, cheek to cheek, flesh to flesh, skin to skin, with hot blood pulsing and burning underneath, and I squirmed in miserable, hurt embarrassment.

Sometimes the thought of Lydia sitting with Troy in the front of his truck made me squirm too. But Lydia still had her promise ring and wore it every day. My Lydia wasn't breaking any rules.

Summer slowly drew to a close, and change was in the air. University classes were starting soon, so we packed up Lydia's room. Bags and boxes overflowed with clothes and tumbled like bales of hay in a heap on the floor. Books were piled like stacked walls waiting to fall. The air smelled of dust from treasures long untouched. And the sun shone too bright.

Lydia's terracotta walls had been painted white by now. White curtains replaced the old dusky pink, their fabric pulled too tightly so the room looked antiseptically clean like a hospital ward, as if my sister were going to be surgically removed. White closet doors hung open. Empty hangers made skeletons inside, where a couple of sweatshirts dangled, and pink bunny slippers looked lonely and lost.

"Can I take those?" I asked, not sure if I meant the sweatshirts or the slippers.

"If you want. If you don't, just throw them out."

We sat on Lydia's bed, sharing the space with three cardboard boxes and a tube of rolled-up posters. Gray dust outlined rectangular shapes of pictures absent from the walls. And bed springs creaked their protest.

"D'you think we're too heavy with all the boxes here? Will we make it collapse?" Lydia asked. Her smile reminded me of happier times, when our beds stood side by side, before the thought of Troy invaded our companionship. I guess that's why Daddy shifted my bed back to my old room, away from the evil influence of a girl who was hanging out with an unsuitable boy. It was all Troy's fault.

I chewed my lip and reminded myself, it was because of Troy that Lydia wasn't departing to some distant state. So I couldn't decide if I loved him or hated him now. Why do people grow up?

Lydia bounced up and down like a child, trying to make me laugh. The bed springs creaked with louder complaints and the mattress swam like the sea. I found myself tossed with awkward memories, the pressure under my seat disturbing me. Was it thoughts of Troy that filled my mind with things I didn't want to remember? Troy on a bed in my imagination, bouncing up and down with Lydia grinding underneath, which she didn't do, because of her promise ring. Perhaps it was the thought of losing Lydia, like losing my childhood again. I picked the scabs of memories and wondered if one day the scar might fade. Then I'd remember how to play. But for now I kept my legs together and sat myself ramrod straight, pretending to myself that nothing hurt.

Daddy's footsteps creaked as he climbed the stairs, and Lydia was suddenly still.

"Why d'you have to leave?" I asked her, for the three hundredth time.

"I need my freedom, Sis."

I needed my security.

We helped Daddy carry the cases along the corridor to the stairs. My reflection staggered in the mirror there, and I stopped to gather breath. I looked thinner, almost as slender as my sister now, with my hair long and dark where hers was elfin pale. My arms were all elbows, legs all knees, with knobs and corners jutting out from me, like a picture cobbled together from broken triangles. I could smash a case into the glass perhaps, then the whole world would splinter as well. But instead I trailed obediently down and carried my load onto the drive, helping Daddy maneuver things into the trunk. As final bags and boxes disappeared, I wondered how a life could be so small. But I felt even smaller, almost ready to vanish away.

Everyone piled into the car. I waited a while, wondering if they might forget and set off without me. But they didn't, so I climbed in. I could have walked it though, to the end of our road, along the next, and out by the Paradise gate. I could have trotted down the street to church, then around the corner and up toward the light. It really wasn't far. But my legs might have refused to take me there, unless the cooling summer air washed my bitter mood away. Still, I'd never find out. Obedient child, I sat in the back next to my sister and stared out of the window without seeing. I listened to her talking, without hearing a word.

Daddy complained there wasn't enough space to park amongst all those trailers and vans of abandoned parenthood. Then he found a place, and Jason Junior, looking as bleak as I felt, walked up the street and found us. Blind walls stared down with empty windows, row upon row, all alike. And streams of girls like grown-up kindergarteners swam toward the doors.

Upstairs we piled stuff into Lydia's new room, loading her desk with electronic devices and snaking a birds' nest of wires to the floor underneath. Mom piled clothes onto hangers and stuffed drawers full with underwear and books. Big brother Jason crawled under the table and buried himself in reams of electrical cables, tangled like tails of cats and mice and raging bulls. Daddy watched. And I read instruction manuals so I could offer advice.

"Plug the big, flat transformer in first, at the end Jason, so there'll still be room." My brother fumbled with the wrong end of a multi-plug, and I sighed theatrically. Jason Junior was really no help at all, but he left lots of threads from his button-holes over the floor.

Chapter 37

A bull bends down to sip water from a pond filled with ducks. His nose is lowered while his horns point wild defiance out of the page. A cat watches patiently from a tree to the left. A crow flies overhead in a patch of blue sky, next to a bright yellow sun. Grass is an almost fluorescent green in front, fading to shadows at the back. Ducks are vividly scarlet and purple and blue. The cat is black, the bull reddish-brown. And a few faint clouds broil restlessly in shades of charcoal gray.

As pictures go, it's rather odd and very childishly posed, unless the animals are meant to have hidden meanings. Comfort and fear in balance perhaps, or stark reality's inherent contradictions.

I think it's time to see my therapist again...

Donald complains it costs too much, but perhaps he's just upset that we're in a new year, working our way through a brand new deductible on the insurance. "You'd feel better if you got a job," he says. "You could get some insurance of your own." I want to hit him but I don't.

The therapist turns my picture over between her long, thin fingers, eyes deep-set in concentration, pursed lips hiding her thoughts under the tangle of iron gray hair. She turns the page, and I think perhaps she's not interested after all. Maybe my tangled animals don't inspire the same sort of questions in her mind. Maybe children aren't meant to be wise to hiding things that matter in cats and cows. But the next painted page shows the cat again with horns and a long forked tongue and snake-like tail. I'm sure she'll comment on that.

Just for a moment I imagine Donald with horns and devil tongue, and tail as well. But that's not fair.

The cat rests lazily on a scarlet cushion. Its fur is gloriously black and smooth as silk. I can almost hear its languid, rippling purr as it watches me. Small ears are pricked with a shadow of horns behind them. A sinuous tail winds around the curled-up body. Sharp teeth shine like daggers over a tongue that's split, just slightly, there at the end. The cat's clean jaw opens in a smile, as if it's catching flies, and green eyes stare above its neatly crossed paws. A semblance of wings shimmers faintly overhead.

"Ah yes," says the therapist with a confident sigh. She sounds as if she knows it all, which she probably does if she's been reading her notes. "Your famous guardian angel cat."

"No, it's not."

Which shows how little she knows about me.

A pastoral scene fills the next page—blue sky with speckled flecks of cloud, green fields with flecks of brown. Dark trees cover the horizon in shades of shifting gray with smog underneath—a city perhaps. In the foreground, neat white picket fences surround a gray farmhouse. There's a bull in a field and a cat sneaking out of a barn, all tidily detailed and measured and well laid out. Everything's peaceful except for a faint touch of mist interspersed with red in the field behind the bull, maybe smoke and a fire.

"The bull's for danger, the cat for security?" my therapist asks.

"And the cat with horns?" I point to the previous page.

"Maybe danger and safety got rolled into one? Could you tell the difference?"

I think I'd rather be safe than in danger any day, but I say nothing. We turn another page.

A white cat stands in the yellow glow of a streetlamp. All around is dark, shading black to the edges of the page. The streetlamp's shadow and the cat's lie close together, intertwined. Paving stones are gray and square. And again there's a halo of silver light, just over the white cat's back, just a hint of angel-wings.

"This one's the angel?" the therapist asks, and I nod. This was my first attempt, my first response when I knew all those rumors were real.

The way Lydia's roommate, Janet, told it, she'd been studying late at the library that night and planned to walk alone across the park. The path was brightly lit so she had nothing to worry about, though the trees must have been dark. And the rumors said...

He wasn't the rumor though, I tell myself, and they… Well, it might not have been him. I never saw his face...

Janet said how she listened to the clock strike midnight just before all the lights went out. A cat had jumped on the junction box they told us later, maybe startled by the bells. Whatever, Janet was left all alone in the dark. Party music blared from university windows behind her. Traffic rumbled ahead. Meanwhile animals, insects, and something else rustled in the undergrowth.

She said a white cat walked past her, with bright green eyes and a red stone in its collar. Maybe she saw it before the lights went out. Would she have noticed the stone if it was dark?

Then she heard twigs crack as if someone was sneaking up on her, so she tried to run. Janet said she was really scared. You could see she meant it by the way she sat on our sofa, like she thought she was going to fall off. Lydia had invited her over for tea, just to help her calm down. Our Mom pretended to be Janet's Mom, since Janet was in her first term here and so very far from home.

"It could have been almost anything," Mom said to comfort her.

But Janet swore it was a man.

She was running and thought she might fall and be attacked, when a stranger appeared in front of her. He had white hair and a red stone in his collar, or something like that, so she thought of the cat and decided she ought to trust him.

Lydia's roommate was weird. Seriously, would you trust a man who reminded you of a cat?

The stranger walked her to safety at the edge of the park, then disappeared. Then the cat came back. Mom said, "How nice," and offered to refill our cups. Meanwhile Janet still looked like she was about to fall off the sofa.

I heard Janet talk about it on TV afterward. Then I heard her when I went to visit Lydia in the dorm. Then I read about her in the paper. I can't remember who started calling it a guardian angel cat, but I liked the idea and started trying to paint one, or draw one, or both, though I wished it had been around earlier.

You'd be surprised how difficult it is to work out where wings grow on a cat. There's the whole crazy question of where all the joints should be. I could hang a pair of wings from its shoulders, above those long front legs, just behind its neck. Or maybe I should fasten them further back, like on an insect, so I'd get more symmetry. Then I had to decide if the wing-joints spring from under the body or from over the back? Does the cat need extra muscles in its chest to carry them? How do feathers blend with fur? Which way does the tail point when a cat starts flying? I must have thrown a million sketches away, but I settled on my design at last and began to paint my cats in class after class.

I brought one home to put on the wall of my bedroom. But the art teacher phoned and wanted it back for some kind of competition which I knew I wouldn't win. Daddy took the call and demanded to know what on earth the picture was about. I told him Janet's story, and he threw a fit. He must have heard all about it by now, but he hadn't realized Lydia's roommate was the girl in the park. Next Sunday we had our family dinner with a side-serving of Lydia storming out. Daddy shouted on and on about safety and how she had to stay in her dorm and never leave except for class, as if Troy were going to *rape* her.

I hate that word.

The white fluffy cat stands ready to pounce, with nose pointing down to those delicate paws poised beautifully in front. Just behind its head two shimmering wings rise up in a pale blue sky, tail twitching between them. White feathers, iridescent with rainbow brilliance, smooth into fur. Green eyes shine bright. A pink nose twitches appealingly, and tiny white teeth smile around the twinkling tip of a small pink tongue.

"So this is the cat?"

I nod.

"And with everyone, even your sister's friend, talking about a stalker, you still said nothing?"

I shake my head.

"You didn't feel maybe you should have?"

"No," I say. It's not hard to answer. Nobody needed me muscling in with a half-baked story about something that happened, maybe, perhaps, sometime in another year. It was now that mattered. And anyway, "It didn't have to be the same person. He might not have been a stalker. And I didn't know who he was. How would it help?"

"So you're still saying you never saw his face?"

I nod and shake my head both at once and feel like she's trying to trap me. I didn't see him and I'm not going to change what I say. Though I wonder suddenly, if I didn't know who he was, why was it so important not to tell? Because I'd led him on? Because my compliance had created the stalker perhaps? Because, in the end, I knew it was *all my fault*?

I shiver and hope the therapist doesn't see. Then I rest my hand on the painting of the cat, my treasure, my good luck charm. My fur-feathered hero gave me strength back then and blessed my silence. She didn't ask questions and never made demands. And she didn't blame me; I blamed her, for not being there on the day I needed her.

I realize I'm crying and reach for some tissues from the box while the therapist watches.

Chapter 38

Where were you when I needed you? Why didn't you tell me to stay away from the woods? Why didn't you guard me the way you guarded Janet? Was I expendable? Littlest sister. Only a leftover child. Nothing I've ever done seems to matter in the end except for that, except that I kept silent when I should have saved.

I recover from my meltdown, tuck the melted tissues into my purse, and turn another page. The therapist has questions in her eyes but I'm not looking.

Tables are spread in a row at a local fair while a church tower stands guard. Trees hang heavy with blossoms, so I think it must be spring, Easter perhaps. The left-hand table's weighted down with cookies and cakes and things. Mom serves behind it with curly yellow hair and a smile pasted on. In the middle, one table stands loaded with books, while another carries knickknacks with white china statues, framed paintings, cups and saucers and fancy plates. If you look carefully you can see some of the paintings are of guardian angel cats. The figure behind them, serving white elephants, just might be me. She's gray as a real elephant, and her dark hair's miserably straight.

Actually, if you look really close, you can see the straight-haired girl's spitting sparks across the page, all the way to the woman on the cake stall at the left. They stand on opposite sides of some vast argument, as if the bakers of cakes don't really approve of angelic felines. "Not Christian," they said. But my blue hairclip's okay because it doesn't have wings.

I laugh and start to tell my therapist how the women would almost hiss at me, like Medusas with snakes. But she isn't intrigued. She turns another page. "Same place?" she asks.

A wedding couple stands in summer sun with trees all around and the church at their back. The bride, my Lydia, is dressed in white, flowing folds of her robe layered like petals on a flower. Her veil drifts like sunshine over hair that floats like silk. Beside her Troy is every girl's dream, James Dean crossed with Sean Connery. Straight hair flops darkly over smiling eyes. His lips part loosely, comfortably, warm, and he keeps one eyebrow raised over flat-planed cheeks and an aquiline nose. I know I said I hated him, but Troy's always been gorgeous, always a heartthrob, always perfect in every way, and I loved him that day for making my sister so happy.

Another picture shows just their faces, the happy couple turned toward each other but looking straight out of the page. I'd almost forgotten the way I mixed color and shade. It's not quite a photo, not quite real, yet somehow timelessly more. You can tell it's a painting of Lydia and Troy even though that's not quite how they looked; air-brushed to imperfection perhaps, until they almost slide to infinity.

Troy and Lydia sat without moving for over an hour so I could paint this. It's not just made from photographs. This is a real portrait, like a real professional might do. At least, it's a first draft, just one in a pile of first drafts, it seems, as I start to flip the pages. They've faded of course, these images, their colors washed and sprinkled with ash, the paper crinkling damply underneath. But I painted it again on more expensive stuff and bought a frame from the art gallery as a wedding gift to them. The picture hangs in the living room of my sister and brother-in-law's house, over the fireplace where it's stood guard for three strong nephews as they grew. I did something worthwhile.

The therapist nods and smiles. She likes me to say things like that, to pretend I'm okay and imagine I have some self-esteem. So we turn the page to see more wedding scenes.

Crowds of figures in bright-colored clothes mill around while one stands alone. There's a white-clothed table next to her with specks of red on it. The figure holds a glass of red wine in her hand while a long line trickles down her skirt.

"Who's she?"

"I don't know. Some girl." We turn the page.

A white-haired young man has his arm wrapped around a luxuriously black-haired woman. He rests one hand on her heavily pregnant belly, while a fluffy white cat curls around their feet.

"They lived near Troy and Lydia. Steve or Mark or something I think. They might still be around."

A small child stands between her parents, an empty mask for her face. She seems unmoving, unmoved while the world spins around. I've painted a stillness in her, eyes blank, not pleading, not gazing nor offering hope or trust, just emptily glazed. Her hand rests on her mother's palm but the child doesn't seem to care. I've painted Amelia, and that was the first time I saw her.

"What's wrong with her?" I asked Mom after we'd shaken hands with the little girl's parents. I pointed to the child, but Mom didn't seem to know. *Something messed up in her head* I think she said, but those empty eyes and the infinite innocent beauty of the face had captivated me. Sweet Amelia.

"Were you afraid of her?" the therapist asks now.

"No."

"Afraid *for* her?"

"No. Why would I be?" But I should have been I suppose, she so helpless, and me hiding my secret from everyone. I did keep looking at her, trying to catch her vacant gaze and see what lay behind.

I glided through the wedding at Lydia's side, a perfect bridesmaid, proudly confident in my task. I greeted strangers as if I'd been doing this for years, training all my life as my sister's hostess. Then the photographer took control, and I let Jason drag me around, introducing me to his friends as, "My little sister. She's too young for you." I didn't mind. The cat ran past, dressed like a bride itself with veil of fluffy fur flung wide—no angel wings though.

Troy's dad sneaked away after a while—I don't have any pictures of him. The other mechanic followed with the waitress, the girl spilling wine in that earlier picture. But Troy's Mom stayed behind. Then Troy and Lydia and Jason went off to visit the old people's home. Lydia worked there weekends, so I guess she wanted to show off to her friends. And Troy's grandmother was there.

I stayed behind with the little girl's image imprinted like a hole in my mind.

Confetti flies, an artificial snowstorm of red, blue, and yellow. It falls on the car, on the bride and on the ground. But I've built the picture from star-spangled speckles, sketching Lydia's face and her dress with a tightening array of dots like confetti-colored fog, unless you focus right. Confetti fog with sharp edges. Confetti triangles.

The next picture worked better I think, where Lydia's wearing her lime green going-away dress. She looked great in green.

Then she was gone. Jason Junior had an apartment in town. Lydia and Troy had a house, just down the road yet a whole world away. And I moved all my stuff into Lydia's room, so I got her view of the street, looking out over flowers and trees instead of our next door neighbor's wall. I was an only, lonely child.

Chapter 39

*P*ictures *of houses and churches and countryside. A bridge over water. A farm up high on a hill.*

These aren't pictures painted at school, I explain. I'd joined an art class with Lydia, who seemed oddly determined to make sure we stayed friends now she was married. Troy was always working at the garage, six and a half days a week, trying to earn enough money to support the baby growing inside her. Mom said Lydia needed the company so, ever the obedient child, I obliged and spent every Saturday morning pretending I might be an artist in the church hall.

It's kind of weird when you're a kid and your big sister's pregnant. I was old enough to know what was going on, but there's *knowing* and there's knowing too many details isn't there? Plus I didn't want to know or even think about what she and Troy must have done to get her pregnant. Do you think that's weird, that I felt so odd about it?

"No," says the therapist. "Do you?"

I was in high school now, still rebelling, still studying art as well as the dreaded math. We did pottery too, a bit of woodwork, and lots of painting of course. We had easels set up all around the room, everyone working in private spaces unless there was a still life or something in the middle for us all to copy—no naked models, of course, not in high school, not back then. The lighting was great, and the teacher was really nice. We even made our own picture frames sometimes.

I saw something in the art gallery once; a picture where the artist continued to paint so the image spread over the frame, as if it were real. I made one like that with my cat, her tail hanging over the edge and a white paw reaching out to catch it. They hung it on a corridor at school but I'm not sure what happened when I left. I really liked that picture.

"Did you make one for yourself?"

"Yeah." I did, in the end. It's one of the framed pictures from the loft, so it's heavy and I haven't brought it here. I remember adding the finishing touches in class, without the frame of course. Then I carried it home on the bus. The paint was still damp so I'd put some blank paper into my folder to protect it. Everyone wanted to see what I'd done and I hated the sound of their chanting, rolling like waves, like leaves over me. But Sharon's big brother Simon was on the same bus and, when he stared at me, I thought I was in love.

"Do you have any pictures of him?"

We turn another page.

Two people stand in the waves at the edge of an ocean. Behind them the sun's red ball is sinking low, sending streaks of light across the sky. Small ripples of water reclaim the sand around the couple's toes, and their hands don't touch. Small emptiness expands the space between them, enough for a thread of light or a whisper of hope.

The girl's dark hair flows over her shoulders, its waves as soft as the ocean's. The guy's long hair is cloudier, with color undefined. It covers his face leaving only a hint of his features, eyes, a mouth, all shadowed and dim. The girl wears a bathing suit. The guy wears a long-sleeved shirt and rolled up jeans.

But our session's done. The therapist tells me to think about how I painted Simon. Why is he fully clothed when I'm not? Why aren't I the one hiding? I tell her the girl's not me but she doesn't agree. Then I go home.

On the way out I check with the receptionist. The insurance payments have all gone through, and Donald doesn't need to worry.

People stare as I carry my folder of pictures along the street to my car. I imagine they're chanting, like the kids on the bus. I imagine they thing I'm strange, and maybe they're right.

Then I imagine Simon as he must be now, going gray or maybe bald, dressed in a suit with buttoned up shirt and tie, hair cut short and fingernails trimmed, shoes shined to a glow. He never was the one for me—just a friend, the brother of a friend, way too close to it all. It would never have worked. I should never have tried...

Simon's aftershave, at the Christmas Prom, reminded me of Daddy's. It was my first high school dance, and the ice in my veins matched the snow coming down from the sky, white on black, stained yellow by streetlamps, soiled like my soul.

I drove there in Mom's old car, feeling so grown up and proud with the artificial freedom of a driving license. Gray-green shadows watched like ghosts from the trees as I circled the park—Paradise Park with its paradise stained by sin and with rumors of hell. Fat flakes of snow covered the windscreen, and Mom's wipers packed up. I had to keep stopping to clear a space to see so I could drive, and I was constantly afraid the car wouldn't start again. I'd be left in the forest alone with my memories. But I reached the town at last, Christmas-lit and bright with people and neon signs. Six-pointed stars twinkled on lampposts where strings of red and green were tethered, fluttering over the streets.

I was late. The school parking lot was packed out, but Mom's car was small enough to slide into a space. Then I tottered on uncertain heels across the icy blacktop, keeping my face bent down to the ground while the wind blew ice in my ears.

I had to show my ID at the door. Somebody stamped my hand with a red Christmas tree. Roars of noise poured out from the hall, loud music, voices shouting, feet stomping on floors. I wasn't sure I really wanted to be here, but Sharon had promised she was bringing Simon with her, just for me, so I took a deep breath.

Lights flashed disco-crazy with scarlet allure. Rippling crowds of bodies washed like waves sloshing to shore. I tried to snake my way between arms that clung and legs that swung.

The drinks table was right at the far side—our meeting place. Then I checked my watch and waited another ten minutes for Sharon to arrive.

"You on your own?" asked the leering face of a stranger, smelling of spoiled fruit.

"I'm waiting."

"Dance with me."

Hands wrapped possessively around my waist, but I stood my ground and wriggled free. "I said I'm waiting."

"Well, sorree." The stranger waved his tongue like a two-year-old, then grabbed a drink and stormed away.

I tried to keep my eye on the door, watching for Sharon and Simon. But I tried to keep my gaze glued to the floor as well, so nobody would think I was looking at them. I didn't want anyone else's hands pawing at me.

Bottles passed around me, smelling sickly sour. I stuck to punch and hoped no one had spiked it.

"You want something more?"

"I'm fine."

"I'll pour."

I covered my plastic glass with my hand and repeated, "I said I'm fine," hating the whine that crept into my voice.

I wanted to run, but of course they arrived just as soon as I stopped looking for them. Sharon leapt at me from behind and I spilled my drink. Simon waited patiently.

"You're very pretty," he said, to her or to me. I tried to smile though I felt like my legs were either going to melt or break into shards of splintered ice. My heart felt the same.

Simon didn't try to touch me. He just took a drink from my hand, shooting sparks up my arm when his fingers brushed so lightly against mine. Then he smiled again, lifted the cup to his lips and saluted me.

At once the room melted away. Lights became a background blur, swirled with a finger and fading into the page. I stared into his eyes—deep, bright, brown, glowing eyes. I looked at the way his blond hair flopped to one side. I traced the hollow of his cheeks in my imagination, thought how I'd paint him, delighted in how the colors reflected from his skin. The supple lips around his mouth lifted softly into a smile then wrapped themselves around his cup to drink. Beneath them hung a wispy yellow beard. I watched his throat, the soft pale skin expanding and contracting again. His collar hung undone. His chest exposed a tiny curl of hair that moved up and down when he breathed. Then he took my hand, and I jumped.

"Sorry. Didn't mean to startle you. Do you want to dance?"

Of course I wanted to dance, except I couldn't remember if I ever had. But how hard could it be? I tried to move my feet to the beat and felt the wooden sculpture of my arms absorb the blow. I wanted to relax but I didn't know how.

Simon pulled me forward while I hung immobile. He placed an arm so gently in the small of my back. Ice ran down my thighs. He stroked my hair with electric fingers, and I felt as if the strands of it might snap, turning brittle with cold. I tried to smile.

"You're so pretty," Simon said and bent his head to my lips. Warm strawberry breath with hints of alcohol blew into my mouth. I swallowed bile, still trying to smile, felt his tongue against my teeth... then I turned and ran.

Chapter 40

Streetlamps leak their yellow light onto a veil of falling snow. In the background, two girls lean low over gray blacktop. One seems helpless, hands outstretched, knees bent, head bowed in pain, or else she's throwing up. The other holds her solicitously, but turns her face to glare over her shoulder, a look of fury jutting out of the page, eyes colder than ice.

It was still snowing as I ran outside. I saw two girls from our class. They looked like they'd imbibed too many of those nameless bottles being offered inside. The air smelled of sickness around them and carried their voices. "What you staring at? Going to report us to the Principal?" I wasn't looking. I didn't care.

I shivered with cold and struggled to make my way toward Mom's car. Then I fought against the keys to open her door, my fingers all thumbs, knees and elbows knocking. Driving home I wondered if the cops were going to stop me. Driving with broken windscreen wipers in the snow—was that an offence? Would I know where all the documents were, or would they think I'd stolen the car? I wondered if I smelled of drink and if I could have breathed enough fumes to fail a breathalyzer test. But I made it home, parked on the drive and staggered into the house.

"You're early," said Mom.

I said yes and went up to my room.

Mom probably thought I'd broken up with a boyfriend or something. That's if she heard me crying. More likely she and Daddy were just proud I'd learned my lesson and wouldn't go begging permission slips for parties anymore. But the only person I'd broken up with was me. I hated myself.

Dancers swirl in bright colors, the background blurred, the foreground bright and clear. Dresses whirl in wide circles of light. Eyes smile. Arms hold each other so very perfectly positioned, balanced just right. All around the border, a jagged edge of red gives way to black. And a small white cat smiles up from the middle of the dance floor.

Colors swirl in facets of bright dancers. Chopped and cut, sharp edges intersect. A broken mirror reflects the hall, viewed from above. Hands clasp and tear away. Fragmented pictures, the music's beat has shattered the glass in the frame, but the cat still remains.

Hands are clasped in one bright triangle, held apart in another. Between them a blur of rainbow colors melds with the red and green of Christmas. Traffic lights and a car and police van hide in broken splinters at the edge of the page. Stars shine overhead and snow reflects their sheen in brittle whiteness underneath.

Sharon asked me why I ran away but I couldn't say. She asked in school, at break, during lunch, during class. She asked as we stood together at the school gate. She asked on the bus. But I couldn't reply.

One day we walked home, arm in arm, through the park. We took the short cut under the trees, stepping past lampposts where Janet had crouched when a white cat came to her aid, hiding from sunshine under the spring-born sprays of dawning leaves. We sat on a bench and listened while children played. I heard their shrieks from the climbing frame and the clatter of feet climbing steps up to the slide. Ducks quacked on the pond and, far away, a dog barked.

"Why?" Sharon said, leaping up from her seat and turning to face me. Arms akimbo, she rested her hands on her hips, like my mom when I've driven her insane. "Why did you do that? Why do you always do that?"

"Do what?" I asked dully.

"Spoil things. Tell me one time you didn't."

I didn't understand, so I twisted my fingers together in my lap and tried to ignore her. Leaves from the long-gone fall crunched under her feet as she stomped angrily. The air was heavy and sweet with the scent of pine. Running water burbled from the pond. And Sharon kept talking, punctuating each sentence with thrust of hands and stamp of foot.

"So we're at the party, right? And there's nothing wrong going on? Nothing our Moms would notice. Everyone's happy. Music. Food. Everything good there, right?"

I nod my head miserably.

"Then my dear Simon, my sweet dear big brother Simon who you've been going all gooey-eyed over forever, who's only there because you asked me to bring him and I promised I would…"

I nod again.

"He asks you to dance and you stand there like a brick. Then he tells you you're pretty and you run away like he's threatened to murder you. What is wrong with you?"

If I knew, I'd still be dancing wouldn't I? Then I started to cry.

Amelia was there, that gorgeous weird little girl from church who had something wrong with her head. I saw her walking past with a rabbit in one hand and a doll in the other. Yin and yang, they made me think of the cat and the bull. But Amelia looked completely at peace while I was battered and torn.

Other children ran along the path, and all I could think to say was, "They shouldn't be here, not in the forest, not without their moms."

I didn't promise to tell Sharon why I was crying. She just assumed I was promising something. I never told.

A little girl in a simple dress stands in a clearing of light under looming trees. She holds a rabbit trailing from one hand and a ragged doll from the other. The doll's red dress is the only bright spot in the picture, all muted colors, vaguely threatening green of forest and leaf with faded sky and pale touches of spring.

Yellow hair frames the girl's doll-like face. Blue eyes gaze emptily. And tiny lips are parted, smiling secrets all her own.

Chapter 41

I've almost emptied the boxes at last. I tip the last one up instead of reaching into the bottom. The card feels soft and flabby in my fingers, making me wonder how it's held up all those years. Scraps of paper flutter out, mingled with dead spiders and other assorted detritus. I slide myself back out of the way in case something's still alive in there. But it's safe, just decay that's gathered with years of neglect. I wonder if memories get mixed up with dust and nonsense when they decay too.

Small pictures flutter up from the floor like confetti when I lean too close. I remember Lydia's wedding, paper snow thrown into the air and floating around Daddy's car. But I think if I can lay these pictures flat, fitting colors together as if they form a mosaic, I'll make sense of it all.

They all match, these tiny squares of paper. Each piece is decorated with a guardian angel cat, white fur and wings set against different colored backgrounds, black, red, blue, green, yellow. Every cat has two green eyes and one red one, where the jewel sits in its collar.

I guess I could have painted those cats in my sleep. I sold so many at church fairs through the years, clipped into dollar-store frames big and small, or painted onto the covers of exercise books to make diaries. I remember the angry chatter of old women as if it was yesterday, and Mom and Daddy too—"Not good. Not Biblical. Not Christian." But Daddy was softening, surprisingly, with the years, or with grandparenthood. I remember him telling Mom that Catholics were Christians after all, and angels could be found all over the

Bible. He even seemed to half-approve my painting, perhaps because I'd agreed to study math, not art, in college.

Math is so much more lucrative, he told me, just like Donald says, so it must be true. Math is *so* much better suited to creating a career. It makes you *so* much more attractive to employers. But I hadn't chosen math for the money or the job, or even to please my father. I chose it for me. I chose it because art keeps changing, good and bad, with the teacher's mood, and math is never anything other than simply right or wrong.

All the same, I wasn't going to give my whole day, every day, to math. I planned on math and art, and science, and English, and something else to round out my timetable for senior year. I wasn't sure which subject would keep me sane, so I read those paragraphed blurbs for senior classes and tried to pick. Then I found metalwork. The caption insisted that students must be detail oriented and equipped with all the skills to measure carefully. That sounded like me. It sounded like practical math and it even fitted with my dreams of art. After all, the teacher had promised we'd try acrylics this year, and they work great on metal. I thought of painting jewelry and decided to sign up, but I didn't tell Daddy.

Rounding my pictures of cats into a circle, I remember my first project in metalwork class: a flat metal plate; that was all; make it flat and make it round, then decorate it. The guys adorned their circles with nuts and bolts like hubcaps for cars, but mine was rimmed with guardian angel cats. I loved that plate, but I never took it home. What would Daddy say?

We made letter racks, and I painted heavenly felines on purple and blue. Business card holders—I knew they were bound to sell well. And finally the girls in the class got to design their own jewelry. I carved small squares, rolled the edges, buffed and smoothed, and painted intricate shapes inside the lines: guardian angel cat bracelets, lapel pins, pendant necklaces and rings. When the boys teased me that I was doing easy stuff, I made pillboxes with delicate hinges and clasps and kittens on top. They stopped laughing at me then.

I got my materials from school at cost, then sold my pieces at the next church fair to raise funds. The old ladies enjoyed much complaining at my expense. But then Andrea Blake, from the art gallery, came to my table in the noise of rushing children and hot-cold commerce. She stopped to talk to me.

"They're good," she said, her voice like gold as she fingered a necklace and bracelet admiringly.

I held my breath—smelled popcorn—and waited in case she needed to back away from the compliment.

"They're okay anyway, not bad." That seemed more like it. "Not marvelous, but I think they might sell."

They *were* selling here, in case she hadn't noticed. In the pleasing atmosphere of raising money and sharing our talents and gifts, I was doing a great trade. But I held my breath again, in case Miss Andrea meant they might sell in her store. There seemed a curious irony to the conversation. I'd finally agreed with Daddy that I wouldn't pursue art, and here was someone maybe offering to pay me.

"Could you keep the gallery supplied," Andrea asked, creasing her face into a frown, "or is this all you have?"

The school supplied me.

"Could you bring them in to sell?"

The school wouldn't mind.

I couldn't speak but I nodded gloriously. Miss Andrea was offering a dream come true. *My* art might go on display in *her* gallery! But Mom was watching and I dulled my response, saying nothing when the next person asked what Andrea had been talking about. It might not happen.

All the same, next day I rushed over to Blake's gallery straightaway, my head exploding with ideas and business suggestions and promises. And hope as well...

I gather the pieces of paper together now, like rings and necklaces dropped on the floor. My fingers twitch, remembering tying those labels with prices written in precious silver ink. Soon I was working at the gallery weekends and vacations, calculating profits and values, putting my math and art to good use both at once. It was the perfect job. Except that nothing's ever perfect, and nothing lasts... as I've learned through the years.

I thought motherhood would be the perfect job as well, when we got married, until the tears and helplessness of knowing I'm no good; until I realized I was wasting my days in what Donald calls *free time*, until...

So I stir the pictures again, mingling memories with dreams. Crinkled paper smells of damp dog. The cardboard box smells worse. And the dog smells of shampoo. I cuddle Tyke and fold the cardboard up to throw away, knowing it's time for a walk. When I come back I'll haul those last framed pictures out of the closet, and my journey's almost done.

Acrylic

Chapter 42

A blue cloth background covers most of the page. It hangs from a small square tack, three fifths of the way along the top. The head of the tack is decorated with a guardian angel cat.

Three-fifths is important to me: math and precision and art blended all into one.

A shiny plate is propped two fifths of the way along one side of the page, three fifths up the other, near the middle of the tablecloth. They're not really fifths though. I measured them. They're golden ratios carefully designed.

Angel cats dance all around the edge of the silver plate. Boxes large and small, all painted in perfect perspective, support its weight. Open lids reveal layers of velvet, while closed ones are sealed with statues of sleeping cats—sleeping cats with wings. Jewelry dangles from a silver tree, where a gorgeously rendered cat pendant takes pride of place.

Everything's well-measured, golden ratio-ed in this picture. Totally lacking in emotional weight, totally planned, and priced to sell, I'm sure, it's carefully, perfectly fitted into its silvered wooden frame.

I wonder how I'll carry the frames from the car to the therapist's office. Perhaps I should just describe the images. After all, we're nearly done. I'm nearly cured. Until another ten years bring me down again.

I smell the dust and anguish of old paint and start to cry, then pull the next frame to the front.

A coffin in dark wood, almost black, is surrounded by wreaths of flowers, just as it should be. Blood red roses, red berries, red leaves of ivy and dour red irises lean against its sides. Red blood drips on the ground and snakes to a pool where reflections slide; etched shapes of a low farm-house with picket fence and field and bull. An ancient truck drives by.

Is the bull really there? I can't tell, and I can't see the cat, but the paint's begun to crack. They may have been lost in the annals of time.

"It's Grandpa's coffin," I tell her, "though I didn't go to his funeral." Lydia was pregnant. I was taking exams or else I'd already gone to college. But Daddy went. I tell the therapist this, and she wonders why I bothered to paint it.

"Were you sorry your Grandpa was dead?" she asks.

But I hardly ever saw him by then. I hardly thought it mattered. Just a picture, painted red and black.

"And your grandmother?"

I didn't paint her coffin or her grave.

"Does that make you sad? After all the time you spent with them as a child?"

Am I meant to feel sad? I hurry on to describe more pictures, proud of how well I've managed to remember them. I'm glad that I have so much to say, because it proves I must be getting well.

A guardian angel cat.

"This one's my masterpiece," I tell her, the one I'd mentioned before and couldn't show her, the one from the wall of my childhood room.

The white cat rests in the center of the page, pink-washed with shadows. Sky bruises purple and blue in bright swirls behind it. I've added lighter streaks over gray-white fur. They thicken and slim to satin, almost breathing, like a cat's soft purr. Feather tips on the wings are flecked with red-lit hints of silver. Green eyes shine warmly and a bright red stone glows like a third eye's secret in the kitten's collar. Silver glitter streaks the small pink nose. Silver laughter wakens in the eyes. And tiny blades of claws are softly sheathed.

The frame is wood. The picture's covered with glass and yearns to be hung back on a wall.

The cat's eyes follow me.

"I'd like to see it," says the therapist. "Can you bring it in next time?"

But I demur and wave my hand. I'm describing another picture now.

An old farmhouse, half-falling down, stands in fields of green and brown. A bull looks over a white picket fence. A cat strolls perkily on weed-strewn paths. And red fire blazes from the barn.

"Very nice," she says, "but I'd still like to see them."

I mutter my excuses, adding, "I'm not sure how long I can keep coming." My fingers twine tighter around each other, twisting my wedding, promise, ring. "Donald's worried about the cost you see; and the time. He says I need a job."

She, my therapist, ever therapeutically, answers by asking me how that makes me feel.

I feel broken and ignored, but tell her I'm fine.

The clock still ticks on the wall of the therapist's office. The sun still glides across the window's square of afternoon sky. Shadows move and time ignores their dance, and nothing's going to change. I'll feed the children, wash and clean, go shopping, cut the grass and weed the flowers. I'll schedule time for doctor and dentist and write on the calendar. I'll answer the phone and make calls, order medications and pick them up. And, all the while, I'll be wife and mother without any time to be me.

"You have this time," the therapist says. "This is your time."

But it's not. This is the time when I pretend to be curable, when I smile and say I'm okay without listening to myself. Nothing changes, you see.

The therapist asks if she can call my mother and check up on the details of childhood days. I guess she wants to know if the fire was in the field or in the barn or if there were two, and I say yes because people who are going to be cured always agree with everything. *I* always agree. And I promise to bring the picture frames next time.

At home I look at the painting of the coffin again. The angles of black and red feel like anger and pain. I wonder whose name lies buried in that grave.

Chapter 43

"Mom, will you, can you, won't you, please." Their words fall like leaves until I'm buried in earthen murk, and I can't remember how to escape. They'll send tractors and trailers to dig me up from the ground. "Mom. Mom!" Dead foliage falling over me.

"Sylvia?"

I struggle to the surface through sheets and blankets tangled around my knees. The air still smells of leaf mold and dirt. My fingernails feel torn from trying to dig. My eyelids are closed.

"Sylvia," says Donald's softly disturbing voice. "The kids need you to get them ready for school. Are you okay?"

I'm not okay, and I know I can't protect them. And I'm glad they're boys, not girls, because... And I wonder if they'll grow up to be evil or good.

"Sylvia. Can you pack their lunchboxes for them?"

I force my eyes to open through the glue of broken dreams. "I thought you said they had to leave."

"They do in a minute."

So of course I can do it. I leap out of bed, wrap a dressing gown around my pajamas, run fingers through damp fibrous hair. I switch myself back onto autopilot and let the rest of me stay buried deep. Let earth fill my nose and my mouth and my silent complaint. Blind eyes will never see *his* face.

I dig the bread from the fridge, smell its glutinous dough, spread slices with mayo like white blood dripping down from the essence of ghosts, and carve slices of cheese. Tomatoes bleed. Lettuce leaves conjure the scents of decay in the ground. I snap the plastic boxes closed.

"'Bye kids. Have fun."

"Mom," they mutter as they pass. They're too old for this, and so am I.

Then I crawl back to bed, escaping the cold of morning's open door. In the distance I hear their school busses roar. In the bathroom Donald runs his shower. But dreams and nightmares won't wash away.

I'm almost asleep again when I feel Donald's lips lightly pressing against my cheek. His breath smells of toast and marmalade. "I've got to go now," he says. "Please wake up, Sylvia."

I don't want to.

"Don't forget your appointment."

I don't want to remember.

"You know the insurance won't pay if you don't go."

He only cares about the money, and I hate him in that moment, hate everything my life's become.

"I love you, Sylvia."

I pretend not to hear.

He doesn't slam the bedroom door, but he shuts it a little too loudly as he leaves. He's just making sure I know he's annoyed with me.

I crawl out of bed and climb into the same clothes I wore yesterday. My hair doesn't look too bad. My breath smells of coffee so I guess I must have drunk some while I made those sandwiches. And my paintings lean accusingly against the wall.

Grandpa's coffin, jewelry, cat, farm, and math—I can't carry any more than that, so I tie a string around them like a parcel and struggle downstairs. Truly, I can't even carry these, but I will, just to prove I'm okay. At least it's not raining.

"Tell me about college," the therapist says, but I've staggered in with these picture frames held like shield over my breast. She's going to have to look at them now. She said she wanted to. And here's one I've never told you about, you see. Yes, it's about college, if that's what she wants.

Mathematical symbols interweave with the shapes of old Greek letters, sensuously sliding and slithering around the page. Folded, distracted, bending around curves and corners of imagined equations, they blend into lines and rectangles of the golden ratio. The shape where they meet might be a man and woman, with bodies entwined. But it's only a hint, like love refusing to be measured, or mathematical formulae that somehow fail to add up.

"Where does Greek come into it?"

"Symbols," I say. "It's symbolic."

"Do you think your guardian angel cat is a symbol?" She tugs my favorite cat picture out and I want to beg her to be careful as she props it up on her desk.

"Symbol of what?" I lean forward, primed to save.

"You tell me," she says, which is really no help at all.

We talk some more, about college, the art club, and how the members' hall delighted me with wide lit windows and shadowed variety. We talk about math lectures in rooms with cramped wooden seating, foreign voices, symbols scratched on a blackboard too faded to read. We talk about dorms and sharing space with a stranger who never spoke to me.

"Did you ever speak to her?"

We talk, and my heart beats too fast, or else it threatens to stop. My pulse chokes me and drowns my ears in its roar. I tell how Donald seems distant these days, and ask if he shouldn't have made the children's lunches, instead of waking me?

"But you needed to wake up for your appointment."

And I should have known. She's ever the voice of reason, my therapist. Maybe Donald's the one who should see her— they think so alike.

But now she's passed me a piece of paper, so I can draw while we talk. Does this mean I've graduated? She used to only offer tissues.

The page fills up with carefully divided rectangles. Then I draw a snail's smooth shell in a spiral that's fitted to all their corners. When time runs out, I tear off the page and throw it with my tissues into the bin. Have I been crying again?

Chapter 44

"Tell me about when you came home from college," my therapist says the next time I see her.

I've brought more pictures but she won't look at them, and I wonder, *what's to tell?*

I used to sneak into the metalwork lab at the high school during my vacations. I paid for stuff; I wasn't cheating anyone. And I got paid. I made my guardian angel cats for sale and worked at the art gallery until the owner died. Then I graduated, not long afterward.

"The owner died?" the therapist asks, as if the event ought to have some significance greater than its words.

"Yeah, she killed herself, maybe. I'm not quite sure."

"Isn't that the sort of thing you might be sure of?"

But really, it's not. Andrea wasn't my friend or anything. She wasn't a kid in school. She was just my boss. And if she went down to the forest every lunchtime, if she ignored the rumors of a predator, or even dared to love him under the trees… "She was pregnant, and I guess she didn't want to keep it."

"So she killed herself?"

"Or did something stupid. Who knows?" I can tell I'm meant to sound more upset, to worry about whether I could have protected her, if saying just the right thing at the right time might have made things different. But how can a kid try to tell her boss what to do? I touch the edge of memory and shy away from it, because it hurts.

Then the therapist asks, "How did it make you feel?"

It made me feel glad I'd never been pregnant I guess. *So what?* And we still haven't looked at all those pictures I carried here today.

A white cat walks across a stage with square black cap on its head. Red fabric trails gracefully behind, neatly positioned over a tail that waves high in the air. A brown bull offers to shake the cat's hand, or paw. A line of mice and dogs and children offer congratulations. The background's black. The edges of the picture bleed to red.

Another painting shows a roomful of cats, all holding wineglasses. They seem to dance, while pastel balloons reflect their souls with wings. Bubbles rise through the air and grow. A bull holds the microphone and stands upon a stage of fallen leaves.

"Tell me about graduation then."

"I graduated," I say.

"Parties? Celebrations?" My therapist points at the dancing cats with their souls caught up in the sky.

"I suppose."

"Drunken orgies?"

"No. Of course not."

Two cats lie together, intertwined, one white-winged, the other black. The white cat wears a rhinestone collar. The black one has a red ring around its neck that wriggles like a snake.

There's nothing left to talk about, and the therapist's really not helping. I'll just pack the pictures and take them home, stack them all back in the attic and wait ten years until the kids are grown. Then I'll talk to another *mental health professional* about *their* graduations. I stare at my hands, clasping and twisting and turning over the sketchpad in my lap. I've drawn rectangles again.

The therapist tears off the page and hands me another clean slate. "Why don't you tell me how you and Donald met? Was that in college?"

"He was in grad school," I say, taking pencil in hand.

"So how did you meet him?"

Two people sit on a wooden park bench. Trees dangle branches enticingly around, making a framework of leaves. The woman sits to the left with hands clasped in her lap. Her face points down but her eyes look across at the man. He stares at her but keeps his body as far away as he can. Legs bend stiffly at the knees while he sits rigidly straight, his back pressed firmly against the wooden slats of the bench. One hand clings nervously to the bench's arm while the other's partially raised as if he's wondering what to do with it.

I tear off the page and draw some more.

Two people sit on a wooden park bench. Trees dangle branches enticingly around, making a framework of leaves. The woman sits to the left with hands clasped in her lap and face down-turned. The man sits in the middle, one arm resting on the back of the bench, the other on his knee. His body leans toward the woman. His face is turned her way. There's tension in every sinew of him, as if he's overbalancing while trying to keep himself still.

Another page.

Two people sit on a wooden park bench. Trees dangle branches. The man has his arm around the woman's shoulders. His body's lightly pressed to hers, but she still faces forward, seeming to ignore him.

Two people sit on a wooden park bench, arms and bodies entwined, faces pressed together in a lingering kiss.

"He always asked permission," I tell her. "That's what I liked about him."

"Only that?"

I start to smile.

Chapter 45

*B*icycles storm the street like a herd of bulls, handlebar horns streaked with the blood of dedication, riders devoted to the task of clearing a path to the next lecture. *A red car cowers, afraid to turn the corner. A white cat sits on a wall and cleans its paws. Gray sky is threaded with silver of late summer light, and a forest glow casts shadows over the frenzy of town and gown. Redbrick buildings hide in faint background lines, cubes and squares like ghosts between the spokes or underneath a rider's arm, until no shape is what it seems.*

I loved that moment after class when I could go back to my room and study, or take myself to the art building and paint something. Painting usually won. The smell of engine exhaust, stale coffee and streets still suffering from last night's booze gave way to paint's astringent cleanliness. The clamor of bicycle bells, car horns, brakes and gears, traffic and radios fell silent. The colors of town would disappear before an empty canvas awaiting the fuel of my imagination. I loved that place.

Brushstrokes whisper their memory on the page. Breathing sighs with the peace of inspiration. Nothing but lines and whispering curls fill the sky, while down below a thin brush leans so peacefully against the blue glass side of a pot. Cool and smooth, bright-colored compatriots stand to attention behind it, while mists of shade and shapeless dreams fall sleepily over them. A picture of nothing—a picture of painting—a picture of pure delight.

We spare-time artists hardly bothered to greet each other in the hall. Sunlight shone through a bank of windows arrayed on the far side. Those needing warmth or light set their easels up there. But shadows filled the corners close to the door, perfect for angst-filled graphics full of angles and mystery and war. Tables invited model makers to practice their trade in the middle, while sculptors labored by the walls.

Hammer, hand and vice hide behind sparks of flashing fire. Cold stone still remembers fractured shapes. Fluid pottery slips and slides around the spinning plate. And sunlight shines through the center. Around the edges, human figures range like the petals of a flower.

I almost recognized him, the bent figure holding a tiny model creature to his eye, thin paintbrush tending to shape and size, dark greens and browns and grays of camouflage in pots at his side. I watched him closely, hiding behind the shelter of my easel. The model was a soldier the size of a fly. Specks of red from a grievous wound adorned his chest and shoulder. Every button was painted. Every fold of his tunic outlined. There was even a visible expression of fear on his face.

I saw the artist add his newborn warrior to its clan, and I wondered what they were. Then he opened a briefcase, lined in red, and drew more figures out. Silver metal turned green and brown under the skill of his hands. Silver statues turned to men. Their blackened weapons shone again with threats of gunpowder's fire. And his fingers flew.

With hair pushed back behind his ears, eyes half-closed intently in concentration, fingers so very perfectly delicate and sure… I almost recognized him and then I knew—he was in my *financial algorithms* class.

Once I knew him, and once he knew I knew him, we started to smile at each other while claiming our spaces in the hall. Soon we even dared to smile outside. We even sat on that park bench together where he learned to ask if he could hold my hand. We chained our bikes to the same dark rail, walked side-by-side into lectures, and sometimes dared sit next to each other there, in full view of everyone. The classes were small and the teacher knew our names. I learned my artist was called Donald before I ever knew the touch of his hand.

A red and white picnic cloth lies over rich green grass. Paper plates are weighted down with bright-colored leaves of salad and chunks of bread. A wine bottle stands half full with a long drip snaking down its side. Two glasses sparkle in the sun.

Behind this scene, dark trees are ranged in a carefully measured arc. Pale undergrowth fills the space between them and the peaceful picnic place. Protected, safe, the image proclaims a need for security, each measured item drawn to scale and laid out by the rules of ratio, my math in art. Nothing is out of position, except the drip's red snake that almost has eyes, that almost looks at you.

The grass smelled fresh-cut, clean, down there by the river. The water carried an oily undertone from its journey through town. Traffic rumbled on distant roads while birds sang overhead. Donald placed the food on plates and offered a glass of wine but made sure our fingers never met. Electricity between us was understood but never had chance to be grounded.

He talked about his model armies and rules the metal soldiers had to obey. Statistics was the measure of it, with corrections made whenever new rule books revealed freshly learned turns of history. He knew the weapons, their names, range, hit rate, deviation, and the weights of every blow. He calculated how much armor they could pierce. One afternoon he invited me back to his room, where tiny squadrons stood guard on his coffee table. He marched them through cardboard streets with building fronts and ruins stapled to matchboxes for support. I rolled the dice, and Donald interpreted. My squadron lost, and the Germans lived to fight another day, while Russians retreated.

I'd never cared too much for history before, but Donald declared I'd done well, and I swelled with pride. Still our hands never touched. His fingers never brushed against my cheek.

My body stirred, unfamiliar feelings growing, and I longed for him, but he didn't respond.

I thought of darkened forests and fumbling hands sometimes. Maybe he saw me draw away. But then I'd look at Donald and know I was safe. That day when he asked if he could his place his arm behind me on the bench, I said okay. Later he wanted to sit a little closer. He checked it wasn't inappropriate, and again I said okay. Could he place his arm on my shoulder because it might be more comfortable? Could he touch my cheek? Could he tell me he thought that maybe he'd learned to love me? And could we kiss?

I said okay, but all the while inside I was terrified. His arm lay soft as fabric on my shoulder, but I imagined heavy hands that pressed me against a tree. I remembered thick limbs wrapped around my waist, remembered feeling crushed. I remembered falling down to the ground as fingers tore at my clothes. He didn't move. When we hugged, I felt his chest so close his heartbeat pressed my ribs. Then I imagined my garments pulled away and the weight of his flesh on me, lips sucking, demanding, fingers groping and sliding into the private folds of me. He didn't try to undo my buttons. He didn't move his fingers underneath.

One day Donald leaned toward me, his face approaching mine. I smelled his breath, clean and minty like toothpaste. I felt the warmth and dampness of his mouth against my cheek, and I tried not to gag. I felt the pressure of his lips, almost dry, warm and gentle, the strangest fluttering touch of a butterfly kiss. His arm slid closer around me. His lips hovered, just in my line of sight. Our breath mingled. We shared the same damp air.

I was frozen somewhere out of time, waiting to land in the present or back in the past. Then Donald's tongue flickered so lightly against my mouth, just the gentlest, softest touch. Smoothly, silkily teasing, opening my lips and sliding his tongue inside... I held him tight for fear, not love, but he didn't need to know. Deep breaths shuddered inside me until I knew I wasn't frightened anymore.

One day perhaps he'd fill that ache that began in my stomach and leaked down to my thighs, that hole of longing growing deep in me. Someday I'd let him run his hands over me as he said he might. He'd lap his tongue against my skin and my flesh might yield to him, might let him in. Someday, but not tonight.

I leaned against him, hip to hip, as he walked me back to my building and left me at the door. My legs were shaking, my body trembling all over, and he kissed me again. This time his tongue plundered deep inside without warning, his saliva filling my mouth, and I tried to pull away. But he'd bought me with his gentleness, so I surrendered to his need. It was okay.

Chapter 46

Far away, back in Paradise, my sister had three sons now with her Troy. Even my ever-awkward ungainly brother Jason had got married. It was hard to imagine. Meanwhile the Paradise Predator still lurked in the dark of the park, but he felt like a story from a children's book read many years ago.

Mom phoned me every once in a while, just to check that I was still alive. I was meant to phone her back between my college lectures, or from the dorm, but I forgot. And Lydia, ever the writer of the family, sent endless letters on paper decorated with drips of tomato sauce, streaks of gravy, and fingerprints of paint and glue.

"Jeremy hates sports," she wrote in one missive. "I think he's going to be a mathematician like you." Poor Jeremy. Math led to computers which led to me feeling felt like a cog in the wheel of progress, condemned to draw flowcharts for computer programs, helping people with useless jobs like designing telephones and cars. It wasn't exactly earthshattering, nor life-satisfying either. But Donald was studying for his PhD. I told myself his job would be far more exciting, and when we married I'd have a much better purpose in life, keeping him clothed and fed.

And bearing his kids? Lydia's letters were filled with the joys of parenthood. "You'd never believe what JC did at toddler group. He sang Three Blind Mice all the way through, and I was so proud of him. Then he threw a fit because Joshua needed his diaper changed."

You'd imagine she'd always dreamed of having kids from the things she wrote. But I remembered her telling me she'd never be a mom when we were kids ourselves.

Then she added, at the end of one long meaningless epistle, "Do you remember that Amelia kid at church who was always getting lost?" I set the paper down, fingers itching to draw the small girl's doll-like features again. I pondered how I'd capture her distant eyes, the way they gazed so far from everyday life, the hints they held of a secret world inside. Then I read on. "The Paradise Predator killed her in the park the other day. You never expect to live where someone gets murdered do you? He never seemed quite so scary in our day. So we're keeping the kids safe, not letting them wander on their own, while the police look for him. Hope you're keeping well."

I felt stabbed through the heart.

Sitting on my bed, door closed, the world and all its bustle far away, I held her letter and listed all the reasons it couldn't be *him*. One, he wasn't dangerous. Two, he never *really* hurt me. Three, he never meant me any harm. And four? Well, it was all so long ago. Plus, of course, at number five, I never knew him anyway.

But you never expect your hand to have touched a murderer's, your flesh to have been pressed to his, your legs pushed apart while his needs intruded on yours. It couldn't be true.

Mom phoned, all in a panic of misery and full of gory details determined to get out.

"He buried her under leaves, just left her there for some dog to dig up. It's disgusting."

I asked how long Amelia was buried for. Mom said, "Not long. Poor Evie was still looking for her. They heard her wandering around and shouting her name, the way she always does. She must be beside herself." Then Mom added, "I hope you don't go wandering on your own in any parks Sylvia. And don't go letting your young man… You take care of yourself."

I could have said I was old enough and my young man wise enough. But it was easier just to say goodbye and hang up.

That night I dreamed the sound of dirt being thrown down on a dead body. My mouth tasted the mold of leaves over me, earthen mushrooms and pepper's gritty tang. I felt my fingers scrabble against the ground that was burying me, saw the sun disappear, and tried to scream. Convinced I'd been buried alive, I dug my nails in the bedclothes until morning revealed the sheets ripped raw and dripped on with speckles of blood. I washed the crusted scabs away and watched them circle the drain like insects crawling around and into and through the holes in me.

If I'd known who he was, if I'd bothered to look closely enough, if I'd stopped him or got somebody else to come with me and stop him, if I'd challenged him, if I'd done any of these things, Amelia Callaghan might still be alive. Instead she was dead.

Chapter 47

Donald's love kept me going. His hands were so gentle, his needs so undemanding. I was employed by a computer firm by then, and we'd moved in together while Donald worked on his PhD. I knew we were going to get married except, being Donald, he had to be one hundred percent sure. He kept saying we should *try out* someone else before getting too committed, as if marriage were nothing more than a new suit of clothes. Perhaps I was over-committed to him. Then Amelia died and, like I said, Donald's love kept me going like a blanket keeping me warm. He held me close when the nightmares woke me screaming and crying my guilt. He slept on the couch when memories made me unable to bear his touch. He didn't ask questions, made no assumptions, and never ever complained. He was just there for me, scented with peppermint toothpaste and spiced deodorant, washed with soap until his skin was as smooth and soft as mine, well-shaven, fine.

They caught the murderer and he killed himself. I'm not sure which happened first. Then Pastor Bill, at our old church, said they had to hold a service in Paradise Park, to cleanse its spirit or something mystical like that. Mom asked me to paint a poster for it.

"And did you?" The therapist points to her empty desk with no pictures cluttering it.

"Yes," I answer, "but I didn't keep a copy." Didn't want one. Didn't need the reminder.

She gives me paper and a pencil again and asks if I'll sketch it for her. I'm glad she hasn't asked who the murderer was. I'm sure it tells her in her notes. But I don't want to remember anymore.

"Why d'you want a picture?" I ask. "What will that tell you?"

Then I fumble with fingers heavy as lead, but find I've drawn it anyway.

"A Call to Paradise. Reclaim our neighborhood. Reclaim our park."

The words stand out from the center of the page, *and I've added a guardian angel cat below them, poised to attack. Its halo's sketched with uneven lines. I carefully count them, thirteen snakes with their mouths wrapped tight around their tails, flecks of light spinning out from them to show they're all glowing and strong.*

"Thirteen." She's heard me counting under my breath and asks me, "Why?"

"'Cause thirteen's unlucky and it's not about luck."

The words tumble out while the image stares accusingly. I know I've said them before, but I don't know what they mean.

She pretends she does. "Because it's about blame and you feel guilty."

I'm crying again.

The murderer was Troy's dad, my sister Lydia's father-in-law. I'd eaten meals with him, shaken his hand, and sat beside him on the sofa at parties. I'd filled his glass with wine. I'd laughed at his jokes. I'd talked with him about children and cars, and I'd waited at the garage for him to say Mom's old banger was repaired. I knew him well, but I still denied it. I still couldn't believe I'd felt those hands on me, still told myself it had to be somebody else. One predator. Two predators. One murderer. They couldn't all be the same.

Even when the police talked about the evidence, young girls' panties stuffed in the back of his closet, broken necklace chains, notes in his diary, even then I was sure it wasn't him. *My abuser* was someone I never knew. *My abuser* was somebody else, and I never saw his face.

So it wasn't my fault, and I shouldn't be feeling guilty, and I don't need to cry.

I rip the picture of the poster to shreds and wad it into my tissue when the therapist tells me it's time to leave.

Red and Black

Chapter 48

So that's it. I'm done. I've looked through all the pictures, tidied them up, stuffed my memories back in the closet where they belong, and it's over. I'm healed, cured, mended, and ready to go; except I'm not. Because there are still those pictures I drew for my other therapist, back when Adam was a baby, back when I was meant to be healed, cured and mended nearly ten years ago. And I don't even know where they are.

She told me to draw them as part of my therapy. She said they'd be something new to counteract the old. She said it would be just like buying new sheets to store on top of metaphorical ones messed up with all the holes in. Clean new sheets, with no painful memories attached. Fresh sheets for a fresh start.

"What if they all fall out of the closet?" I asked her.

"They won't. But if they do, you'll just look at the new ones and put them away."

"So I'm okay?"

"Do you feel okay?"

I remember saying I guessed I did, but it was a long time ago. Adam's not a baby now.

And I'm wondering where I hid them.

I've emptied the boxes, tidying their contents away into prettily decorated tins. I run my fingers over the lids and think how tins can't fall open unless you drop them, not like closet doors. But my mind's running wild, searching for all the hiding places I might have used back then, as if the missing images hold the keys, and I can't be cured until I find them. I open doors, closets, kitchen cupboards, chests in the family room, boxes and drawers, and I slam them all shut. I drag out blankets and strew them over the floor. I don't even remember what's in those pictures, and trying to see is like tonguing a broken tooth or pulling a scab, tearing holes in my knee. Reluctance falls over me like a black and red blanket, black earth to bury me, and red of fire, or autumn leaves. Then I put the bedding away, stack knives and forks back into their drawers in the kitchen, put letters in a pile on Donald's desk, and go out to my session.

"I have her notes," my therapist says as my monologue on searching comes to a close. It seems I gave her permission to ask, one of those many papers and forms I signed. She even shows me a copy of my signature. "I have copies of the pictures too." She offers the file to me.

I reach for it and watch my fingers tremble. Do I really want to know what's inside? But I'm sure *she* knows. She must have looked. Somehow I feel as if art's betraying me.

"Okay." I start to pull the pictures out.

Leaves cover the page. Black leaves and red hide scraps of dirt in between. And two small eyes, wide open, scared, peer out.

Leaves cover the ground and a single arm reaches out from under them, hand open, fingers spread to catch the breeze. Dark trees keep watch behind and hide the sun.

Black leaves and brown cover the ground where a small child lies, all white, slashed red, while a pool of blood like a snake flows between her thighs.

Hands morph into leaves into hands again, crossing space like an Escher image etched in blood.

Leaves cover his face. It's not clear which came first, the washed out features or dark autumn's fall.

Leaves cover the page except for a blackened hole, red around the edge, where the bullet turned his mouth to mud and slime.

She picks the one that almost shows a face and asks again, "Are you sure you didn't know him?"

Am I sure?

But I didn't tell anyone anything, not then. I wept with the best of them over the phone and echoed their refrain, "How could we have known?" Soon the words had morphed into, "How could we *not* have known?"

"I always thought there was something odd about him," my daddy said.

I always thought he was my sister's father-in-law and the garage man. Truth is, so did everyone else. There was nothing to give him away, but memories change.

I used to see him at the garage, the old clock ticking, me wrinkling my nose at the smell of gas and oil. Creaking metal and crashing hammers clashed behind his recital of charges and fees. I remember his hooded eyes when he stared at me.

He came to our house for Sunday dinner sometimes, with Lydia and Troy, but he seemed out of place. Dark dungarees hung over his knees while we wore our Sunday best. His shambling voice rose up to stridency in our soft-toned, ever-perfect symphony. His blunt-ended fingers stroked the silky metal of knives and forks, beard twitching as he spoke.

I remember him at the wedding, half-hidden away. His wife, Troy's Mom, was there with somebody else and I liked her better—liked the guy she was with better too.

But I told myself over and over it couldn't have been him. I'd have known his face. I'd have recognized his voice. He would've reminded me of Troy, so it had to have been someone else.

And anyway, in the end, it really didn't matter who'd attacked me. My job was to get over it, to tidy my memories back on the shelf and tell my family and friends how to help me keep the door closed. Which meant I had to tell them what had happened to me first. Which I couldn't do. Which meant...

"Did you tell them it was him?"

"No. It wasn't, I mean... They might have guessed, some of them, but I just said I didn't know."

"Did you mind when they guessed?"

I spit the answer angrily at her. "Yes. I minded. I was there. And I should know." How dare they tell me differently? It wasn't him!

"What happened when you told?"

Chapter 49

I find another picture of leaves in the stack.

Loosely scattered around the doorway of a barn, red splashes on green, leaves cover the dregs of hay and faint sprays of grass. The barn's painted yellow and outlined in thick jagged black. Wide doors reveal a small girl standing inside holding onto a cat. White cat. Red dress. Featureless face with just a hint of a smile.

I was back in Paradise, without Donald, without the babies. I was *telling* as I'd promised the therapist I would. So I went out for coffee with Lydia then thought, how stupid—I couldn't say anything in a store. We carried our drinks down to the park where I thought, how stupid—how could I talk with the forest still watching. Then we wandered the quiet streets back to Lydia's house. I imagined I'd wait until we were inside, but instead my words just tumbled out.

"In the park. When I was a kid. This guy kept touching me."

"Why didn't you just say no," said my sister, her voice as brittle as saccharine poured into coffee. "It's what *I* did." And I wondered what she meant.

That's when I learned about Grandpa, and why we'd moved so suddenly all those years ago. He took Lydia to the barn, she said, and wanted her to touch him. He let his trousers down and asked... She waited until his feet were tangled up then ran away. And she said "No." Then she told Mom and Daddy, and we moved out of the farmhouse that very same day. So that was why we didn't go back for so long. That was why Grandpa grew silent and thin, why his voice turned strange and he started to shrink as if he were suddenly dying. That was why. It was Lydia's fault.

"No," she said, taking my flailing arms in hers. "No Sis. It wasn't my fault. It was his."

The street was empty which was just as well, though I wondered if some curtains didn't twitch. Of course I knew it wasn't really her fault. Lydia had done the *right* thing. Lydia was good. She stopped his mistake right there at the start, so Grandpa hurt nobody else.

I was the one who said nothing, and Amelia died.

A blue coat, threadbare, lies among leaves. Buttons hang by spiders' legs. Red stains like wine or blood or disease bloom over the broad lapel. The leaves are black and green.

I told my brother and he hugged me and said, "Poor you. Did you know our Lydia got abused too?" So I wondered if you can measure depth with the number of times it occurs, and define who's more hurt.

Leaves fall from the sky and beneath them a red car sits with its door opened wide. There's no one inside.

Mom didn't want to believe me at first. I sat beside her on the sofa and we stared at the TV's empty eye. She said she would have known. She would have noticed it. She said I couldn't have got home late from school so many times. She said someone would have told her. My school work would have suffered and the teachers would have said. I was never any good with secrets so it couldn't be true.

Mom said they talk about recovered memories and so many times they're false. Auto-suggestion, she said, and it's all the psychiatrist's fault. So what had my therapist said to me?

I said I never forgot, so I didn't need to remember, and it had to be true.

She said I'd forgotten his face.

I said I never knew it.

A black page carries an image of farmhouse and barn outlined lightly in red. The old bull stands behind his picket fence. A cat strolls carefully on top. A line leading out from the door might be a snake or a path.

If we'd stayed with Granny and Grandpa it would never happened, Daddy said.

If we'd stayed there, Lydia would have suffered.

Instead of me.

Daddy cried.

I could tell when Lydia told Troy because of the way he looked at me, as if he was trying to imagine his father's hands on me, or else his own. I was glad I didn't live in Paradise now. I was glad to get in my car and drive away, back to Donald and the children, back to the safety and secrecy of my home.

The therapist asks me, "What about when you told Donald? What did he say?"

Donald said men have needs and he was glad our children were all boys.

"What did he mean?"

I didn't ask. I think he meant he loved me and it wasn't my fault.

Chapter 50

The therapist wants to know how my relationship with Donald is now. I tell her it's great. It really is. He's kind and considerate, and he wants me to get well. He always asks how my meetings go with her. He wants to know every detail, what she said, what we discussed, what I told her and why, and whether I think it was wise of me to say it. But I won't tell him this bit. He doesn't like to think I might talk about him behind his back, so I always say I don't.

"'Cause I don't really, do I?" I ask for confirmation, forgetting her profession.

"Do you?" she asks.

Donald laughs with me about how therapists always answer questions with a question. When we watch TV, if there's a psychologist there, we'll joke about what she's going to say, but only if the kids are in bed or if they're upstairs. Donald wouldn't want them to know I'm seeing a shrink. After all, they might imagine me covered in shrink-wrap and ready for sale. He likes making jokes like that, like asking if I'm still breathing under all this. And he doesn't mind the pictures all over the floor anymore, not as long as I tidy them up before he comes home. Because he doesn't like mess. And he worries about money, still, all the time.

"Does he?" she says. "How do you know he worries?"

"Because he keeps telling me I need to get a job."

"How does that make you feel?"

She passes the everlasting tissue box, while I wring my hands at her like a supplicant. But I ignore the call to cry this time. I'm better than that.

"I feel like he doesn't appreciate me. Like he thinks I'm lazy because I don't earn anything. Like money's all that matters."

"Is money a problem?" she asks. What about money for appointments? Is the insurance still paying our bills?

"There's still a copay," I tell her. "But it's not a big deal. Donald just worries."

So she asks me what else he worries about.

I feel Donald's cold breath down my neck and imagine he's watching me now. His eyes narrow as he waits to hear what I'll say, that worried frown appearing between them, the one that makes me think he doesn't trust me. Can't we just change the subject? Then the therapist adjusts her chair, and the room comes back into focus. Donald's not here. Donald's never going to meet her. He'll never know.

He worries a lot about the kids, I say—the subjects they choose in school, their chances of getting scholarships to college, and the jobs they might aim for. I sigh theatrically. Sometimes I wonder if he's turning into my father. But Donald's an engineer. He's into numbers and details. I always knew that.

"So… Would it help if you had a job?"

I know it would. It would help pay for after-school activities that would beef up the kids' applications. It would give us a chance to save for college fees.

"But you don't want to do it? Why not?"

"Because…" I stare at my hands in my lap. They lie still suddenly, like fallen leaves. Then I look away, and they twist and turn in the breeze. The skin around my fingers is red from cleaning and all those tears dripped into tissues. The nails are chewed.

I try to imagine going out to work every morning, not being there to pack lunches or make sure the boys leave on time. I think of the afternoon phone calls I get when one of them misses the bus. I remember frantic shopping trips for things they've forgotten they need, washing PE kits at the very last minute and flinging them, soddenly, sullenly, into the dryer. I think of time spent making sure they have enough shirts and ties and pants and jeans. I think of cooking and dinner and buying food fresh to keep my family well fed. How would I do all this if I went out to work?

Then I think of afternoons walking the dog, coming home to pictures strewn on the bedroom floor. How will I ever find time for Tyke or for painting or the pictures in my head? My fingers ache to draw.

The therapist sees through me of course and passes pencil and paper across her desk. Am I as transparent as this when Donald talks to me? Will he know I've been foolish this morning and talked about him? I draw pictures of hands.

"How does it make you feel when your husband wants you to go out to work?"

I'm too busy drawing to even think.

More hands. They spread across the page until they turn into leaves with just one hand, disembodied, lying bloodless on the ground.

I start on another sheet of paper.

More hands crawl up the center of a page. This time they morph into a tree. A black form holds a smaller figure pinned against its trunk.

More hands and in between them they hold a snake.

"I feel like when he pushed me on the ground. Like when he forced me. When I couldn't make him stop." Blind fingers drop the pencil now and reach for the tissue box. *This voice isn't me.*

"You know; your husband's *not* your abuser, Sylvia. He's not trying to abuse you."

"He's trying to make me do something I don't want to do."

I'm whining. I sound like Adam, refusing to carry his dishes back into the kitchen. This voice isn't mine, but the stranger's wearing my skin.

"He's trying to make me turn into someone I'm not. He's not asking what I want."

I think I'm screwing up tissues to throw away, but I've rolled the pictures into a ball as well. The paper feels brittle as fallen leaves. The pencil smells of damp and earth and dust.

"Does that make you feel better?"

"Does what?" I feel more like myself.

"Drawing your memories on paper, then throwing them away?"

I suppose it does, but not much. And now I'll go home with reddened eyes from crying, and Donald will sigh. Been there. Done that before. Why aren't I mended yet?

I'm not a computer program, I think. I'm not a technical drawing or a sum on the calculator. You can't add me up and define what I want to say. I want to be me.

I go home. I cry. Donald asks why and I don't tell him.

Chapter 51

Am I better yet? Do I think I could get a job yet? Will I at least consider it?

Can I stand on a bridge over the freeway and shout at passing cars, "I'm not good enough"? Does he wish he'd never married me?

Donald asks all his questions aloud but I keep mine silent, keep pretending to be proud wife and mother and there's nothing wrong with me. Nothing wrong with pretending anyway.

I ladle dinner onto plates, smelling the warm scents of cooking and safety and home. When the phone rings, I use my spare hand to pick it up, still slopping gravy over vegetables.

"Hi Sis." It's my brother Jason. At once I'm afraid and wonder why he's calling because Jason hates phones. Jeannie's the one who makes all his calls for him. Is something wrong with Lydia and Troy, or their sons, or Mom and Daddy?

Jason hears my silence and continues. "Is Donald around? I just wanted to tell him something. Can you put him on?"

"Why not tell me?" I challenge him. "I'm putting dinner out."

"Then you're busy. I'll not keep him long. Just pass the phone to him."

Jason doesn't sound worried or annoyed, just quietly sensible, which is perfectly normal for him. So I carry the phone in one hand and ladle in the other. I'm trying not to drip, and I find Donald bent over his computer. He doesn't look up.

"Jason wants to talk to you."

Donald turns around as if I've said it's Christmas. His face brightens, and I wonder how long he's been wearing that midnight frown. When did I last see him smile?

Peas, potatoes, carrots, and meat. Back in the kitchen I make sure each plate has a healthy mix of each. Boys' voices compete with the blaring television. I wish I could hear my husband's voice as well. I wish I knew what Jason's calling about.

Carrying plates to the table and laying them straight, I remember last Thanksgiving at Mom and Daddy's house. I sat sketching by the dresser. Jason and Donald stood together in a corner of the room while Jeannie shot wary glances at them over her shoulder, clearly not included. They were plotting something, which doesn't make sense because my big brother's not a plotter. Straightforward, totally boring, destroyer of button-holes and general drip, standing up like a question mark waiting to fall on someone... but he's not a plotter.

No matter. Donald finishes with the phone, and we all sit down to eat, though the boys complain their programs aren't finished yet. "That's what videos are for," says Donald. End of conversation. It's clear he's not planning to tell me anything about what Jason said, not at the table anyway. I wonder if it's some business opportunity for me. Donald will say how easy it'll be for me to work from home. Then he won't understand when I tell him I'm already working. I can't be that busy. I have time to look at pictures—oh, how often he's told me that. So I must have time for a job.

The boys head off again after their meal. I load up the dishwasher, slamming plates and dishes into place, pouring powder from the too-heavy box, and smelling acrid cleanliness as dregs spill to the floor. Donald's arms surprise me when he snakes them around my waist.

"What's this?" I ask, wriggling around to face him.

"I love you."

Oh so innocent Donald looks, like a child who really didn't break the dish for all I watched it happen. I wish I could believe him, but I wonder what's brought this on. The smile in his eyes makes him look suddenly younger, wild and full of vitality. If he tells me what's wrong I'll probably fall apart, but half of me feel like I might just fall in love with him over again. *Keep holding onto me.*

"How d'you fancy living back in Paradise?" he asks, and all my hopes come crashing down. The warmth and need that spread from stomach to knees is turned to ice.

I hear leaves in the wind outside, smell mildew and mold, and choke on the darkness of earth falling into my throat. Frost drips in my veins as I step from Donald's clasp. The bright blue kitchen wavers, disappearing into shadows of trees and gray. The clock ticks too loud.

"Paradise?" I ask, my voice growing thick as it struggles to climb out of me. "Why would I want to live there?"

Donald strokes my hair. I feel hands touching, probing, gliding over me, and I pull away, my body shuddering. "There's a vacancy at Jason's company. He says he can get me in."

"But you've got a job." I almost shout the words. Not only has Donald got a job, but he's forever telling me I should get one too. What's going on?

"I've got a job until the end of the month, Sylvia." He reaches forward to hold me again, but I step back, trying to work my way around the table in the center of the kitchen.

"What do you mean?"

"Come on. I told you."

He didn't, I say. I'd know if he'd told me his job was going away.

"I told you over and over again, but you don't listen to me."

Yes I do listen!

I've backed myself into a corner of the room, and I lean against the wall. Smooth swatches of paint touch my back, not brittle trees, no crumbling bark falling like snow at my feet. I try to drive the memories away, then push myself down onto a chair. "When? What?" I'm shaking, cold as a winter tree, and my words fall like leaves.

Donald paces like a lecturer in front of me. He tells me in carefully measured tones that they're closing down his office. His job's been outsourced, and he's just there to finish training replacements. Everyone's gone. The reason he's begged me to get a job is because we can't afford our health insurance when his paycheck's gone.

"Who'll pay for my therapy?" I ask, my voice like a child's while I try to process the thought. I watch my fingers bend and twine in my lap.

"Who?" Donald thumps the wall with his fist and I jump. His face is screwed up as if he's trying not to cry. "It's not all about you."

So *I* cry instead.

He's told me so often, he says, his voice forgiving and soothing, trying to be kind as he makes allowances. He knows I've had a lot on my mind, and he never wanted to hurt me. He needed me to sympathize, but I never seemed to care. So he turned to my brother.

I remember him asking when I'll finish therapy, as if it costs too much. I remember him telling me I need to get a job, as if he didn't value the things I do. I've heard him complain about expenses; I thought he meant it was me that was spending too much. I've heard, and I've not listened, or else I've listened and not heard.

"How long have you known?" I feel defeated, as if it's already decided and we're destined to leave.

"Since before Thanksgiving, before our trip back there. Jason promised he'd keep an eye out for me, and I guess this means he has. It's just what we need."

But I still don't want to go back to Paradise.

Chapter 52

"Why not?" the therapist asks.

Well, there's the hassle of selling the house and packing up and buying another place to live. That's just a start. There are boys who might not want to lose their friends. There are credits that might not transfer from one school to another. And there's no guarantee the job will work out either. Of course, in my quest for guaranteed perfection I realize I sound like my husband, so I'd better stop talking.

"Is that all?" she prompts into my silence.

I don't want to say more. I don't want to remember how I hated leaving Granny and Grandpa's house, or how long it took before my new home felt like home. You don't just move children and expect them to agree. You don't plunk them down in a new place where nothing tastes right and nobody knows what they like or who they are.

"So you're worried about the children then. It's not that *you* don't want to go?"

Of course not, I think. I'll go wherever Donald needs me to go. But suddenly I'm sitting on that low wooden bench in Paradise Park again. It's last Thanksgiving and Jason's wife Jeannie is chattering empty nothingness at my side. A cold wind blows the green, green darkness of memory over me.

Jeannie looked so neat and petite and calm while the forest buried me. So no, I don't want to go. I don't want to face all the memories hidden there. But, I will, of course.

"Just worried about the children. Really," I lie. "I mean, it was all so long ago."

When Donald suggests we visit and look at some houses, I can't find a decent excuse. I tell him okay, though I can't think why he wants us to go at Easter. My heartbeat throbs in my ears and my hands feel clammy, but it's okay.

"Let's leave the boys behind," Donald says, a smile of triumph in his eyes.

"No way. Thomas is only fourteen."

"Leave them with friends I mean."

"But it's Easter weekend."

"Leave them with friends at church."

Somehow I find it's all arranged, though I didn't know Donald knew half so much about who the boys hang out with. I don't even have to help them pack. "Mom, it's only a weekend. I'm not a baby." Then we rush from house to house dropping them off. I feel like I've dropped off bits of myself—arms, legs and feet perhaps while the rest of me is waiting to fall apart. If I don't watch them, I might not see how they stroll so contentedly away, as if they don't need us.

I pretend to sleep while the taxi takes us to the airport. Then I won't have to talk. But all too soon we're dragging our bags across the crowded concourse. Security's a scramble, dropping shoes, picking up shoes, forgetting to take my phone out of my pocket; but at last we're through and can settle to drink some coffee while we wait at the gate. Its warmth soothes me, until Donald piles printed papers into my lap. They smell of ink. They're covered with square photographs of houses, windows, doors, tables and chairs, long driveways and paths. If I look closer I might see the addresses and remember locations perhaps. Too near the park. Too far from the city center. Things like that. But reading the small print feels like too much effort. It will cause too much pain.

They call our flight and we stumble along the aisle to find our numbers. "Take the window seat," says Donald.

"No, you take it."

"No, you want it more."

I demur, and a crowd gathers behind us, so Donald sits down. I'm still fastening my seatbelt, trying to match up the ends, while he reads safety checklists and the inflight magazine. A muffled voice makes announcements. Then engines roar. I lean back, wishing I could change into somebody else. If I run fast enough from my thoughts, do you suppose I might fly?

"Our first trip without them," Donald says, smiling expansively and stroking my hand. He looks as if the cares of the world all fell away with the ground, eyes bright as the clouds. I can't answer him.

The window's small, and the world outside is empty, white, unpainted, waiting for life. As a child I might have seen pictures in the clouds—here a dragon, there a castle, a bull, a cat? But now I see only canvas, devoid of dreams, and I turn away.

"Magical isn't it?" Donald's bright eyes reflect blue and I can't answer. I turn away from him too.

I tug my book from my bag and try to read. But the seat keeps shuddering as if it wants to express the way I feel. They offer food and Donald says it's good. I still can't answer him.

"You need to change the time on your watch," he says.

I change it in silence.

Eventually he just stops talking to me.

When it's dark, when I'm more than half-asleep, we land and stumble back down the aisle from our seat. Mom and Daddy meet us at the baggage carousel. They bounce with excitement, hug us too tight, and proclaim how wonderful it is. I can't answer them either.

Chapter 53

A realtor drives us around in the morning, and breakfast feels like a leaden ball in my stomach. Donald has organized it all; Donald the wise, the efficient. Paradise is full of wondrous homes that we're scheduled to view. I should know my way around I guess, but the streets seem strange from the back of the car, with the landmarks all gone awry. Houses stand too empty, too square, arrayed in long blind rows. When we get out to look, they smell too dusty like cardboard cutout models with plastic inside. I feel like a visitor in the history of my life.

"Is this anywhere near the school you used to go to?" Donald asks.

We walk down yet another green-trimmed footpath to a blue-painted door. I don't know. I don't even remember going to school. I'm not that person now—not the schoolgirl, not the daughter, not the sister, mother nor bride. I'm a child in a forest of shadows, and a figure's walking toward me, too fast and too dark, and I can't see his face.

We go to Jeremy's church in the afternoon, and sit with Mom and Daddy like prized awards brought down from the mantelpiece. It's Good Friday, though I never understood what's meant to be good about somebody dying on a cross— Easter Sunday and resurrection might be good perhaps, but Friday's just sad. Pastor Jeremy, my dear little nephew, all grown up, leads us through prayers for this and that and the needs of all the world. Then we, the people mix "Hosanna" with "Crucify," in endless Bible readings for the day, and send Jesus to die. It feels like saying *Yes* to the shadow in my dreams.

The church is so cold my hands start to shake in my lap. I wrap myself tighter in my coat and lean against Donald's sleeve. Jeremy's just getting going with the sermon, but really, it's been a long day, so I close my eyes to houses with blue doors that open onto forests and green. The shadowed man still waits for me.

"Father, forgive them," Jeremy intones.

But if that shadowed man really is Jeremy's grandfather, Troy's dad, Lydia's father-in-law, it's me that needs forgiving. I'm the one who didn't see—didn't say—I'm the one who did nothing and Amelia died, so it's all my fault. The sleeve of my coat gets caught in my mouth and I'm choking on fallen leaves.

"Jesus didn't say, 'I forgive them,'" Jeremy intones.

Who didn't? What? I fight to find my way back to his words. Is he talking to me?

"Jesus didn't forgive. He asked his father to do it for him instead."

Really? I look up at my nephew in the pulpit, wondering if I heard him right.

Then Jeremy raises his hands to encompass us all. His face seems to shine. "When we struggle," *I'm struggling*, "when we think we can't forgive," *I know I can't*, "we should remember that."

Father, forgive them. They know not what they do? I've heard the words before. But I tell myself, *he* knew.

"So, who do *you* need to forgive?"

I make a list, trying not to touch the hurt that's bleeding inside. I need to forgive Donald of course, for moving us, for not understanding why I can't come back. And Daddy too? Should I forgive him for the move when I was a child? Or for not knowing what was wrong with me when I was a teen? And the shadowed man?

"Ask God to do it for you. Don't keep trying on your own."

I smile bitterly, smelling candlewax mixed with bile. Still, Pastor Jeremy's not really talking to me so I stop listening. *No need to ask God to forgive if I'm not trying.* Instead I stare around a room that's growing dark with the afternoon gloom. I wish they'd turn some lights on—heating too.

"But you know who's hardest to forgive, don't you?" says Jeremy. "The one Jesus never had to forgive, because Jesus never needed to be forgiven? Can you forgive yourself?"

Goosebumps prickle along my arms. *Switch the heating on, please!* Meanwhile Jeremy's telling us all how Peter couldn't forgive himself for saying he never knew him. Then Jesus never told Peter he was forgiven. "Feed my lambs," he says and, "Feed my sheep." And feed my kids and my husband, and anyway, I really don't need forgiveness 'cause it was never really my fault. The only reason I'm shivering is because I'm cold.

"'I should have noticed,'" says Jeremy. "Is that what you tell yourself? 'I should have said. I should have made a difference. But it wasn't my fault.' And then we can never forgive ourselves, because we can't admit that we need to be forgiven."

He lifts his hands again in benediction. "Admit it today, this day, when the price is paid."

But it wasn't my fault.

"Admit you're not perfect, and know that God still loves you anyway. Let him forgive you. Be forgiven."

But it wasn't my fault, not really.

Jeremy goes on and on about Jesus carrying our sins and paying for us, but I've paid for myself. And she paid too, poor dead Amelia. We paid, and the world moved on. Cold clammy air settles down on me like leaves. Voices turn into whispers in the trees. The shadow stands, his arms outstretched to hold me, offering peace. But I still don't know his face.

Donald jokes as we leave, telling me I fell asleep during the sermon. Jeremy smiles and shakes my hand. When I look at him I see his father, Troy, and his grandfather too, looking out through his eyes.

Chapter 54

We walk down the street to buy coffee after church, giving Mom and Daddy a break. Donald says we can discuss houses on the way. He has them all memorized and categorized by mathematical detail, square footage, average heating bill, taxes and fees. I ask him which one had the blue door and he doesn't remember.

"And a really big yard."

"There were three with a third of an acre," Donald offers agreeably.

"I didn't measure it."

We follow the same route I took with Jeannie last fall, ending up at the entrance to Paradise Park. The path leads down through trees to the duck pond, sparkling blue water reflecting an azure sky. Donald leads and I follow, trying not to see.

"Let's sit down on this bench."

Yes, of course. Let's sit down. And *"Why do you always do that?"* says my friend Sharon in memory.

"It's beautiful," says Donald, arms outstretched as he leans back comfortably. I try to switch on my artist's sight and imagine painting the colors, the gentle sweep of the hill, shadows and shades all billowing in the clouds. Then I agree, though my eyes are still closed.

The coffee's too sweet and coats my tongue with glue. It weighs like lead in my stomach, so I lean back, giving room to digest. Then Donald slips his arm into the gap between me and the bench and holds me tight, tugging me to his chest. The shadow held me that way too, and I want to push him away.

Open your eyes. See his face.

I see a gray cloud overhead. Ducks quack, and I turn to the sound. A white cat runs past.

"Hey! Isn't that your Jeremy's cat?" Donald asks.

I don't know but it could be.

"D'you think it's okay?"

"It's lived here long enough."

We fold the coffee cups together now and toss them in the trash. *Okay. Let's go back.* But Donald steers me with his arm, forward to the climbing frame and on to the track under the trees.

Children's voices echo in memory. Jeremy, Jay and Joshua; when they were small, they used to play here. Amelia too. Would she have learned to play real games with friends if she'd grown older?

My feet sink in the mire and won't move on. My arms are pinned by shadows falling on me. My mouth can't breathe for the leaves that cover me.

"Sylvia?" Donald asks, still holding too tight.

"I don't want to," I mumble against his shirt. "I don't want to go back there. Please. I want to go home." I think of what Jeremy said in church, and I raise my voice to add, "I don't want to forgive him."

Donald's chin feels heavy on the top of my head. The breeze of his speaking flutters through my hair, while his arms keep hold of me. But the words don't make sense. "Doesn't what I want matter, too?"

What does he mean? I try to pull out of his grip, then twist my neck to look at him.

"You're not the only one that needs to forgive him for what he did," says Donald.

"Why? What would you forgive him for?"

"He hurt someone I love, Sylvia. He stole something from you. Don't you think I've hated him for that?"

I try to think it through. Isn't Donald the one who said, "Men have needs," when I told him what had happened? I thought he didn't care.

"Of course I cared! I understood. That's not the same as forgiveness."

I *never* understood.

Somehow we've walked further under the trees anyway, like a three-legged race with the blind leading the blind. The sun has vanished in a canopy of leaves. The air's damp, redolent with life. Donald keeps his arm around my waist, but gently now. I come to accept it as protection, not betrayal after all. My footsteps get lighter, while the forest gathers its darkness all around.

There's a clearing ahead of us where the sun breaks through. Light shines like a golden waterfall pouring down over green. Could this be the place? I step forward, almost lightly, almost forgiven, almost as if I imagine he's waiting for me with kindness and thanksgiving. Is he here?

"Thank you," he said. I hear his voice again. "I'm sorry," just before he left.

Donald follows me. We stand together in the clearing and I bend to pick up a red leaf from the ground. Bright red, it's fresh as the first leaf-fall of autumn. I turn around and of course he isn't here. Just me and Donald and the whispering breeze and the twittering birds in the trees.

But a twig cracks.

I stare at the shadows. Now. I'm waiting for him.

Donald holds me from behind, his body pressed to mine, his arms stretching over my shoulders, hands together in front of my chest. He's gentle, at rest. But my body stiffens in wary expectation. There's nobody here, but I see him still, that shadow in the trees. I see him slowly stepping out. I see him run to me. His coat flaps like bat's wings, never an angel's, propelling him on. The baseball cap's pulled low over his head. Sunlight catches the faded blue of his garage dungarees, then he's holding me.

I raise my face to look at him carefully now. It's not really so dark. It isn't so impossible to see. At first I think he's Lydia's boyfriend, Troy, but it's the beard confusing me. It's really Troy's dad. He presses his lips on mine and I taste garage smells of metal and oil while he sucks on me. I fall forward, helplessly into his arms, enraptured, enslaved. He's captured me. I'm an innocent bird scooped up from cupid's bath by a giant's clasp. I can't escape. But I've seen his face.

"Don't tell anyone," he says, "or it'll cause trouble, too much for you to bear."

I don't like causing trouble.

"This is our little secret." Then he tells me I'm beautiful.

I'm a cuckoo learning to be a swan, and I mustn't say a word or I'll break the spell.

Donald holds me, even as I lean forward. Even as I make to fall, my husband holds me back. When I start to cry, he turns me around and clasps me ever so gently to his chest, where I make his jacket wet.

"I saw him," I say but my words are crushed to silence in the fabric of my husband's clothes. I saw *him* and all the images come back. The black scab's torn away. Eyes dull and slack while his fingers probe into me. Tongue thick and hungry as he aims his mouth for my throat. Face filled with violent anticipation as he throws me to the ground. Clasping hands with the marks of grease from cars, with the smell of engine oil; his rough unshaven untrimmed beard; his eyes so much like Troy's yet different; his hungry appraisal of frightened quivering flesh; and his violent thrusting into me. It all comes back.

I pushed him away and stared at his raptured face, then slammed the door on my memories. I could never say. Not this. What had I done? What had I made him do to me? And how, oh how had I led him on? My sister loved his son. It *was* all my fault.

The picture flickers in my mind, blank shadowed face unfeatured, blind, but the memory's real and I know, it really was him.

My silence killed Amelia.

Donald holds me still, letting me cry into his jacket. I see my dark tears soak through to his shirt. He holds me still as I feel myself broken in pieces, shattered like memories, torn apart on a mirror's shards in my mind. He holds me, whispers honest love, blowing words through the hairs of my head, blowing comfort over me. And slowly the warmth of the sun breaks through the cloud. My ice starts to melt.

I'm shivering.

Donald adjusts his arms.

I'm crying. He offers a tissue but I need a whole box.

I'm ready now.

Chapter 55

"What happened back there?" Donald asks, as we walk through trees to reach the path again.

"I remembered," I say. When he doesn't ask, I tell him I remembered who it was and everything. "Peter Markham, the garage guy, Troy's dad, it really was him. And it's true, isn't it? If I'd said something, if I'd told someone, he might never have killed Amelia."

"D'you think you're the only one he ever touched?"

"No, of course I don't."

"And nobody else said anything?"

"I guess not."

"So are they all to blame?"

"No, of course."

"Then neither are you."

But I am, and I don't understand how I hid it away, how I forgot the look of his face. Why didn't I draw him then, so I would've known? So everyone else would have known.

I am to blame after all. But then I remember what Jeremy was trying to say, that we're all guilty, and everyone needs forgiveness. Did he tell us how to forgive ourselves? I can't remember the rule. But does all this mean I'm cured?

The trees don't feel so threatening now. They've opened the doors on their secret and let it out, so the sun can shine. I listen to rustling leaves under our feet. I watch a bluebird flit from twig to twig. Then something cracks. We turn together and watch as Jeremy's cat leaps after a squirrel.

Children race on the playground with happy shrieks and dancing feet. We walk past them and stop at our bench again by the ducks and the pond.

"Have you forgiven him?" Donald asks.

I shake my head but really I don't know. I'm mulling memories around in my mind, the poster I made for Amelia's memorial, thirteen halos, thirteen snakes, and saying, "It's not about luck." Mom said Lydia gave some talk about how you can still love someone without forgiving them. "Wasn't that wonderful?" Mom insisted, while I filed it away as pious irrelevance. Not that I want to love him either, but perhaps that's what happens when you leave the forgiving to God. I turn to Donald. "Have *you* forgiven him?"

"I'm not sure." He tightens his fingers around my hand. "I think I learned to feel a bit better in time, about knowing who he was, and about you, but it took a while."

I thank him for being there for me. I rub my thumb against his hand while other images fill my thoughts—Donald afraid of what the future might bring, Donald worried for us, Donald caring for me. I'm sorry I imagined him to be unkind. Perhaps I'll show him I'm sorry tonight, in that slightly small bed in the slightly small room in Mom and Daddy's house. Life is good after all.

Chapter 56

Donald moves to his new job, but we stay behind so the boys can finish their year. I'll deal with end of term conferences at school and try to sell the house. Somehow I'll pretend I know what it's all about. As for being cured, I know I'm not. Happiness lasts about as long as sunshine between clouds, then I want to cry again. But Donald's new health insurance doesn't work back here, not in this State. It won't pay for mental health here anyway, so who's going to pay for my therapist?

She says it's okay. She'll meet me in the morning in the park and pretend we're just friends. "I've got something to tell you," she says and, of course, I need to tell her I've finally remembered his face.

We meet at the coffee shop and set off to run, pretending we're joggers. She's not pretending, but I am. And it's not Paradise Park. It doesn't have a forest or even any trees. Still, I look warily off the paths, search for strangers hiding in the grass. I stare at the duck pond as if there might be somebody listening there.

"No one listens to joggers," says the therapist when I complain. "We're here one moment then gone away. No one stays close long enough to hear a conversation."

Her breath comes easily, so relaxed, and I know I'm holding her back but she doesn't complain.

"So tell me," she says.

I'd look at her face if I could, but I'm afraid I'll miss my step and fall flat on the ground. Is this like talking to kids in the car, when you can't see their expressions, so they tell you stuff 'cause they know you're not able to react? I've already told her I saw his face. I've told her everything. "I thought you had something to tell me."

"I've been finding things out."

Our feet repeat their rhythm on the ground. "Finding what things out?" My chest is tight. I cough to breathe again.

"I talked to your mother."

"No!"

"You said I could."

I don't remember what I said, but I guess it does make sense. Who'd know me better than my mom?

"I didn't tell her anything; don't worry. I just asked some questions. I wanted to confirm some things. You know the way it goes."

I don't know much, but her voice sounds light and casual enough, the phrases spaced to fit the thump of her feet. I ask what she found out and try to balance my breathing to match with hers.

"Your Grandpa didn't have a bull."

I stop, then stumble forward again because she's running ahead. She didn't even look at me when she spoke, but what does that mean? Grandpa didn't have a bull? I've shown her all those pictures of the bull. Does she think I made it up? I remember the warm air over his back, the way his eyes switched strangely from gentle to wild, the smear of blood on the end of his horns. I loved that bull.

"He rented one, to service the cows. Your Mom said you were a toddler, two years old." Thud go her feet. "You liked to look at the bull, but your Grandpa didn't keep it. That field, the fence you sat on—there was no pen, no bull."

I know she's lying. I pant and search for words. Of course there was a bull. Then I ask her, "What about cats?"

"Oh yes. Your Grandpa had plenty of cats. They lived in the barn and you used to go all the time, you and him, to look at them."

I only remember going there once, but I smile in memory.

Then the therapist adds, "But it's the snakes I really wanted to ask you about."

"What snakes?" There weren't any snakes on the farm, but she says she saw them in my pictures. "No." I deny it.

The therapist asks about the cat with bull's horns on its head and a snake's forked tongue, a snake's long tail. I remember that, seeing the picture superimposed on long green grass and rough gray path. "I was thinking of the devil," I muse. "With horns and a tail and all that."

"And a snake's forked tongue," she repeats. Her feet thud forward, moving ever on.

I catch my breath.

"What about the halos made of snakes? In the poster you made."

"They just looked like snakes. It was just…"

"You're sure there were never any snakes?"

We jog in silence, the path like solid rock beneath our feet, the morning air like milk straight from the fridge, and no snakes, not anywhere. I can't get around the bull not being real though, and eventually I ask her, "What about the fire?"

"There was no fire," says the therapist. "Just a coal that fell on the living room rug. You were only a tot and your Grandpa put it out. Your Mom says it scared you. But what about the snake?"

I hear flames crackle in the sound of mounting traffic, see fire in the sun, and I want to stop this running but my body keeps hurrying on. A yellow building reminds me of the barn. A white picket fence has a small dog barking behind it. Someone shouts, a sharp, insistent command, and Granny's complaining in memory. If I listen harder, will I catch her words?

"You put that trouser snake away. What if the kids came in here?" My legs won't move.

A tiny tot, crouched in the hall, wonders why Grandpa would carry a snake in his pants. I'm not running anymore and the therapist's stopped as well to watch.

"D'you want to talk?"

I don't answer.

"D'you want to sit down?"

There's a bench beside her and we sit while memories pour in.

My therapist, ever ready, has a sketchpad in her shorts and a pencil in her shirt. I start to draw.

The picture begins with a bed, big and old, wooden framed, thick blankets flowing like snow over it. An old man sits on the edge of the mattress, denting it heavily. His legs splay awkwardly apart, and a little child rides on one knee, as if his hand beneath her were the saddle. The bulge in the old man's trousers starts to rise underneath my pencil and I'm asking him...

"Do you really have a snake, Grandpa?"

"Yes. Do you want to see it?"

"Does it bite?"

"Of course it doesn't."

He unfastens his zip so the hairy creature flops out and I think it's ugly, more like a warty toad than the shiny snakes I've seen at the zoo.

"It's a very clever snake," Grandpa says and shows me how it wriggles while his fingers twitch under me. His fingernails are sharp on the elastic of my pants. "Look what it can do."

The thick snake stiffens, growing longer, and I'm entranced.

"Do you want to touch it?"

I pull away, but Grandpa holds my hand, tugging me toward him until my palm's cupped over the snake's slick end. It's smooth and damp. This trouser snake is spitting at me.

"It looks more like a stick than a snake," I say, nervously searching for words.

"Ah yes, like Moses' stick. Do you remember?"

I shake my head.

Grandpa tells me how Moses had a stick in the desert. It turned into a snake when he threw it on the ground.

"Like magic, Grandpa?"

"Like power. My snake's got power like Moses' snake."

I ask him if I have a snake and I struggle to slide off his hand. It doesn't feel right.

"No. Little girls don't have snakes. They have holes instead."

His finger's in my hole and I hope there's nothing else in there. Where do moths and spiders go? So I ask him, "What kind of a hole?"

"A hole for snakes to go in."

At last I pull myself free of him. I scramble down from his knee, feeling dirty and itchy underneath. I imagine snakes and spiders and centipedes crawling all over me. I wish I was a boy.

"But it's our little secret," Grandpa says, putting his snake, much shinier now and more snakelike, back into his pants.

"What is?"

"My snake. You must never tell anyone. Never at all." His voice is suddenly firm and sharp, the preacher's voice that promises hell for sinners, and I know I'll obey.

I nod my head. I'll never tell.

I turn the page.

This time I'm drawing a child's small hand pressed down beneath the larger, scraped and wrinkled hand of a man.

We used to go to the barn. The hay scratched under me as I climbed onto Grandpa's knee. Bits of dirt and straw were caught in his fingers. I hated the thought that he'd leave them behind in me. But it was our secret, known only to Grandpa and me, and the cats.

Lydia said no when Grandpa tried to touch her, then we moved away. But I didn't say no. I was a child obeying my elders, honoring the Bible, doing what the preacher says. I thought I was being good, and I didn't understand why it felt so wrong. So I hid it away.

"You learned to hide your memories didn't you?" the therapist says. "From a really young age."

I learned to hide my secrets in symbols and pictures on a page.

Grandpa, the bull, the hairy creature, hypnotic, dangerous.

Granny, the cat that should have been keeping watch and protecting me.

Fire when I wished I could turn all my problems to dust.

And a guardian angel because they say there are angels watching over us.

It hurts still, touching the place where these memories are stored, as if my brain's hard drive is scratched, and searching there might make the whole file structure fall apart.

"You're not going to fall apart," the therapist says. "You're stronger than that."

Then I wonder how much I've said aloud? But I'm suddenly very tired. All I want is to sleep.

"I'll drop you off at your house when we finish our run," the therapist says.

She holds my arms and pulls me up from the bench. I wonder if I'll fall when she lets go. But she turns me around like a rag doll following the path. "You've got some serious thinking to do, Sylvia. But, for now, let's just wear you out a bit. Exercise helps."

The earth doesn't move. The ground thuds contentedly beneath me. The air doesn't freeze but grows warm enough for summer to blink on the horizon. Strangers run by and don't see us. We scarcely see them. And memories hide in the solid square shape of a sketch pad on my therapist's thigh.

Chapter 57

Donald phones from Paradise. I curl up on the bed to talk, pretending the weight at my side is him when really it's just the dog. The bedroom smells like morning. I haven't even bothered to tidy the sheets or open the curtains yet, for all that I ate lunch an hour ago.

Donald asks how my meeting went, and I'm not sure I want to tell him. So I stroke Tyke's back and imagine it's the hair on Donald's head. "It went okay."

"Yeah, sure, my love. And what aren't you telling me?"

I mumble into the pillow and hope he won't give me the third degree.

Then he says, "Poor love. I'm sorry."

"Sorry?" I ask. "It's not your fault." I laugh because he's saying my lines—I'm the one that's sorry all the time.

"Ah but it is my fault," says Donald, his voice like honey pouring over me. "It's my fault you're dealing with this on your own. I should be there with you."

My body tingles as I stretch luxuriously, enjoying his voice. "Why? What would you do?" And it's a good job the boys won't be home for a while. But how did our conversation take this turn? Does absence really make the heart grow fonder?

I feel Donald's hands glide over me as his tongue whispers the words. A fire burns in my chest, and this time I don't want to run away. I lick my lips and taste his sweet caresses while we languidly talk, while my fingers languidly walk where I want him to be. When Tyke lifts his head, I almost drop the phone.

"I should be packing," I say. Moments drift, and I'm not ready to move.

"It'll wait." The ever efficient Donald is telling me something will wait?

"But I should…"

"What did the therapist say to you?"

I tell him now, my body warmed and soothed by his distant love and the languor of his voice. I tell him how it wasn't just Troy's dad in the woods that hurt me. The reason I couldn't tell. The reason I wouldn't remember his face, even though I saw him and knew exactly who he was. It was Grandpa too. And it wasn't just my sister he tried to touch.

"Oh Sylvia."

For a moment I'm afraid Donald might need me to comfort him, and that won't be fair. But suddenly he's talking again, sweet murmurings, sweet gentle meaningless nothings that make me feel better. I want his body next to me.

"Oh Sylvia. So much has happened to you. My poor, sweet thing."

So much, I think, like a tower of ills upon ills. I feel like I've staggered around trying to carry it all, while the balance kept shifting, persisting in making me fall. But what happens now?

The pieces start to fit together, I think. The tower's not so tall. It's not so awkward after all. Like a jigsaw of jagged triangular shapes, once it's done it hardly takes any space anymore.

"I wanted the therapist to make you feel better, but now she keeps adding more stuff for you to deal with."

"No," I whisper. He doesn't hear, so I whisper it again. "No, she's not just piling stuff on. She's making the pieces fit, so it all makes sense, like I've got the right equation, like the answer might work. I think it's good."

And I do. I don't think I realized it until then, but I do think it's good.

Donald hugs me again with his words, and I wait for the boys to come home.

Chapter 58

No. I'm not permanently mended, but I'm better than I was.

The house feels more broken than I, and it's no wonder the boys prefer to go out all the time now school's over. They're at friends' homes, playing with friends' computers, watching friends' TVs and reading friends' books. Meanwhile I watch Tyke slink into corners, while I put off getting suitcases out. I guess I'm thinking somehow I'll manage to keep our precious pet from being too upset, but he's upset already. I've packed all our books and DVDs and half our pots and ornaments away into boxes from a liquor store. Thomas says we look like alcoholics. But I keep the curtains closed so no one can see. Of course, I'll have to pack the curtains soon.

Now I stand in a memory of a room, red-shaded, fabric-swathed, with walls that look too bare—all the pictures all gone. Tables and chairs are there, but it's like a sketch before the painting's done. Dust drifts through the air as miserably as Tyke drifting into the hall.

I'd take him for a walk except I've just remembered I really ought to empty the loft. There's space on top of the other boxes now, the floor turning into a computer game of blocks balanced over blocks. I drag the ladder to that spot outside our bedroom, wrap a scarf around my head so spiders won't get in my hair, and plug Donald's light into the socket by our door. Tyke lies by the bottom step so I have to climb over him. I hope he might move before I come down.

The panel over my head's as stiff as before. I lean back on the ladder to push with both hands, hearing dust and splinters grate as the wooden plate starts to move. Tyke snuffles, and I whisper down to him, "Hush. It's okay." Then I push the panel sideways out of my way. With arms hooked over the square's empty hole, I lift myself up, then hang the lamp on its beam. The light sways dizzily. Seasickness rocks with shadows over me then settles again. Shapeshifting boxes meander like ghosts, while reflections in an ancient mirror form an army of angels to defeat them.

The hole I took the carton of pictures from has filled with dust. You'd never know there'd been anything standing there. But other boxes have multiplied in my absence, so many more than I remember. How will I manage to carry them all?

I look down at Tyke and wish he was one of the boys. They could help, but I don't like…

"They could help," says the therapist's voice in my head, decisive, driving me on. "Don't forget, Sylvia. You're important and your feelings matter." My fingers matter too, and my bones I might break if I fall. But I'm not used to this. Asking for help feels like failure. "Failing to ask for help is failure." Perhaps I should take her advice.

I switch off the light but leave it dangling from its beam while I climb down the steps. The square hole gapes behind me in the ceiling. *Here be dragons* the fables say. I wonder whether a cobweb might be a moth and fly into the hole inside my ear.

"You don't have holes in you," says the therapist's voice. "You're just as complete and real as anyone else."

I leave the ladder and lead the dog into the kitchen. His leash and treats lie amongst things not yet packed, not yet sealed into those incriminating, intoxicating containers. I pull the curtains wide and laugh at the sight. Let the neighbors draw their own conclusions. We're displaying wine boxes in our window, and we're off to get some fresh air.

"You don't have to hide," says the therapist's voice inside me.

So I tell Tyke, "See? We're not hiding," and I wonder if this urge to dance is what triumph feels like.

Thomas phones when we get back. He wants to know if he can stay out to dinner, but I ask him to come home and help me pack. Soon all three of them serve as my laborers. The therapist's voice declaims, "You're not their servant, Sylvia." They slide the boxes across the loft, pass them down to each other through the hole, and glide their backs along the wall as they stagger toward the kitchen.

Part of me wants to say *Be careful* and grab things from their hands. But, "You've got to let them grow up," says the therapist. "You've got to treat them like grownups." So I busy my hands with sorting and labeling.

Old cards and letters, I write as the lid slides off a crumbling crate. Should I dig out the ones from Grandpa and throw them away? If I've not forgiven him I'll burn them and pretend they're his effigy, scatter ashes on his grave. But then I remember God's doing the forgiving for me. Why stir up memories when I have sons to love me and all these other things to busy me?

Donald's old models are stacked in layers of plastic in the next container. Still gorgeously painted, though dusty, they eagerly await new rules to govern them. I run my hand over their sharp edges, smiling at the loving rows of them, laid out layer upon layer, with weapons to the fore—beauty and war. Another box is light as a feather and filled with model buildings glued to matchbox supports. They look too cool to ignore, so I spread them out on the table to check they're okay. "I thought you were packing things away, Mom, not getting stuff out," says Thomas, but he can't resist coming closer to take a look.

"Hey, these are neat." He holds a soldier to the light and turns him around.

"They're your dad's," I tell him.

"Seriously? What do you do with them?"

I dig into more boxes until I find a book of rules. It's easy to recognize from pictures on the cover and symbols and numbers and tables ranged inside, long glorious lists of probabilities. "You play games," I say, offering the hard backed volume to my son.

Thomas carries it over to a chair, clears a gin box from the cushion, and settles down to read. When his brothers pass through the living room, they have to stop and see. Soon all three are gathered around the book. Adam finds dice and they roll them on the floor. Michael gets a pencil and paper from the kitchen to keep track of scores. All they need now is a father to call out the moves.

Suddenly I realize I'm looking forward at last instead of looking back. Donald will recover his misspent youth when the boys demand to play at our new house. I'll recover my painting time. Tyke will have a whole new park to walk in, and I won't be afraid. The moths and spiders, and bulls and snakes and cats will fade into patches of dust on the floor.

Chapter 59

I don't want to talk about loading up the truck and driving to Paradise. Some memories are best left hidden away or never even stored. But we made it. We're here. And this is our home.

I walk the streets with Donald on a warm summer evening. Benson's restaurant still stands, where Mom and Daddy used to take us out. Donald says we'll celebrate there if he ever gets a raise. The art gallery where I used to work is empty, its vacant window covered in dust. Some new shops sell toy soldiers and games that recreate historical battles, the sort of thing Donald used to enjoy. But the boys are hooked on a fantasy wargame, with model orks and goblins, and Donald doesn't mind. He's teaching them to paint.

I imagine getting a job in school as an art teacher perhaps, but nobody's hiring. Maybe one day. And we walk on.

At the edge of Paradise Park, Donald pauses. "What do you think? Can we go in?"

I check the shadows to make sure they're behaving themselves, and I answer, "Yes."

It's peaceful under the trees. Sunlight dapples into patches of gray-green shade, bright and dark forming patterns that whisper and glide. Birds sing. Squirrels rustle in the undergrowth. Leaves sigh in the breeze as we walk past. And insects flutter by.

This green, green world is cool and peaceful and shady. Time rests here. Nothing rushes. Life waits awhile.

We hold each other where no one can see, and Donald kisses me. I kiss him back. No shadows jump out. No memories warp the taste of his tongue or the touch of his fingers lightly, ever so gently, tugging my tee shirt and flickering under my bra. I press close to him, and no ugly voices whisper about the secret under *his* clothes. I lift my face and pull my mouth away so I can lean back and stare into his eyes. Then I tell him, softly, "Donald, I love you." I really do.

Mom and Daddy have invited us to dinner tonight. We cross the park arm in arm toward the duck pond and the church. It's nice to walk instead of driving everywhere. It's nice to be here. It's nice to know I'll be around to help my parents too. They suddenly seem so much older than they were. I wonder if Mom was so gray or Daddy so frail last Easter or Thanksgiving. Was I really wrapped up in myself so much that I didn't see?

I tell them how happy I am when we arrive. Mom doesn't look convinced. She gets the sherry glasses out, and Daddy pours. Meanwhile I assure her that life is good, and I really enjoy walking down the old streets again. Can we take them to Benson's someday, I ask, for old time's sake? And do they think the art gallery will ever be opened again?

Six weeks later, Daddy dear Daddy has bought it for me.

Complete

Chapter 60

I have a room in the back of the gallery, half for painting, and half of it set out for playing board games. Donald runs a kids' club every Saturday afternoon. I teach art to students after school. I can hardly believe how well this suits me, like finally coming home.

Sometimes I sit at the counter in the store and wonder if I can hear my old boss's voice. I imagine her gliding forward from one of the walls on silent feet. "The name's Ohn-Dray-Uh," she used to say, as if Andrea were somehow too plain and boring for such a fascinating profession. Now I'm the boss.

The doorbell jangles, and I jump up to greet a visitor. "Hi. Welcome to Guardian Angel Arts. Are you looking for anything in particular?"

"No. Just looking."

"Well, let me know if you need me for something." I'll not follow my visitor around. I'm busily sketching on a pad stretched over my knee, well-hidden by the counter while my fingers grasp the pen.

Trees line a clearing in a thickly wooded park. Outstretched branches shed their autumn leaves, as soft as snow, with each one carefully outlined from delicate edge to traceries of veins to quivering stem. The leaves in front are large, almost obscuring the view, but behind they shrink, to fractured specks, to dust.

Sunlight shines like a waterfall, and a small girl stands with her hands upraised to the sky. Her feet dance lightly above the ground, and her shadow undulates on the dry earth beneath her. I add tufts of dust until it's clear she's really dancing on air. Then I flare her skirt out wider, fly her hair in wild abandon, and I smile.

It's a happy picture. It's the way things ought to be.

"Excuse me," says the customer, leaning over the counter so her shadow distracts me. I wonder if she's already asked me to help, and I've not heard her. "Are you an artist?" she says, staring down at the sketchpad on my knee.

"Sort of," I answer. "I've got a little studio behind the shop. But these aren't all mine." I stand politely, putting my sketchpad down, and wave my hands.

"Some of them though?" says the stranger, staring at the pictures on the wall. "Some of them are yours?"

"A few." I ought to be proud, but I smile sheepishly. I felt so nervous putting my own stuff on sale, not sure I can really call myself an artist yet. Can artists have math degrees? Can they wait until they're mothers of teenagers before they make the grade?

My customer asks what sort of prices I charge. She leads the way across the floor, and I follow obsequiously. If I'm not careful I'll start wringing my hands like the dreaded Ohn-Dray-Uh. But there's a kind of certainty in the steps my guest is making. She doesn't meander. She's chosen something and wants to know more about it. Will this be my big sale? Then I see where she's going.

Clasped hands, empty hands, open hands, closed hands, blunt-nailed hands, short-fingered hands, all colors of hands have flooded over this picture—ever, always, only hands. They pass through, over, under each other, ghost hands and solid together, some bits erased while others still remain. Impossibly twisted, tortuous, grasping hands. There are hands everywhere.

Underneath them, covered, hidden away, pale lines like broken memories scar the page. Something almost invisible has been painted and almost lost. A girl, like the girl I've just sketched in the clearing, stands, square pack on her back, dark hair cascading in a shimmering veil, short skirt, with hands raised in the air.

"I like this one."

"Why?" I ask—perhaps not the wisest question if I'm trying to make a sale. But this woman seems nice, and I really want to know her answer.

"I like the imagery I guess." She waves her own hands lightly in front of her face. "Those hands all over the place in front of the woman, the way there are always so many demands on our time. Do you see what I mean? But there she is, that girl, in the middle of it all, finding time to look up at the sky and just be herself. In spite of it all, in spite of everything the hands all make her do, she's still herself. It's such a hopeful picture."

I nod and smile, thinking it really would be hopeful if you look at it that way. And I make my first sale of the day.

The store's called Guardian Angel Arts now. And the sign over the window matches the picture on my stationary, a fluffy cat like my nephew Jeremy's, but with tiny angel wings.

I'm not sure how my accounts will stack up when we do the taxes next year, but I do know this. My store is more than the money poured into it. And my life is more than the sum of events behind me. What's in front is what matters. What's in front is an infinite sum and an infinite future. And that's more than math, memory or art.

I hope you've enjoyed your visit to Paradise.
If you want to learn more…

discover the neighborhood in **Divide by Zero**
and meet Amelia's absent father in **Subtraction**.

If you want to help the author, please recommend this novel to
your friends and leave a book review.

And thank you for reading **Infinite Sum**.

www.ingramcontent.com/pod-product-compliance
Lightning Source LLC
Chambersburg PA
CBHW050606190726

48283CB00007B/2299